Praise for *Where t[he Truth Lies]*

'A gritty tale full of twists, *Where the Truth Lies*
is a page turner packed with compelling characters.
An exciting new voice in Australian crime fiction.'
**Jane Harper, author of *The Dry*, *Force of Nature*,
*The Lost Man***

'A complex and compelling debut that's impossible to put down!'
**Christian White, author of *The Nowhere Child*,
*The Wife and the Widow***

'A clever, explosive thriller that twists and turns through
Melbourne's gritty underside, with complex characters
and chilling secrets at its core.'
Petronella McGovern, author of *Six Minutes*

'You will be spellbound . . . Death comes vividly to life in news
reporter Chrissie O'Brian's chilling search for *Where the Truth Lies*.'
**Joanne Drayton, author of *The Search for Anne Perry*,
*Ngaio Marsh: Her Life in Crime***

'For all those fans of rural Aussie crime, come spend some time
in the big city, you won't regret it . . . Kilmore has delivered a
twisting thrill ride of a book.'
Aoife Clifford, author of *Second Sight*

'Chrissie O'Brian is a terrific new character in the crime fiction
pantheon. Broken, tenacious and uncompromising.'
Mary Martin Bookshop

WHERE
THE
TRUTH
LIES

KARINA KILMORE

**SIMON &
SCHUSTER**

London · New York · Sydney · Toronto · New Delhi

A CBS COMPANY

WHERE THE TRUTH LIES
First published in Australia in 2020 by
Simon & Schuster (Australia) Pty Limited
Suite 19A, Level 1, Building C, 450 Miller Street, Cammeray, NSW 2062

10 9 8 7 6 5 4 3 2 1

A CBS Company
Sydney New York London Toronto New Delhi
Visit our website at www.simonandschuster.com.au

A catalogue record for this
book is available from the
National Library of Australia

Cover design: Luke Causby
Cover images: Miguel Sobreira/Arcangel (woman); CazzJj (back cover Skyline)
Typeset by Midland Typesetters, Australia
Printed and bound in Australia by Griffin Press

The paper this book is printed on is certified against the
Forest Stewardship Council® Standards. Griffin Press holds
FSC® chain of custody certification SGS-COC-005088. FSC®
promotes environmentally responsible, socially beneficial
and economically viable management of the world's forests

For my one and only

PROLOGUE

She was slipping away. The further she fell, the closer the clouds seemed to come. Wispy transparent slipstreams of white. *Cirrus.* Pain smashed her head. *Floating.* Her life snapped as her body folded in two. But still she hung in the big city sky, like a seagull in an updraft. She could smell the harbour, feel the winter sun. The pain began to ease. *Going home.* Hands lifting her. False hands. Falling again, down through metal and men and power, to regret.

CHAPTER 1

Gulls screamed and wheeled, diving around the towering metal cranes that stood as a silent guard between the land and the sea. Tall and proud, they stretched almost through the blanket of grey that hid the morning sky. The cranes' splayed feet set solid, crucified by rusty bolts and rails to the concrete wharves.

The rain had stopped but droplets still hung from the wire security fences, a glitter of water shook loose with each gust of wind. Chrissie pulled her coat tight, not just from the cold but also to cushion the memory. Childhood. Her grandfather. The rumble of trucks vibrating through her feet, the constant whistles and sirens of caution, the shouts and cheers of working men. It was the same in every port.

The picket in front of the main gates had been going all night. Portable generators chugged, tent canopies were tightened, digital sign boards reprogrammed with new messages: 'Safety first'. 'People not profits'. There were about forty men, some with drooping banners held loosely in tired hands, others with slogans stretched tight across t-shirts on strong chests and pot bellies alike. Chrissie had been there for about an hour, still and unnoticed off to the side, leaning against a car. She could see the anger as she watched the men, it wafted off them like steam.

Finally, she stood straight, took a slow deep breath, clenched her jaw and stepped into their midst.

They quickly jostled around, a hand pulled on her shoulder from behind and spun her around.

'You're with that right-wing lot. The fake news brigade,' he said as he yanked on her media ID tag. Outrage in his eyes. Spittle in her face.

Another tapped her notebook so hard it almost fell to the damp gravel but her fingers kept a thin grasp on the spiralbound pages. It was her red cross of neutrality. Her shield.

'How you going to twist this one, then?' the big mouth added. Chrissie pulled the notebook to her chest and took a step back then lifted her face to them.

'Why haven't you been down here before this?' A new voice.

'No celebrities or footy stars, that's why. Bloody workers don't rate! Just another story too boring for the likes of you.'

But it wasn't just another story. The wharves had once been part of Chrissie's life, her old life. She had been following the snippets of information about the picket from a distance; it was not her round, it was no one's round, *The Argus* had other priorities. But like these men, she knew this change would be their last. Ghost ships already roamed the oceans, automated ships with just a handful of crew. Ghost wharves were next.

Chrissie stood her ground among the men and did her job. She listened. Centuries of shared tradition between ships and men were at an end. The wharf was being automated, workers were no longer needed. The media, too, she knew, faced a godless future. Algorithms dictated assignments, traditional news judgement now optional.

The dispute had been going for almost six months. The news cycle had long moved on, but she had gone straight to the wharf on instinct this morning and slowly worked her way through the men and their need to be heard. Perhaps she had been drawn by the memories. Perhaps she had come to test her resolve to block out the past. Or maybe it was just a story that needed to be told.

'Here she is,' someone called as a grey four-wheel drive pulled up. The passenger door opened before it even came to a stop. Chrissie guessed who it was as the picketers sent up a round of cheers and whistles, moving forward in a good-hearted surge. Helen Carter, the maritime union's scrap-loving state boss. Chrissie had only seen photos and footage of her until now: shouting the odds at rallies, walking out of negotiations, slamming her fist at news conferences. She would stop at nothing for her members.

In person, Carter was more rumpled than her TV image. Her shirt threatened to burst its buttons as she leaned back to give her pants a much-needed hitch, a big mop of grey curls bounced around her face. Chrissie knew Carter's reputation. A ball breaker, a pub fighter. Hel on a bike. Hel the dyke. She had earned her passage through the union the hard way. At forty-two she was at the top of her game.

The men soon pointed Chrissie out and Carter hitched again and started to roll towards her.

'Hi, Helen. Chris O'Brian, *The Argus*.' She took the greeting up to the union boss. They had spoken on the phone just yesterday about the latest injury, a man's legs crushed.

'Gidday, nice to see you here.' Carter's hangdog face wrinkled upwards, her eyebrows offered a warm welcome. But then she pounced. 'I barely noticed your piece in the paper this morning. Thought you could have made more of it.' She tilted her head back. 'Dangerous shit going on down here, people's lives.' Her voice a coarse mixture of highs and lows.

Chrissie looked down. She had checked the story early in the morning, it had been slashed. The quotes from Carter deleted, the background to the dispute gone. Now it was just a handful of words at the bottom of a page, a few paragraphs on the website, a tweet to help meet her quota for the day.

'I'm sorry. No space. But this is good timing.' Chrissie stepped closer. The noise around her was ramping up, the men were cheering as the morning trucks started to rumble through the wharf gates. Her palms started to itch. 'I'm keen to do something in-depth about the docks. A behind-the-scenes piece.' Carter maintained a smile but it came with a pause. *She wants an out.* 'I'm happy to be steered by you,' Chrissie added. 'What do you think are the issues for a modern workforce? How many generations have you still got working here?' Chrissie switched to automatic, giving COQ, as her old boss would say. Control. Opinion. Question. Let them think they're in control. Encourage an opinion. End on a question.

A truck horn blasted extra loud but it was a sudden percussion of air brakes that forced Chrissie's hands over her ears. *Breathe.*

The picketers lifted their clicker rattles high in the air and spun them loudly in response. Panic rising. Chants: 'Safety first. Safety first.' She shook her head but it only made the sounds fade in and out on a sickening wave.

'Okay, why not?' Carter finally replied. 'Yeah, let's do that . . . you all right?'

Chrissie fanned herself with her notebook. *Got to get out of here.*

'Tail end of a flu.' She feigned a cough. 'I'll be in touch, thanks. I'm late and I'm busting.' She indicated towards the toilet block at the tram depot and rushed off. She felt Carter's eyes on her but didn't turn back.

Safely away, now she walked across the ancient metal pedestrian bridge that linked the sea to the city, high above the rail lines. Chrissie gave a last look back at the wharves and the solid grey clouds, *stratus*, before she was swallowed by the deep skyless valleys of the city's office towers.

CHAPTER 2

'O'Brian! What the hell's going on with this wharf piece? Supposed to be a news story, not a bloody novel. Cut it back. O'Brian!'

Chrissie jumped up and glared across the newsroom. Dare she argue back to the news director, again? She walked towards him, sidestepping waste paper bins and navigating crowded desks, all eyes on her. She swallowed, lifted her chin.

'Harry, it's worth the space. The wharf's hot news. Everyone's got a piece of this story, the strike, the city, big business. Whole place is a fire cracker.'

'Forget it.' He held up his hand to silence her, a glimmer of white where a wedding ring once was. 'It's me who decides. You've got 170 words. Get rid of the fluff.'

Chrissie threw her hands up and turned back. *A short show tonight, folks*, she thought as the heads popped back down behind their partitions. They had become used to her being hauled over the coals; they probably even looked forward to it.

She gave her colleague James a look and slammed her hand across the desk as she sank hard on her chair.

'Why do you bother?' James asked quietly. 'How many times, Chrissie? Play by Harry's rules or end up in the dog house.'

'Woof, woof!'

He was right of course. She stared at the screen, her hands curled and ready on the keyboard but unable to type. Harry's dismissal had got to her. She flicked back and forth through her notebook.

The newsroom was loud. People, desks, tables and partitions were jammed into every spot. Journos, subs, producers, editors, assistants, they all worked on top of each other. Televisions blazed different channels on every wall, radio stations were monitored and constantly tuned in and out, phones rang nonstop.

The noise didn't usually bother Chrissie but tonight she couldn't shut it out. She shook her head to clear her thoughts but it only heightened her senses. Voices grew shriller while the thumping bass of the newsroom amped up even more. Two people argued at a sub's desk, the chief of staff shouted for copy, a mobile phone rang, over and over, the same irritating tune. And all the time Harry prowled.

'Do you want me to do it?' James broke her thoughts. 'I'll cut it for you.'

She smiled. Her one friend since she'd arrived at *The Argus* a year ago. Despite being from an old Melbourne family, a toff slumming it with the ordinary folk, he seemed genuine. He'd latched on to Chrissie from day one, god knew why. Perhaps the stray dog syndrome. He'd thrown her a lifeline amid a storm of resentment. A year later, he still shielded her from some of it. He invited her to drinks when the others didn't. He put her forward to work on joint projects. He even signed her name on farewell and baby cards when no one passed her the envelope.

In turn, Chrissie toughened him up. Showed him how to go in for difficult questions, how to hit a story hard and run with it. James was already a good journo but he was too polite. He had the best contacts in the city, 'access all areas', but his natural instinct was to politely step back.

'Nah, I'm okay. Just need to shake Harry off. His pacing is doing my head in. Cup of tea, that'll fix it.'

'Hey, you're in Melbourne now, remember? Coffee capital of the world,' James called after her.

Coffee was the last thing she needed for her jangled nerves, now or ever. Chrissie walked straight past the kitchen and into the bathroom. She locked one of the cubicles and leaned against the grey laminate. She stared at the hook on the back of the door, anything to avoid another inspection of the grubby walls and the cracked lino. Even in here the noise buzzed in her ears. Her skin itched. Sometimes her medication made her extra sensitive, on edge. But so too did Harry. The meds she could tinker with, adjust her dose to slow things down. Harry was constant. There was no turning him down.

He'd resented her being hired at a time when he had to let other staff go. He'd said as much on her first day, a withering put-down loud enough for everyone to overhear.

Chrissie unlocked the cubicle and stood over the basin. She splashed cold water over her face, two hands working to cup it over her nose and mouth, her eyes, her forehead, as she held her breath for as long as possible. She looked into the mottled mirror. Dark shoulder-length hair plastered around her neck as water dripped inside her collar. People had told her that she had a strong face, beautiful even, but she could never see it. Intense blue eyes framed by thick black lashes and ruffled eyebrows, despite her almost thirty years her nose still had the evidence of a childhood sprinkled with freckles. She saw only ugly in the cracked reflection. The fluorescent light hollowed her cheeks and greyed her pallor. Fractured, inside and out.

She practised in the mirror to set her mouth to a determined grin. 'Stuff him!' she said to the reflection, then walked back to the newsroom. She dropped a teabag in a mug, filling it from the boiling tap. What was this stuff? 'Essence of tea'. Not even real tea anymore. When she neared the main news desk she slowed her walk and absently dunked the teabag as she passed Harry. *That'll piss him off.*

Chrissie had thrown herself into work that morning and as usual she ran too hard. The stories became too important. She was always determined to outdo her rivals. Different angles, extra comments, paint a bigger picture. She had just one speed at work, full throttle. Now, in this new job, she had to work even harder to prove herself. Tonight, with another story spitefully rejected, she hated that she cared so much. It's just a job; just another story, she chided herself as she deleted line after line of type.

CHAPTER 3

'Who's for a drink? Chrissie, you finished?' James flashed his best grin. Mid-thirties, he still had his twelve-year-old face, cheeky and privileged, unlined by the hardship that wealth had allowed him to avoid. James was a 'lucky' journo, Chrissie had realised soon after arriving at *The Argus*. He was good, but his success had been from luck more than skill. He often had trouble with his social filter. He could be side-tracked to think that someone was untrustworthy because they lacked his social niceties, the polite practices that were ingrained in him.

Chrissie sometimes wondered why he even wanted to be a journalist. The pay was lousy and the kudos was dubious, yet silver-tails had always been drawn to the job. The first time Chrissie had met James, she thought he looked out of place in the newsroom. He didn't move quite fast enough; wasn't hungry enough.

His appearance, too, said it all, even though he tried to keep it low key. His handmade shoes and no-label clothes stood out, even his watch, a see-through Hublot, a brand Chrissie had only seen in glossy magazines. A timepiece, he called it.

'A present from my fiancée,' he had explained when Chrissie first eyed the watch. 'And yes, I know, she could have bought a small Pacific island for the same price.' To entertain her, he had slipped the watch off and had made Chrissie try it on. They had laughed about it ever since. It had become a running joke and now he regularly turned and asked if she wanted to know the time, shaking his 'nude' Hublot at her.

At first Chrissie was wary; most at *The Argus* had given her a frosty welcome. But James was easy to like, unconventional in a conservative way. He made her laugh. Unlike Chrissie, he wasn't competitive: another reason she liked him. And he was popular, despite his background or maybe because of it. He was the office toff. The 'thar thar thar' Melbourne Club footy supporter. And importantly, for Chrissie, he knew how to handle Harry.

'Harry's a good man in a bad way. It could happen to any of us,' he had said once after Harry had doled out another public dressing-down. His comment cemented her liking for him. Not because it excused Harry but unbeknown to James the description could just as easily apply to her. Yet as the months went by she realised James was too forgiving, in both his assessment of Harry and his approach to stories. His upbringing had meant a life of open doors. In turn, he didn't know how to make trouble. He avoided controversy. Not a good trait for a journalist, Chrissie decided. He preferred the easy route.

But somehow, she appeared to be James's project. He refused

to accept her excuses for not having a drink after work. Introduced her to his contacts. Insisted on bringing her treats from his favourite bakery for lunch or an afternoon snack. He was like a giant golden Labrador, Chrissie thought, always bounding up to her with a big smile.

Despite the open offer it was just the two of them that headed off for a drink tonight. Chrissie pretended not to notice sideways looks as they left. Rumours of more redundancies had started up again and so had the resentment towards her.

They walked a few blocks, their coats buttoned but not so cold as to make them hurry. The weather had started to turn as the last of Melbourne's winter retreated. New leaves had already sprouted on the plane trees. Chrissie kept up with James's long stride. Her hands pushed deep into her pockets, head tilted down, she was used to walking fast.

A handful of people were in the bar. It was a bit swankier than their usual watering hole. Gina, James's fiancée, was already at a table sipping a pale-yellow wine. She smiled and stood to give them both a hug. Chrissie reluctantly accepted Gina's huggy ways.

Most of Panama's regulars were corporate types, lawyers like Gina, accountants, traders. Unlike Chrissie in her black pants, white t-shirt and black blazer, not quite a suit, Gina fitted in perfectly with her smart tailoring.

They made a good-looking couple, Chrissie thought. Like James, Gina had tucked Chrissie into her life quickly and easily, even though Chrissie preferred to keep her distance. They would feel betrayed if they ever found out about her.

Chrissie started to talk about Harry but Gina skilfully interrupted.

'You know he's a jerk. I know he's a jerk. So please, let's have a fucking jerk-free night,' Gina said. Her Californian accent was still a novelty to Chrissie. Gina's swearing didn't fit in with her sweet-mouthed image and she expertly rationed it for maximum impact.

They chatted easily as they filled Chrissie in on their oddball families. Gina's parents were arriving within weeks for their wedding, along with a bevy of other crazy US relatives. James's home-grown Toorak pedigree had been exaggerated over the years to become Melbourne elite. Both of their backgrounds were a dramatic contrast to Chrissie's puddle-splashing rural New Zealand childhood.

Just as the three were about to call it quits, the doors pushed open and Harry bowled in with one of the night editors. His mean walk, straight to the bar, signalled his sour mood.

Chrissie immediately turned her back and slunk lower in her seat.

'I know how this is going to end,' she said and started to gather her things.

James had seen how this had played out before too and nodded. But Gina's striking looks always grabbed people's attention, including Harry's now as he scanned their table.

'Hey James,' Harry guffawed, 'perhaps you'd like to introduce me to your blonde friend here?' He put a clumsy hand on Gina's shoulder.

James stood instantly. 'Harry, this is Gina, my fiancée. You've met before, actually.'

Gina blasted him with her brightest smile as she expertly brushed his hand away.

'I hope you're feeling better next time we meet,' she said to Harry in her slow lilt and began ushering Chrissie away from the table.

'Come on, Harry, you're out of line,' Chrissie heard James say and she risked a look backwards. 'I mean with Chrissie too. It's getting out of hand –'

'James, you think you know everything, but you don't know shit!'

Harry slammed his hand on the table. The empty glasses jumped and thudded.

'You don't know *shit*,' he repeated, pointing his finger in James's face. Then he turned and stormed back to the bar.

CHAPTER 4

The trip home that night passed in a blur of graffiti until Chrissie got off at North Richmond station, oblivious to the seedy surroundings.

When she'd first moved in, she hadn't realised how deep the problems in the area were but the cheap rent and the quick commute to *The Argus* were drawcards. Close enough even to walk through the clean calm streets of East Melbourne, passing the suburb's historic iron lace facades and balconies, every front garden a manicured treat. Then across the grand English-style parks that breathed clean air into the city and buffered the city from the inner east. The contrast between the cramped threat-filled pockets of Richmond and the genteel wealth of East Melbourne always made her pause.

Now, walking through the neon and noise of Victoria Street and into the alleys, the addicts, dirty streets and busted lights meant nothing to her. She'd stopped thinking about it. A year on, she knew it was no accident she'd ended up in Richmond. It was another way to take risks with her life. Instead of trying to creep timid and unseen through the streets, she had taught herself to walk without fear.

But she had learned the hard way. At first the creeps just watched, tried to freak her out. They probably couldn't believe their luck, a weak fool in the wrong pace. They snapped the thin handle of her computer case in a snatch-and-run the first time. The next time they grabbed her leather jacket, slung over her arm.

During the first real mugging she knew she had to fight. When someone pulled her satchel, she refused to let go. Chrissie didn't scream or shout, she just held on in a speechless tug of war. He won, of course. She was pulled along the street until she fell on her knees, but, still, he had to turn and kick her to make her finally let go. Her defiance must have struck him equally as hard. Instead of running off with the bag, he tipped its contents out on the bluestones. Chrissie, still brazen, grabbed her wallet and threw it in his face.

'Take it, you fuck,' she shouted, scrambling around for scattered keys and phone and stuffing them back in the satchel. The rest she could live without. He looked like he was coming down. He'd be agitated, in need of another hit, she thought. But he was amused. He grinned with a near-toothless mouth as he took the money and threw the empty wallet back in her face, just as hard. He walked off almost cocky.

Chrissie had seen him several times since and he'd seen her. He would come out of a shop doorway or step from one of the lanes. Often, he was with a woman. After months of traipsing

Victoria Street, he realised Chrissie was one of them. Different but accepted. She too learned to accept him. If he passed too close, his bad breath was overpowering, he only breathed through his mouth. His clothes filthy from constant wear. Every cent spent on crystal, or E, or scag. But it was the woman who always caught Chrissie's eye. Her vulnerability showed in every cringing body movement. Her bones threatened to poke through her wrists, she was so thin. Greasy blonde hair plastered to her head.

Instead of shying away from her, Chrissie slipped her whatever money she had. On a good day, the woman – Demi, she would later learn – would nod an unspoken truce. On her hard days, she would stand silent and desperate knowing, now, that Chrissie would volunteer some money.

Despite the tough neighbourhood, Chrissie's flat was her haven. The Victorian house had long been divided into four apartments, two up, two down. The big front hall, once the home's grand entrance, was now crammed with a row of aluminium letterboxes constantly leaking unclaimed mail and advertising flyers. Still, the black and white marble tiles made a fine statement as they led to the timber staircase which curved up to the units above, including Chrissie's flat. Just two huge rooms, the lounge with its kitchenette and the bedroom, plus a small hall and a bathroom, but the high ceiling meant she never felt trapped.

Chrissie tried to shrug off the day, the wharf visit, the story she was later assigned to about a private school principal sacked for making racist comments. But her thoughts turned to her fight with Harry. *Another failure.* Her suggestion to take on the wharf as a news round had also been brushed off, instead she was asked to write a column of briefs from leftover stories. A junior intern's job.

She poured a glass of wine and walked around tidying, straightening, wiping. She poured a new glass. Rinsed a few dishes.

Harry the bastard. Her thoughts jumped. She wiped the small table and sorted the empty bottles. And all those other bastards at work. After a year, a year of trying, why wasn't she accepted? She rinsed the cloth, rinsed it again. Another glass of wine. It was Harry's fault; he deliberately made it difficult to fit in.

'Listen, I've lost good people, people who should have kept their jobs. I didn't agree with you being hired,' he'd told her on that first day.

He picked on minor issues with her copy, assigned her the shittiest jobs and made no secret that he wanted her gone. He ruled the newsroom through fear. No one wanted to be on his bad side even when he was wrong.

Chrissie stared at the white plastic bottles on the shelf above the kitchen bench. She reached for one, tossed it in the air a couple of times then twisted the lid off.

She swallowed one, two, three pills between bites of an apple and deep mouthfuls of wine. Wine, dine and doze, she thought. Harry would be delighted if she spat the dummy and just walked out. Or took another way out.

In the bathroom now, she adjusted the towels on the rail, pulled the sleeve of her jumper and gave the mirror a quick polish. The tiles were cold on her feet, the fluorescent light above the cabinet fizzed and hissed angrily at her. She took another two tablets from a new bottle. She flicked the light off and slid the plug into the bath.

Finally relaxed. Warm, safe, sleepy. Chrissie nestled further down into the water. The dim light from the hall gave out a soft glow. The pills would kick in soon. She soothed herself. Closed her eyes. Let the darkness fill her mind. It flowed gently into every space. Back to black. She began to float as she welcomed the creeping loss of consciousness. *How long would it take?*

But then the knife-sharp panic was back. *Fight it.* Small white explosions were calling her back. *Fight it.* Her eardrums threatened to burst. Pain ripped across her chest and her body, a power of its own, forced her head out of the water. Forced her to sit up. Forced her to gasp a desperate ragged breath, followed by another and another. Forced her to keep living.

She sat in the cooling bath and hugged her knees, her mind a familiar peaceful wooze. Just seconds from oblivion. *Had Dave felt that peace?*

Chrissie stepped out of the bath. Water dripped over the tiles. There hadn't been any need for a bathmat because she wasn't supposed to be getting out. Now she wrapped herself in a towel and padded across the hall.

Here again, she thought, as she collapsed on the bed and stared at the ceiling. Its centre rosette a white swirl of flowers and leaves. She pulled up her quilt, a rare keepsake, worn with the years, and her neediness, its soft fabrics easing her raw hands. Finally, she rolled towards the bedside cupboard and reached far in the back for her timer: 33 days, 1 hour, 17 minutes. She stared numbly for a few more minutes. Tears slid as she gently pressed the reset button to zero and pushed the clock back in its hiding place. It had been thirty-three days, one hour and seventeen minutes since the last attempt.

CHAPTER 5

The noise was like a truck in reverse. *Beep beep beep*. Chrissie's hand slapped the top of the bedside cupboard until she found the phone and turned off the alarm: 9 am. She groaned. The sun squeezed a narrow slant across the room and onto her bed. Last night's beige towel in a damp heap on the floor.

Get up. Get dressed. Go to work.

Black pants, boots, white t-shirt, leather jacket; she was still too groggy to know if it was hot or cold. Her body temperature swayed from one to the other.

It looked like a warm late winter day but she had learned to over-prepare in Melbourne. A hot morning could have you shivering by midday. A winter's day could quickly turn on a stifling afternoon. She stuffed her phone, key and wallet into her satchel and grabbed a scarf, avoiding the mirror as she left.

—

Chrissie felt the rush of adrenalin every time she arrived on the newsroom floor but the mornings were her favourite. Not knowing what lay ahead each day was one of the best parts of the job. The mornings always crackled with the promise of a new story. *Another chance.* The *Argus* newsroom was a huge grey space. Desks, filing cabinets, sofas and broken office chairs spread haphazardly. Bits of dusty paper hung from ceiling ducts in attempts to modify the failing air conditioning. Windows were blocked by slimline venetian blinds, set at odd angles, their cords tangled and locked in place long ago. Even the daily conference room, once the lavish inner sanctum with its closed-door debates and whispered confidential sources, was now just a large bench in the middle of the floor. No privacy. Everyone forced to stand to make sure they didn't linger.

By late morning the floor was alive, phones rang, televisions danced and flickered, computers cranked up, emails checked. The smell of coffee overpowered the permanent stale whiff of the old place. The historic corner building on Elizabeth Street had long seen better days but it had been home to the paper since the 1920s. The Chicago-esque and Beaux Arts architecture was a crazy rich mix of history and styles just like its occupants and the newspaper's fortunes over its 180 years.

'O'Brian.' Today's chief of staff, Sam, stopped briefly mid-stride as Chrissie cleared a spot on her crowded desk. Small and pointy Sam was whippet-like, constantly racing around the newsroom corralling reporters and feeding storylines. 'I've got you down for a 10.30. US ambassador, the tech agreement follow-up.'

Another follow-up. The tech agreement was a patsy handout from the government. No one was interested in real stories anymore, journalists were being used as mouthpieces for the powerful.

'Grab a photog and head off. Not much in it, sorry, meat and potatoes, caption story.' Sam handed her the details and was off again, racing towards the conference table.

The other section heads scrambled to print off their news lists. At 10 am on the dot, Harry rose from his desk and strode, ramrod straight, to the head of the conference table. Chrissie watched as he began conducting the meeting ahead of the editor's arrival. On his approach, the section heads stood more upright, held their news lists higher or put their heads down and wrote unnecessary notes to avoid eye contact.

Chrissie pulled the keyboard towards her, deflated by the assignment, and searched up the original story. The main angle, a new digital security agreement, had already been splashed on the front page. *The Argus* had been given the drop two days ago. In return, few questions were asked and the story ran unchallenged – and that's how the political galleries worked. They took their turn. Those who missed out this time were forced to do low profile follow-ups, so as not to trumpet that they had been beaten to the punch. Or, rarely, they would go extra hard, raising all the problems and issues with the deal that had gone unchallenged in the drop story. But that was a risky move. If they went too hard, they might not get their turn for an exclusive next time around. Governments and bureaucrats now had more spin doctors than the media had journalists. Chrissie's job this morning was for barely a hundred words, mainly to remind readers that *The Argus* had already scooped the rest of the news pack.

In New Zealand, Chrissie had won attention for several stories early in her career. There had been the exposé of a rugby club scam. That most sacred of male sports. She had worked hard to break the code of silence to reveal false invoices for supplies that were never delivered. She'd followed up with a feature about teenage motherhood, interviewing the now teenage children and fledgling adults of those young mothers. Their stories, one generation on, were compelling. Their tough start in life had taken them in many directions. It had won Chrissie attention, even award nominations.

None of that success, however, had translated to Australia. Most of the staff thought Chrissie had been shuffled out of her old job in New Zealand quick-smart because of an affair with someone high up and then hired as a favour. How else did she get hired when others were being fired?

Chrissie now felt she was being cut out of the good stories. Assigned to cover middle page fillers, vox pops of people on the street, follow-ups. 'She shouldn't get too cosy, her sugar daddy won't save her here,' she had overheard one of the subeditors sneering to Neil from the business section not long after she arrived. But then she had been surprised to hear Lou, the glam young fashion editor, shutting down their sniggers.

'Typical sexist comment,' Lou had bristled back as Chrissie stood unseen at the vending machine.

'Only joking, Lou,' she heard Neil say. Chrissie imagined his slow thin smile. 'What's wrong, can't you take a joke?'

'Fuck off. That fake joke crap doesn't hide you,' Lou replied before Chrissie had heard her heels clack their way across the tiled floor.

Even James had once awkwardly mentioned the rumour, in a bumbling, polite way.

She had invited James and Gina for dinner. A phone promise to her dad to try harder to fit in. But Chrissie had drunk too much before they arrived. Her lamb shanks had been dry but the mashed potato was a winner, heaped with butter and salt. They had laughed their way through the food and more wine.

Chrissie had just smiled at Gina's sharp elbow that night after James's awkward attempt to tell her about the rumour. But she hadn't corrected him. She hadn't corrected anyone.

One part of the rumour was true. She had been hired as a favour.

And if her colleagues discovered the truth they would hate her as much as those back home.

Anyone who had searched Chrissie's name on the internet would have found only the public, professional version of her life. She had always used her maiden name for work, O'Brian. Her journalism career and achievements were well documented. It would take small-town knowledge to connect her married name to what had happened in New Zealand. The court records. The snippets in her local paper. The shame.

Despite her difficulties fitting in at *The Argus*, she couldn't resign. She loved her job. Her sense of justice and truth had been instinctive from an early age and her good instincts made her a natural journalist. The excitement of the chase, the sniff of a story, she later found, was an addictive bonus. Journalism was not just a link to the past; it was her only way forward.

CHAPTER 6

Chrissie took the slow way home that night, walking almost the full length of Victoria Street, past the noisy bars and restaurants. Bursts of music and sweet and spicy fried food smells surged onto the footpath with every open door. Orange-roasted ducks hung pride of place in front windows, gaudy signs flashed restaurant names, always double-barrelled: Vinh Vinh, Thy Thy. A newcomer, The Africcane, yellow, red, orange. New colours for the street. She dodged the last of the daytime shop owners as they packed up their footpath displays, winding back their awnings and pulling down roller doors. They were handing over the street to the nightlife. Chrissie shunned the brightly lit glass-fronted cafés and kept her head down past the gym despite her boxing gear stuffed in her satchel. If she missed a morning run or her waking darkness was too heavy, she would take herself to the gym at night, but tonight she had other plans.

Like most days, Chrissie had thrown herself into work and as usual she'd overdone it. She was trying too hard to prove her worth. To lose herself in her work. The unscheduled trip to the wharf yesterday; her pushy questions at the cyber press conference today.

'Ambassador, how many data breaches did the US government detect last year?'

The cyber security agreement was a political sore point. Australia had been reluctant to sign because the US had insisted it also include expanding their desert satellite bases. Chrissie had manoeuvred herself to the front of the small embassy meeting room to get the Australian minister's attention but he'd quickly sidestepped her questions and signalled the meeting was over.

Now, instead of a workout, she pushed open the wooden door of the old corner pub with its dark green painted facade and small high windows. Built in the era when drinking was secret men's business. She had become a semi-regular, enough for most of the old people inside to know she drank to forget. She sensed they kept a watch and a worry over her, she felt their sideways glances and turned heads when she left. But she never looked back.

A few hours later, not for the first time, she fumbled with her front door, the key kept turning in air as it refused to find the hole.

The door burst open to reveal a skater boy in ripped jeans and a grunge band t-shirt.

'Keys still not working, hey?' He was almost laughing at her.

'Very funny, Mike.' Chrissie stumbled into the building.

'Hey lady, you fancy eating? I did a big batch of duck soup.'

Chrissie shook her head, but Mike was already slipping his arm through hers and directing her towards his door. 'Come on. Not taking no for an answer.'

The first time Mike had let her in, Chrissie had clocked his clothes and pinned him as a student or a musician. Another misfit like her with something to hide.

Now, however, she knew she was wrong on several counts. Not a musician but a computer nerd and at least ten years older than his wardrobe. He had fixed her modem one night after she complained about the slow internet. Afterwards, he invited himself to stay for a drink. Since then he had also linked her phone to her laptop and set up a network between her laptop and her desktop at *The Argus*. It allowed Chrissie to work long into the night. Those times, too, he had helped himself to the fridge and her sofa.

His unit was identical to Chrissie's and directly below. His main room was dominated by three mismatched desks, pushed against a wall. A big squishy sofa and three wooden stools took up the rest of the room, as well as a small dining table in the big bay window at the front. The place often smelled like an old wardrobe full of clothes and shoes but tonight the soup filled all her senses. As always, the desks drew Chrissie's attention, they were laden with computers, screens and gadgets. Bleeping boxes, lights – green, amber, white. Cords running everywhere. A big whiteboard above had equations all over it.

'What are you up to this time? Looks like space command.' She nodded to the equipment.

'I'm running a diag.'

Chrissie screwed her face up.

'You heard about those recent lightning strikes?' Mike tried again. She shook her head.

'Blitzes. Big data breaches.' Mike rolled his eyes. 'Security companies run them. Get people like me to find a crack, get through the walls. Big fat bonus each time.'

'How do you know all this hacking stuff anyway?' Chrissie picked up what looked like a fluffy toy panda. It turned out to be a computer speaker.

'I'm no hacker! I'm very precise. I fix things, find stuff, retrievals mostly.' Chrissie pulled over a low stool and sat down. As he tried to explain, it was like watching a comic book of faces. He'd make a terrible liar, Chrissie thought, and she liked him even more. He ladled out the steamy soup and Chrissie felt her mouth water. 'Here, try this, bet you've never had it before. Polish.'

Chrissie stared around the room. A family portrait from the early 90s – the pink and brown smudged studio backdrop a time-capsule giveaway. The mum, part Vietnamese from what Mike had told her, black hair teased high and wide, tucked behind her ears. Two older kids behind and a baby, Mike, propped on her lap. The dad, a tough guy Polish immigrant.

'What are you doing in this dive then if you're such a hot shot? Wouldn't hurt you to open a window every now and then.' She shifted on the wooden stool, rubbed her nose, then blew on her porcelain spoon.

'Hey, what about beating around the bush? Don't they teach journalists social niceties?'

Chrissie smiled but regretted her bluntness.

'Man, this is beautiful.' She swallowed hungrily. 'Thank you.'

It was the first thing she'd eaten today, she realised.

'I don't need money,' Mike continued. 'I've got it when I want it but I don't need it.' He took Chrissie's bowl and ladled in more soup. 'Anyway, what did you do today, Miss Fancy Pants Journalist?'

'Ah, well, something up your alley, I think. What do you know about that new cyber security agreement? Bit controversial.'

'Course. But it's bullshit, like all of them.'

'Do you think that someone can actually prevent a security breach, like one hundred per cent, guaranteed?'

'Nup!' Mike shot straight back. 'Temporarily maybe but not for long. That's how I earn my millions,' he said with a wave around the bare apartment.

'I was at this presser today, the signing with the US ambassador.' Chrissie finally slowed down with her soup, savouring the tastes.

'I'd like to get a look at that agreement. More about another land grab, than a cyber deal,' Mike cut in. 'Ah, nah, second thoughts, it would be pure rubbish. Nobody's ever going to know what's really going on. Doesn't matter anyway. The White House doesn't rule shit anymore. It's the tech giants who call the shots these days, they run the governments.'

A loud meow suddenly crept under Mike's front door. Chrissie quickly sat up and twisted around.

'That must be Skinny,' she said.

'Skinny? Is that what you're calling it?' Mike got up and opened the door and a grey cat slowly stretched its way into the room. Tail high, eyes narrowing when he saw Chrissie. Neither of them knew who owned the cat but it visited both of their apartments.

'It's not skinny. Like, it's not starved,' Mike said. 'That's how it's meant to be. Burmese or Persian or something. An aristocat – ha, get it? Exotic, just like me. I'm a Polish-Asian superstar, he's Asian aristocracy.'

CHAPTER 7

Chrissie took a deep breath; the gauntlet, as it was known, seemed extra crowded this morning. She pushed both hands deep in her jacket pockets. Head down, against the cold, she sidestepped through the throng of angry and desperate people at the entrance to the newspaper.

'Please, can you take my flyer? The police have stopped –'

'In the name of God and Christ Jesus, they will judge the living and the dead!'

'You've got to do something, they've sent us bankrupt and –'

The steps outside the big corner double doors of the paper were a popular spot for people to wait. They had usually already been ejected by front desk security but they hung around. Holding their signs. Folders of photographs. Old clippings. Trying to be seen or heard. Their grievances would not let them rest.

Chrissie hadn't become used to the gauntlet yet. She still had to concentrate to avoid eye contact, not like the other journos who did it automatically each day. Today, however, the small group was a sharp reminder of how few stories were being told. Instead of ignoring them, she slowed, took some handouts; she would read them later, she indicated with a nod and a quick glance, but she didn't stop to talk or look in their eyes.

—

'You're in luck today, O'Brian, your wish came true.' Sam the whippet was back in front of her desk.

Chrissie quickly shoved the notes she had taken from the gauntlet into her pocket.

'Harry wants you to take another look at the docks,' he said. Chrissie couldn't help but smile. Harry must have reconsidered her suggestion. *At last a decent investigation.*

'They've got some hot shot female crane operator,' Sam said, 'only one in the country. It will make a nice profile piece, keep our women readers happy.'

Chrissie slumped into her chair. The last thing she wanted was to do a puff piece about the wharf.

'Right up your alley,' Sam continued. 'And you can thank your desk buddy here too,' he nodded as James arrived.

'Oh crikes, Chrissie,' James said as Sam walked off. He off-loaded his bag and scooted his chair towards her. 'I know you hate those profiles. Just thought with the cuts to your wharf piece the other day, well, you know . . .'

Chrissie shook her head. 'They know too well that's not the sort of story I want to do.' She watched Sam walk back to the news desk then motioned towards Harry. 'Bet it was his idea. He's been trying to get rid of me since day one, just because he didn't have a say when I was hired.'

'Harry doesn't like anyone, it's not personal, you have to earn your stripes first with him,' James turned to his screen. But Chrissie's gut told her otherwise.

'Yeah, well, this woman in a man's world crap. It's not a friggin' man's world, nothing's a *man's* world anymore.' Chrissie glared across the newsroom at the news director. 'I've never met a woman who wants to be interviewed like that.'

—

Masina Weber immediately caught Chrissie's eye as she was escorted across the wharf's cracked and lined concrete forecourt. Black hair in a single long plait, like a ship's rope. Tall and strong. But after their introduction, 'Call me Mas,' the crane driver had hung her head, took a step back. Shy, Chrissie recognised and mirrored her body language.

'It looks high up there. But I'm in your hands,' Chrissie said as the small group, the two women and two company minders, walked towards a row of giant yellow metal giraffes.

'Top's about seventy metres, some are one hundred and twenty, one hundred and forty even.' Mas hid her wide brown Polynesian eyes. But Chrissie had heard the pride in her voice.

'What sort of training do you need for one of those cranes?' Chrissie kept her talking.

'It's called a portainer. I've got tickets up to here.' Mas lifted her hand to her forehead with a laugh then looked down again, shoved both hands in the pockets of her yellow vest. 'I'm no one special.' She scuffed a boot out in front of her as they waited at the bottom of the metal stairwell for the others. 'There's been other female operators, US, couple in Amsterdam, but think I'm the only one here.'

No one special. Chrissie had heard it often, women playing down their ability to help them fit in with the men; not too smart, avoid being a target.

'I'm pretty sure you are special,' Chrissie said quietly. Mas looked up, a big grin spread across her face.

—

How much higher? Chrissie's knees hurt – too many years crammed under cheap desks. The front of her thighs burned with each step. The force of the wind had increased, their safety vests filling and billowing with the cold air as they climbed the metal stairwell. The higher they got, the whistles and shouts from below faded. She stopped, tilted back her safety helmet, the strap loose under her chin, escaped hair blowing across her face. She looked up past Mas to the endless crisscross of steps still to go. The woman ahead of her now looked almost identical to their two male chaperones in the narrow metal stairwell. Only her long plait differentiated her among the bulky blue cotton overalls, identical vests and jackets. Matching hard hats, orange, with a large blue letter G. Grange Industries. The big multinational terminal operator was transforming wharves around the world. It also had the worst safety record in the country.

Chrissie leaned out over the railing. Unafraid, willing to take risks, push boundaries. An eerie quiet settled around them as the clanging of their footsteps stopped briefly. The two company minders were catching their breath. Mas hopped from foot to foot but Chrissie was grateful for the pause. She was eye-level with a hulking stack of containers balanced on an impossibly small ship opposite. A patchwork of red, blue and grey corrugated boxes, their secrets stencilled in code on their salty skin. Chrissie took the next step and pulled herself along by the handrail, cold and smooth on her rough palms. The stairs shuddered again with their climb, back and forth up the giant crane's leg. Mas ahead, her thick black soles and turned-up hems setting the tempo, step by step. Mas had done this climb many times before. 'Crane fit,' one of the company chaperones had said admiringly, as they had rested on the stairwell. All the new automated portainers would have lifts, Mas told her with a shake of her head, but they were for maintenance crews only, as no operators would be needed. Finally, at the top, they gathered their breath. It had remained a cold drizzly morning, thunderous skies. *Nimbostratus.* One of her favourite formations. The wind blew the clouds straight at them, a south-wester, hard and steady. Chrissie looked straight at the source, a thin dark horizon line squeezed flat between a big angry sky and a choppy blue sea.

Mas snapped Chrissie's safety rope to the walkway, while the men remained on the top landing, and led her to the control box. Through the glass floor, Mas lined up her target. A dark blue container on the back of a toy truck far below. Using the levers and buttons, she clamped and lifted it. Heavy from its own weight, the container hung steady on long rope wires as it whirred up towards them, beneath their feet. With a jolt the cabin flew through the air attached to a rail under the big boom arm, the giraffe neck, which had been lowered horizontally, to hover above the ship. The container flew along beneath them held by the wires. A sudden stop and Mas whirred the container down into its allocated slot on the ship and the cabin with its two women occupants flew backwards to land again.

'I couldn't do your job,' Chrissie said after a few more lifts, looking around the glass cabin. 'Isn't it sort of claustrophobic crammed in here, even if we're almost in the sky?'

'Never thought of it like that, but yeah.' Mas gave her a wide grin. 'Just another glass ceiling, eh?' She tilted her head towards the men. Chrissie laughed out loud, for the first time in weeks.

'I'm sorry about this profile piece,' Chrissie said quietly as they clambered out of the control box. She leaned closer as Mas hitched them to the safety rail again. 'I know Grange probably wants a puff piece but I'd love to include it as part of a bigger story about the wharves and all the changes, new workforce.'

Mas's eyes dropped, her shoulders rolled forward.

Chrissie pushed. 'Maybe we can catch up away from these guys?' She swivelled her eyes to indicate the company minders.

'Yeah, I'd like to but . . . tricky.' Mas looked at the huddled men, now also roped onto the walkway. 'I said I'd do this interview months ago, before . . . but, well, then I couldn't get out of it.' She almost whispered now, 'You know, it might look suspicious.'

Chrissie slipped a business card from her pocket and Mas buried it inside her bulky jacket. 'I'm leaving,' she said, almost under her breath, 'but no one can know.'

CHAPTER 8

The train home was almost empty, except for a group of girls who screeched at private jokes. Their noise travelled as a single soundwave down the carriage and straight into Chrissie's ears. High-pitched and irritating. Her breath started to come fast and shallow. The train was in the underground loop and her neck and shoulders tightened in the confined space. It was only when she felt the train start its gentle climb back above ground that she started to relax again.

On the lounge floor, propped at her coffee table, wine and microwaved pasta carbonara, Chrissie looked through her search results: Port of Melbourne, safety, Grange Industries, maritime – forty-seven hits from the newspaper's archives which she had downloaded onto a USB. Several times a year there had been an accident worth reporting in *The Argus*, which meant that there was probably twice that amount that nobody bothered with or had room to publish.

She switched to the internet and the Maritime Safety Bureau's website: in the previous two years there had been more than six hundred and fifty serious injuries and five deaths across the country. Bulk carriers, livestock transporters, massive roll-on, roll-off container vessels competed against new computerised equipment, fewer workers, dangerous cargo and a macho workforce. A recipe for disaster. The wharves had always been a dangerous place and progress had done little to change that.

The research showed that working on the docks was the most dangerous industry in the country, outstripping construction and even transport for the percentage of workers killed and injured. But the accidents at Grange seemed out of proportion. She went back over the numbers. About forty per cent of serious incidents had been at Grange, when it should have been only about twenty per cent based on workload. And Grange already had one fatality. Grange alone would account for almost the average of the whole country. Shocking, she thought, but a good hook to hang her investigation on. She was determined to broaden out Masina's profile piece to a more in-depth story.

She glanced at her phone, out of battery, she'd been too focused to notice. Plugged in now it showed one missed call and a message. Chrissie switched from the floor to the sofa to listen to the message. She would go to bed soon, her eyes were stinging from looking at her laptop screen.

'Chrissie, hi it's Mas, Masina.' Chrissie smiled to hear her voice so soon. There was a long pause but a steady hum of background noise sounded like Mas was in a noisy pub or restaurant. 'Um, from the wharf. I wanted to tell you . . . something's wrong . . . it's dangerous.' Chrissie sat upright. 'Can we catch up? It's confidential, right? No one can know. Call me, tomorrow? But not till late, they switched my shift.'

Mas could be the perfect insider, Chrissie thought, replaying the message as she quickly checked the news wires before going to bed, 2.15 am. Another suspected terrorist driver in London; peak-hour pedestrians injured on their way home. Midday in New York; stock market down sharply, more computerised sell orders. An earthquake off the coast of Peru; a tsunami watch spread west across the Pacific as the islands began to wake for a new day, as the sun crept towards New Zealand then Australia. *Get some sleep.*

She backed up her laptop and closed the lid. Her kitchen bench held two empty wine bottles; she'd hardly noticed drinking them. She smiled when she saw the furry grey circle curled on the kitchen chair.

'Hey, Mister Skinny.'

When she'd first moved into the unit, the cat had found his way inside her flat through the fire escape. Now Chrissie kept the small upstairs kitchen window locked open just wide enough for him to fit through. Despite what Mike said, she thought the cat still suited his name.

Skinny lifted his head, twitched his whiskers and tucked back down. Chrissie jotted a final list in her notebook:

GRANGE: CLASS ONE INCIDENTS
Hand amputation, Theo Podgornik
Multiple leg fractures, Owen Anderson
Partial paralysis from fall, Howard Bryant

C6 spinal crush, Michael Eastern

Burns, Daphne Weathering

Foot crushed, Darryl Pilker

Lower limb fractures, Peter Gregory

T7 fracture, Gerry Raymond

Knee fracture, Con Christoff

Multiple finger amputations, Peter Verner

And this week's accident: lower leg amputation, Joseph Turner.

DEATHS

Ivan Pinder – fall, drowning (two years ago)

And Hank Timmons – vehicle collision, 5 months ago (not yet in stats)

As she wrote the names, she thought about the survivors. She knew 'dead' was the easy part. It was the living who were left to suffer.

CHAPTER 9

Harry's voice boomed across the newsroom the next morning. 'Jesus wept! A total fuck-up.'

Chrissie and James both looked up to see him standing over Steve, one of the crime reporters.

'I've just had the lawyer on the phone; you had the wrong name on the court appearance. You were supposed to check everything. Big fat expensive mistake!' Harry jabbed with a pointed finger to reinforce each word.

'I'm sorry, I asked the intern to doublecheck, I had to rush to that bail hearing.' Steve stood, then hung his head. 'What do you want me to do? What's going to happen?'

'Churn that fucking intern out. Cheap labour, my arse. More bloody trouble than they're worth. How they think they can man a newsroom with kids, Jesus!' Harry stormed off.

Shouting and swearing was normal in newsrooms. Tension was always high, more so in recent years with all the cutbacks. People had to cope with 24-hour rolling deadlines, tweet quotas, Facebook posts, guest radio spots, video broadcasts, podcasts, digital publishing and then still meet the major print deadlines each night for the morning paper. But Harry was the loudest bully that Chrissie had worked with. Despite this, she knew most of the staff gave him leeway. They had known him in better times.

'Got to head off,' James said as he pushed his chair back, stretched and stood. 'A multi-car crash on the West Gate Bridge, morning traffic. A guy trapped. And, I'm – *ta-daa* – getting a lift in the Channel Two helicopter.' He puffed up his chest in mock importance unaware of Chrissie's reaction. 'It pays to have friends in high places, O'Brian, eh?' He disappeared across the newsroom.

A guy trapped. A guy trapped. The smell overwhelmed Chrissie. She rubbed her nose, trying to be rid of it. But the sour, sticky smell of blood spread into her lungs, followed by a waft of burning metal and the chemical foam of fire retardant. She scrabbled in her satchel for mints. Where the hell were they? *Don't breathe.* She tipped the contents of her satchel out onto the desk, until she found the tin and shakily flicked the lid open. She tossed two mints into her mouth and crunched through them. Then she took two more and sucked. They helped block out the smell and the taste and the memories. She carried them everywhere.

She could deal with the visions, the flashbacks, but her other senses remained raw, like bear traps the smells and sounds would jump out of nowhere, crush her throat and screech in her ears.

She sucked even harder on the mints. *Count,* she told herself as she looked around the newsroom, nobody was watching.

Her hands slipped under the desk. She pressed her thumbnails hard into each finger pad. Methodically. A constant rotation. *You're here and now. Feel the pain. One, two, three, four. This desk, this room. Here and now.*

—

Chrissie could never explain why she was driving that night. She'd had too much to drink. And besides, Dave always drove. There were many other hows and whys that she still didn't know. The explanations were locked away. No matter how desperate everyone was for her to remember, she couldn't. Instead she was left with patches and flashbacks, sounds and smells that triggered panic attacks. Always the crippling guilt.

According to the accident report, the driver of the milk tanker said Chrissie and the male passenger were looking at each other, laughing, as she drove through the intersection despite the stop sign. Then they disappeared under his bumper.

The force crushed Dave's legs and lower body against the console between their front seats. His chest smeared against her, his head bowed, slightly above her. Dave was dead. She didn't need to look. She knew. Instead she kept a robotic gaze on the yellow halo of a streetlight out her shattered side window. She sat in the driver's seat unable to speak or move, conscious the whole time, and covered in him.

The paramedics arrived within minutes but she stayed trapped in the car. His blood seeped over her, it didn't flow or pulse. She would never see his big smile again. Never feel his gentle arm rub. Never have his kiss. Chrissie sat in the wreckage, as everyone around her did their job. She nodded when asked to respond, but did not say a word. She remembered the flashing orange and red lights, the stream of cars that slowed. The faces of the drivers and passengers, open mouths and hands that quickly flew up in horror. But most of all she remembered the smells. Burning, petrol, metal, fear. Loud smells.

A man, a first responder in a dark jumpsuit, with a red rash across his cheeks, crouched beside the driver's door and talked to Chrissie through the empty window. He had a whiff of deodorant about him, fresh and spicy. They had removed the glass to get a drip into her arm while they worked out what to do. He told her, this paramedic, through his pudgy lips, that his daughter was starting school next year. He flipped a photo of his girl, as a baby, in front of Chrissie and asked her to look at it. It was laminated, worn and curled at the corners. Chrissie memorised every detail, the dimple on one cheek, the tiny nails poking out of a fluffy sleeve. She even knew the smell of that baby. The paramedic moved the image to the side and watched her eyes follow. He asked her what colour the baby's blanket was.

'Would you call it pink or orange?' He scanned Chrissie's face for an answer. None came. He talked about his mother's garden, how the drought had reduced all the blossoms on the apricot trees. They expected a poor crop this year – not enough to make the annual supply of jam – the neighbours would be disappointed. She could remember the photo and the lack of jam, but almost nothing else.

Eventually they cut her out. The firemen had put earmuffs on her but they weren't enough. The petrol saw screeched and the steel vibrated her seat as they ground away at roof pillars. Loud cracks signalled the last was done with bolt cutters. Then they pulled Dave off her, prompting one long last glug of blood to spread across her lap. It must have pooled inside his chest, around his heart, waiting to be with her. Then she blacked out.

Pelvic hairline fracture, left tibia, multiple ankle fractures, left collar bone snapped, left shoulder dislocation, cracked ribs, pierced left lung, concussion; she was in a bad way. Dave had crushed her, broken her, but she had killed him. The hospital put her in a coma and then slowly brought her out as the worst of her injuries were patched and the swelling in her brain subsided. But she fought against the light, against the pain. She thrashed and beat herself back to oblivion, back to black. They put her under again but, on the second day, they made her stay with them. Time to face the world.

Her world broke all over again as soon as she saw her father's face.

'He didn't make it, bub. Dave died in the crash.' George told her straight, as he stroked her face. She could see him trying to hide the worst pain he had ever felt.

She wished she could die. Grief grew everywhere in her body.

Later that night she was forced to do a police interview where she learned about the impact on the milk truck driver, her blood alcohol level, the eye witness at the intersection. The evidence damned her. Everyone did.

And so did she.

CHAPTER 10

Chrissie jumped on the afternoon tram and headed back to work. She was already pissed off. The midday press conference, about a toxic waste fire during the night, had been whitewashed. *Nothing to see here, folks.* But the warehouse had been exploding in fireballs for hours during the night, popping barrels of who knew what into the air and across the low-income western suburb. Sheer luck no one was killed. The Environmental Waste Board and the fire department, however, had stuck to carefully worded scripts. Chrissie, like the other journos there, hadn't been able to get anything extra out of them. The official line would have to prevail, for now. Meanwhile other reporters were gathering accounts from shocked neighbours and staff but Chrissie had been diverted by a phone call from the news desk. She had to cover a ribbon-cutting ceremony for a new department store. Unlike the fire, with the officials trying to contain the news coverage, the department store assignment was all about the company getting as much coverage as possible.

Chrissie was told by the news desk her story would hang on the tentative hook that city retail was prospering. An angle she doubted. The only good part of the job was a brief catch-up with Lou, before the fashion editor carefully perked herself up and separated off to search for inside information about which labels and designers had been signed to the store. Neil was there too, the story had a strong business angle. He barely gave Chrissie a nod but she felt him keep his eyes on her until she deliberately slipped out of sight. Three journos. *The Argus* wanted a show of strength at the event. Big potential advertiser, while more worthwhile stories went unreported.

The ribbon cutting story would be quick to write, although she would still dig up the latest statistics on vacancies and shop turnovers which she already knew showed an ongoing decline. But as she walked across the news floor, Harry stood and waved her over.

'O'Brian, get on the blower to Grange. I've got reports of emergency services called to the wharf. Sounds like another accident.'

Chrissie spun around and raced to her desk: 4.45 pm. She punched in the number for Grange's media office. It went to message bank. She phoned Hel Carter at the maritime union. She was bound to know if something had happened. All the safety reps on the wharf were union members. No answer. She worked methodically, on automatic: ambulance media, Port Authority, union, Grange. She tried them all a second time, bypassing mobile numbers this time – too easy for them not to answer – instead going through their office switchboards. But still no luck.

She rang *The Argus*'s police roundsman; Danny someone, she didn't know him properly, he was based offsite near police headquarters. He had received the initial tip from the cops but no further details.

As she hung up she saw James walk back in from his helicopter ride, taking his usual long slow strides, hair ruffled. He was always so relaxed.

'James, who do you know at Grange? Got anyone on the inside?' Chrissie jumped straight on him.

'What? What do you mean? Why?'

'Looks like another accident at the wharf,' Chrissie said. 'And everyone's stonewalling me – again!'

He took his jacket off and swiped through his phone. 'Actually, I might have the perfect contact, well, Gina's contact really.' He started to write out a number on a post-it note. 'Geens did her final year of law here in Melbourne with this girl, Suri.'

'James, please.' Chrissie didn't have time for one of his networking stories. 'Harry's given me the gig so I want to get on it asap.'

'Yes, yes. But just saying, Suri, well Suri's dad is the head of the transport union, Graham Parenta. Transport's got a lot of members on the wharf, they sort of love-hate the other lot there, have to share the power.' James handed her the number.

'Well, union contacts, that surprises me. Thought you'd have someone but not in the blue-collar end of town,' she retorted.

'Glad to be able to impress you, oh doubtful one.'

Chrissie googled Graham Parenta. He'd had a recent but high profile career in the union. Then she quickly searched Suri for a bit more background. All smiles and long black hair on her Instagram account. Her eyes, the deepest dark brown. In a recent photo her hands were covered in brown swirls. Henna. 'My baby sister engaged!' the caption read.

The number James gave her, however, rang out. No answer. No voicemail system. Instead, Chrissie texted the number and introduced herself. But within minutes a press release bounced into her email. Grange Industries. Four lines.

Grange Industries sadly confirms a staff member has been involved in a fatal accident this morning at the Port of Melbourne. No further details are available. All inquiries should be directed to the police and emergency services. A formal statement will be issued after the authorities have informed the family.

Another death! *Breathe.* Her hands flew under the desk. Her thumbnails immediately started stabbing each finger. One, two, three, four. Repeat. Repeat.

The habit had started when she'd first woken in the hospital after the car crash. Braced and strapped because of her broken bones, to still her mind, she pushed her thumbnails into each fleshy finger pad. She counted slowly over and over, as hard as she could, the thumbnail strong and sharp, then moved on to the next one. *Focus on the pain.*

She grabbed her phone and pressed Mas's number, her fingertip soothed temporarily by the glass keypad. The call went straight to voicemail.

'What if it's her?' Chrissie turned to James.

'Her who?' He stood and leaned over Chrissie's shoulder to read the email. 'It doesn't give a name. Her who?'

'Mas, Masina.'

James still looked blank.

'The woman in a man's world. The profile piece.'

'There are hundreds of people working there, it's not likely to be her.'

'I can't sit here and wait. I'm heading down there.'

Chrissie took the tram and ran across the old pedestrian bridge this time towards the sea, the familiar oyster smell getting stronger. The crane necks were at attention, spotlights lit up the wharves like a movie set as dusk set in. But there was something different. Something wrong? Chrissie searched the scene as she hurried towards it. *No noise.* The whole place was at a standstill. Silent.

Grange security had already erected a cordon outside the main gates. Even the picketers were quiet, standing respectfully, waiting for the news. She searched for Hel Carter but couldn't find her. She recognised a few faces but when she asked no one knew who the victim was.

'Ghoul,' someone spat out at her.

'Ambulance chaser.'

She heard their anger but weathered their pain. The next-best option was a tall plain-clothes policeman giving orders. Dark suit pants, predictable blue business shirt, no tie, a bomber-style jacket. His boots, however, gave a slight jolt. It was a while since she had seen a pair of polished Blundstones. Out of towner, like her. *Farm boy?* She needed access to the people inside the gates, a way through the cordon. But despite his smile the detective was unhelpful.

'We haven't set up an incident room in there yet. You're a bit ahead of everyone,' he said after she flashed her media ID.

'Yeah, well, that's my job, isn't it?' She shifted her weight from foot to foot. 'Look, I was just here yesterday at the request of the company,' she tried again. 'I'm sure they'd be okay with it. Can you get a call through?' She waved towards the other side of the security fences.

'Sorry, no can do, be at least another hour.' He shoved his hands in his pants pockets, dismissing her. 'One of my officers will take your details.' He half-turned his back and signalled with a sideways toss of his head to a uniform. Chrissie's face flushed red.

'No, I'm giving *you* my details.' Chrissie stepped around in front of him and looked up to read his badge. 'Senior Detective Jason Bannister, and I've taken your details. What's a detective doing here, anyway, at a workplace accident?' Chrissie didn't understand why she was so annoyed. It was just the usual cop brush-off. He smiled at her feisty reaction and stepped closer. *Too close.* But Chrissie couldn't back down. He nodded again and pulled out his phone.

'Here, put your contacts in this.' He brushed back a wayward flop of brown hair that threatened to fall across his forehead and passed his phone to her. 'I'll give them to incident control.' This time his smile spread to his hazel brown eyes as he almost towered over her. To her shock, her shoulders dropped and her eyes softly half closed, she wanted to lean into him, to push her face into his shirt. In horror, she forced a stumbled step backward, instantly wretched, hating herself for this sudden betrayal, this burst of weakness. She kept her face down, and tapped in the contact details, deleting the mistakes and wrong letters until she got them right. Then angrily thrust the phone at him and took another step back.

'Thank you.' He looked down at the screen and read: 'Chris O'Brian from *The Argus*.' She gave him a twisted grin, then turned just in time to see one of the paper's photographers, Frances, arrive and wave her over. Frances would stay onsite but Chrissie had to get back to the office and file. It was almost 6 pm. She glanced around as she was leaving. Bannister, taller than most at the scene, was busy fielding other media but he glanced across and caught her staring before she could look away. She gave no response and turned her back.

—

It would be rare for anyone to get the name of the victim un-officially – that was one of the few things that no one ever leaked. It was something of an honour point among the murky world of informers and the media – family finds out first. But she went through the motions, anyway.

'It won't be your puff piece crane driver,' James tried again to make her feel better. 'What are the chances?'

But they didn't have to wait long.

By 6.30 pm the information was confirmed. 'Masina Weber, Australia's only female portainer operator, has died in a fall' the Grange statement read. Chrissie's stomach twisted in pain. *Mas.* She pictured her big wide grin.

'O'Brian, three hundred words.' Harry was in front of her desk. 'It looks like it's your profile woman but hold off on any info you got from her.'

'But Harry,' Chrissie stood up, 'we'll be the only –'

'I said hold off!' He swallowed, controlled himself and added: 'We have to figure out how we're going to use it. Make the most of it. But not tonight.'

'But it'll be stronger if we include some of it now.' Chrissie sat back down but leaned forward hands on her hips.

'Jesus, O'Brian! This is not a debate, just do as instructed!'

Chrissie wrote and filed the story, clinical, factual, no sign of the warmth or admiration she had felt for Mas or the dread that stuck in her throat as she was forced to put this young woman's death into words. Cold and emotionless words. Everything that Mas was not.

She wondered what Mas's family were going through right now. *Harder for the living.* She finally slumped back in her chair. James was finishing writing up the car crash fatality.

'The photos are incredible, the guy had to be pulled out the back window, while the car was still hanging half-off the bridge.'

She swallowed away the nightmare that filled her thoughts. The car crash would get priority. It had shut down the West Gate Bridge. The traffic chaos had lasted for hours. Both deaths equal but the commuter chaos would touch tens of thousands of households and readers. Mas's death was less newsworthy.

—

Chrissie squinted through the crooked venetian blinds, the newsroom was emptying and the light had long gone, when her desk phone rang.

'Chris O'Brian? Hello? Ah. I'm a friend of . . .' The male voice broke in a sob. Chrissie's skin prickled.

'She showed me your card. Mas, Masina, you spoke to her.' Chrissie took a slow deep breath. 'I was her . . . My name's Remi, Remi Basill, I work, worked with her.' She didn't know the name but she half-recognised the voice – could it be one of the loudmouths at the picket; thick, dark hair, angry? 'Can we meet? Say Sunday? Vic Market? Mas was scared. I need to know what she told you.'

CHAPTER 11

Bone weariness and a sickening hangover forced Chrissie's mind where she didn't want to go this morning. *Dave.*

Her throat ached as she heard Dave's sleepy murmur, smelled his love. She curled herself around her stomach and lay still, eyes screwed tight, carefully sipping the air until she willed Dave away again. *Mas.* Another death on her hands. She knew the empty bottles from last night would show she had polished off too much wine again but her horror and disbelief about the crane operator's death had so far kept her away from the sedatives. She had to find the truth. She stared at the ceiling, her drishti, her focus point. The cornice with its rhythmic concave and deep mitres settled her. *It's Sunday, meet Remi. Get up. Get dressed. Go to the market.*

She swung her legs out of the bed and within seconds her head was thumping, her vision blurred from the pain and her stomach cramped. She knew the signs and sprinted to the bathroom, her head over the sink just in time.

Usually she stayed in pyjamas on her days off, watched trashy TV or read biographies and survival stories. Eventually she would slouch off to one of the Vietnamese cafés. Crispy squid or campfire beef? She could never decide between the two. Or she'd walk along the Yarra River, watching the school rowing teams, their long sleek strokes, their synchronised calm mesmerising. But on days when the pain would not budge, she would punish herself with a long run to the botanical gardens then sprints up the Anderson Street hill. Twice more around the Tan Track and back past the MCG to Richmond and exhaustion and a different pain would take over. A trip to the Queen Victoria Market today would mean some of her favourite cheese to bring home, maybe a new teapot so she could stop using teabags.

She pushed her phone into her jacket pocket but it was full. The forgotten gauntlet notes from outside the office. She quickly read through them. A printed quote: *How beautiful upon the mountains are the feet of him who brings good news, who publishes peace.* Religious. She screwed it up and tossed it in the kitchen bin. The second, pale green A4 page, handwritten. *Data breaches, geo blocks – smoke and mirrors. Rare to be safe. It's coming in under dark. Check the hardware store.* Something to do with the new cyber security agreement? Why is everyone so cryptic? She folded it neatly, Mike might know. A third; stiff white paper, almost card: *Why aren't you reporting on the power play at Trades Hall? The infighting is breaking the unions apart. Someone should be writing about it.* Potential. The fourth; a copy of a photograph with a headline: Paedophile. *This man assaulted our son.* Chrissie looked at the picture. Thin fair hair, mid to late twenties, early baldness, sports top, a whistle around his neck. Police rounds, she decided, and folded it with the green paper and card beside the mail pile on her table.

The meow sounded as soon as she walked onto the landing. Skinny came running, making her smile.

'Hey there.' She bent and scratched around his ears as he looped between her legs. The loud purr washed away her tension. The thrum of it made her feel connected to the world, grateful that she could make another being happy.

'Sorry, mate.' She smoothed a hand over his grey head and along his back. 'I'm headed out.' But Skinny had plans too; when he heard Mike's door creak open, he flipped his tail at her and was off. Chrissie followed him down the stairs.

'Just out. Work. Catch ya.' She smiled and lifted her head to Mike.

'Dumplings for lunch? You know you love them.'

'Not sure, might be late.'

'Late's okay.' He ushered Skinny through his door. She smiled at the two of them.

—

As the train pulled into the station Chrissie saw the seats were already taken, people were standing in the aisle. It was over-crowded, especially for a Sunday. Damn, she thought, it must be the early footy fans. Everyone, regardless of team, was desperate to see one more game before the season closed. Chrissie hesitated. Her palms itched as she paced beside the carriage's open door, unsure what to do. The next train would be more crowded, she worried. Before she could change her mind, she stepped across the gap and into the carriage. She searched for a strap to hold and mentally paced out enough space around her to keep her panic at bay. Just as the doors were closing, a group ran in laughing, bustling her deeper into the carriage. She was surrounded, no room to move, no air to breathe. She tried to stay near the door. Close to the exit. The train moved forward as the first sweat sprang across Chrissie's forehead. *Breathe in; one, two, three. Breathe out; one, two, three.* She turned to the window, to the space and light. A magnolia tree in someone's backyard was full of large pink and white flowers. The bright green leaves had just started to sprout. But the murky smell of people filled her nose. Everyone forced to stand too close. Voices growing louder. More footy fans got on at the next station. She felt them suck up her air. She kept a low steady gaze out the window, the station master's building, its bluestone windowsill and red door, red brick walls. Conversations piled on top of each other. People pushed closer. Their striped footy scarves and coloured jumpers started to scream at her.

Chrissie's work hours – late starts and late finishes – meant she usually managed to avoid the suffocating peak-hour crush. Big city living was hard to get used to. She certainly hadn't expected the crowd today or she would have steeled herself. Practised her breathing. Put in earphones.

She held tight to the overhead strap and kept her focus out the window. Glimpses of bright sky flashed above fences and scrappy trees beside the track. Only one more stop and the crowd would get off at the Melbourne Cricket Ground. The MCG, the gladiatorial home of Aussie cricket, and during the winter, Aussie Rules football. Its massive light towers, heads bowed, stood in awe above the action.

Chrissie tried to slow her breathing in time with the train as it came to a long stop. *Just a few more seconds and the carriage will empty.* The doors opened. Fresh air. But people didn't get off. Instead more got on. Chrissie's palms itched uncontrollably. She rubbed them against her leather jacket, switching hands as each needed relief. She was forced to let go of the strap to scratch them both, her nails dragging against damaged skin, then lurch for an overhead strap just in time as the train started up again.

'C'mon the Pies!' The black and white Collingwood Magpies supporters shouted their dominance to the newcomers to the train: St Kilda fans in their red, white and black. The game must be at the Docklands, Chrissie realised. *Two more stops. Could she last? What if I lose it here on this train, in front of all these people?*

'We're going to smash you Saints.'

'Smashed avocado and Saints on toast? You'll be a hundred before you win a premiership.'

The banter was loud and good-natured but Chrissie cringed at the shouts. She tried to cover her ears but the train was rocking and she couldn't let go of the strap again. *The window, look out the window.* The view had changed to railyards and weed-covered sidings. *Breathe. Keep it together.*

'Pity about those shop-lifting charges,' a Saints supporter returned fire.

'You guys out on parole?' Another quickly followed, taunting the Magpies. But they were soon drowned out.

'Coll-ing-wood.' *Clap clap clap*. 'Coll-ing-wood.' *Clap clap clap*.

Chrissie started to shake in time with the chant. Her headache throbbed a different rhythm. Her breath was faster still, her chest a thumping mess. She wasn't going to make it. Everyone was staring at her. She looked around again but they were all smiles, looking straight through her. They were enjoying the rivalry. More people got on at Flinders Street.

She tried to shrug off her jacket but there was no room. She let go of the strap, held in place by the crush, as she scratched her palms again. She needed air. *Breathe in, slow; one, two, three. Breathe out, slow; one, two, three.*

At last, the train pulled into Southern Cross Station and people surged out the doors. But the chanting and sledging ramped up. Kids jumped excitedly, pushing and ribbing each other as they raced to get off. Men puffed up to almost twice their size. The women remained small in their tight jeans and long hair. Then, outside the carriage, voices amplified under the station's wave-roof high above the platform. The excitement of the two tribes crackled as they marched towards the stadium. It was going to be a tough game.

Chrissie collapsed into an empty seat as the train jerked its way under the ground into the city loop. Would she ever be rid of these crippling attacks? She watched desperately for each dim wall light as the train sped along the black tunnel. She felt the brakes and the train shakily slowed. Flagstaff Station. She jumped up and stood at the carriage door. Shuffling from side to side, she pressed the button again and again to open the door. At last, the coloured ring lit up and the doors slid open with their welcome beeping. A rush of air from the cold tiled platform spread over her face and cooled her hands. She took the escalator two steps at a time, up into the daylight. Made it.

But before she fully realised, Chrissie was swept along in a new herd. Determined, jostling market shoppers.

Not again. The anxiety was back. Worse. As if someone had ramped up the volume. She looked around the market as she was funnelled into the narrow alleys; a thumping bass came from an impossibly small speaker, a child screamed and arched its back trying to get out of its stroller, the mother leaned over and hissed 'no'; loud and menacing it lingered in Chrissie's ears. She twisted at the sound of a deep bark, a dog brushed her hand, its fur like wire against her skin. People backed away from it, clearing a path. Chrissie tried to follow the clearway behind the dog but she couldn't keep up and the path quickly flooded over again. People and bags and children and hipsters and shopping trolleys overwhelmed her. Her nose exploded – fish, cheese, coffee – she could barely hold it together. Men shouted prices, the squeaking wheels on someone's shopping cart screamed in her ears. She rushed both hands up to block the sounds.

Got to get away. She pushed her way to the edge of the throng and lunged between two stalls, throwing herself among the boxes and stock. Her feet finally still, she bent over, exhausted. Her hands and head rested on a stack of cartons. It's just noise, just people. *Breathe in; one, two, three. Breathe out; one, two, three. It will end soon. It will end soon.*

'Oi, what you doing back here?'

She jumped, patting her chest, signalling she was not feeling well.

'Sit down. Sit on this, miss.' The old man slid an empty wooden crate forward. Beetroot stamped on its side.

Chrissie sat reluctantly. She didn't want to, couldn't, speak to him, to anyone.

To her shock he lifted a wrinkled, red-stained hand towards her face and she instinctively pushed it away. But he forced his hand onto her forehead.

'You're hot, you got a temperature.'

Then he took one of her hands, palm up, and examined her scarred fingertips and her cracked and raw palms. She tried to pull away. But he was strong, caressing her palm with his hand, holding tight, while he searched her face.

'You clammy, love. You gonna pass out? Don't you pass out, okay?'

Chrissie snatched her hand back but the stall-owner was not easily dismissed. He placed both his hands firmly on her head and stroked her hair down each side, over her ears, then spread his strong, bony hands across the top of her shoulders. She could feel the static from his touch through her hair and clothes. She let her shoulders relax. The weight of his touch prevented her from moving but so too did his face. He stared right into her eyes, past her blue irises, past her lenses and along the nerves to her brain. His earthy sweet smell swirled through her nose. She felt the word coming before she heard it.

'Death.'

What?

He released her arms and stepped back, his eyes had travelled back to the surface of her face.

Chrissie stood and twisted, unsure which way to run. She pulled her jacket around her, a barrier against the word.

Shock triggered her into action. She stumbled through the rubbish and the merchandise. Other stall-holders looked at her, puzzled. The growing gasps made even more look. Chrissie heard the word 'thief', as more people watched her run. But everyone stayed out of her way. At last she burst out to an open car park.

Gasping for air, Chrissie looked around, eyes still wild. She expected chaos and faces staring at her. But she was invisible to the people busy opening boots, piling in shopping. Sunday morning at Victoria Market.

Leaning against a white delivery van she told herself she had misheard him. In the crowd and the noise, her hangover, her anxiety, the old man didn't say death, he said breath. Take a breath, yes, that's it. Or stress. He said stress, too much stress.

No. It was death.

How could he know?

She should have died, not them.

CHAPTER 12

A phone was ringing. Dull and irritating. The noise was coming from her jacket pocket. Her hand fumbled, finally grasping the phone as she looked around the market car park again.

Remi flashed on the screen. Can't talk yet. Take a breath. Slower. Take another. She could hear the music from the buskers in the distance. Pan flutes. She breathed in and out on every third note.

A ping, as a text flashed across the top of her screen.

Are you here yet?

Another breath.

Yes, she typed, her fingers slow and unresponsive. **Where can we meet?**

Near the music. On the bench. Blue beanie.

Chrissie stood taller, breathed deeper as she walked to the spot. The area was full of children with bright flushed faces. An early spring had arrived for the afternoon.

Two anxiety attacks in a row. She was getting worse not better. *Still falling.* Just when she thought she had started to get them under control. What if it happened at work? Her greatest fear. What if the whole newsroom saw her panic one day, bent over, as she struggled to keep calm? Or worse: if she lost all control. Started screaming or running.

Chrissie joined the queue for the food van. She could see Remi. Slumped, black jeans, reefer jacket. Dark hair poking from around the edges of his beanie. Yes, he was the one who had grabbed her arm at the picket, spoken too close. His spittle on her face. She kept watch as she inched down the queue to buy her tea. Tea: the only connection she had now with the country kitchen she'd grown up in. The teapot permanently on the timber table. But the thin cardboard cup she was given squeezed inward when she took hold. Hot water spilled over the rim but she leaned forward just in time to let it splash on the ground. She stood to the side of the van, dunking the teabag. She finally walked to the bench seat.

Remi seemed smaller today, fidgety, eyes scanning the crowd. Perhaps nervous, impatient? He had been big and aggressive at the picket line, looking for someone to blame. Today he looked beaten, his shoulders slumped. He stood as she crossed the road, shook her outstretched hand and pulled her down to sit next to him. *Too close.* Chrissie forced a smile. She was back in work mode. She gently shuffled backwards on the seat and faced him, creating space for their words.

'I was having second thoughts,' he blurted. 'Haven't had much sleep. I keep thinking about Mas – I can't tell Allegra, my wife. I can't tell anyone.' His voice trailed off and he looked away.

Chrissie sipped her tea.

'What did she talk to you about? What are you going to write?' He leaned towards her, the aggression back.

Chrissie stayed quiet. She sensed he had more to say.

'Mas's death wasn't an accident. Maybe it's karma. You know, God's intervention.' He slammed his hand down on the seat.

Just what I need, Chrissie thought, *a God botherer*.

'For what?' she finally asked.

'For me being a two-timing bastard. I was, we were – with Mas. I loved her. We were going to go away. To her home, to Samoa. Now she's gone, both gone.'

Chrissie pricked up.

'Both?' She leaned closer. 'Who else?'

'Ah, I meant Mas. Both . . . both of our plans, gone.' He hung his head.

Chrissie shifted on the seat. She could still hear the vendors shouting their vegetable prices. She looked down at the shopping bags spread at Remi's feet. Beetroot. It reminded her of the old man and his red wrinkled hands. She breathed deeply again and kept her focus down. Fluffy green carrot tops, a bag of fresh ground coffee beside them. The smells threatened to make her sick again, the buskers annoying. *Those pan flutes! Don't they ever take a break?*

'They're saying she fell during the shift change. From the top.' Remi sat forward. 'But she couldn't have. She was too careful.'

Chrissie recalled how Mas had attached and reattached them both to the safety rails. Mas had owned that crane.

'I'm fucked up about it. A mess. Sick with grief,' Remi continued, 'but I can't show it. I'm barely keeping it together at home, at work.'

Chrissie put her empty cup on the ground and moved a little further back from him. *Or sick with guilt?* This guy can't decide if it's about him or Mas, she thought.

'What did she tell you?' His voice cracked. 'She's been climbing that equipment, lifting containers on and off for years. Worked around the world. There's no way she could fall.'

He moved closer again. Chrissie leaned back as he spoke at her. His words came faster. 'Mas thought something was wrong. She – we were going to leave. She said something was wrong.'

Chrissie replayed Mas's phone message over in her mind. Mas had said things were dangerous. Was she afraid of him? Had the wife found out about the affair?

'What do you mean? I don't get it. Was she being threatened?'

Remi continued. 'She was convinced someone deliberately ran into Hank, earlier this year, killed him.' *Ah, he did mean both!*

'Hank Timmons?' she said. 'Vehicle collision, a container dislodged.'

Remi's eyes widened, he drew back.

'I looked up a few archive stories. But there wasn't anything suspicious. Safety Bureau report was straightforward.'

'Mas and him were tight,' he said. 'Not an affair.' His face grew red but he tried to cover. 'She was keeping an eye out for him, thought he mighta found something, before his accident.'

Chrissie watched Remi carefully, the way his rough hands gripped the bench seat. Was it anger? Why did he keep asking what Mas had told her? Maybe this other death was a red herring?

But two people *had* died. *Breathe.* He seemed unstable. Either a nut case or dodgy. How could Mas have been involved with this guy? She seemed so in control. Professional. Maybe he was lying. Maybe he was suspicious? Or maybe he had just really loved Mas. Chrissie refocused, tried not to ask too many questions.

The sun was strong. She slipped one arm out of her leather jacket, then the other. Her cup of tea long empty, she desperately needed another one. The painkillers were wearing off, she moved her tongue around her dry mouth.

'I think someone warned her off. We were going to skip through, a new life, but I kept putting it off – I've got two kids, you know. Now, bam! She's dead. Family's taking her body on Tuesday. I've got nothing.' *All about him.* 'After Hank, she told me, lotsa times, if something happened to her, tell the cops. But I can't.'

'Of course you can.' Chrissie sat up straighter. She needed something to eat. Her head thumping again.

'I can't!' He slammed his hand down on the seat between them. People nearby looked at them in surprise. 'If I did,' he said more calmly again as people turned back to their conversations, 'I'd have to tell them about us and then Al would find out. I heard you were writing a story. You can investigate it.' Remi took a deep breath then let it out in a rush. 'I shoulda believed her. I shoulda got her out of there sooner. No matter how I spin it, it isn't right. It's playing on me, real bad.' He hung his head. Chrissie knew all about keeping secrets.

'I'm sorry, I understand about your wife. But you have to go to the cops. I'll go with you,' she offered.

'Nup, absolutely not. I can't lose Al and the kids now. And I can't put them at risk, what if . . .' Remi's eyes squinted at her, tears threatened. His jaw clamped tight as he stood suddenly and scooped up his bags. He loomed over her and jabbed the air with his fists of groceries. 'What if they come for me, for my kids? It's your job to find the truth, isn't it? That's what journos are supposed to do.'

'Hang on, it's –' Chrissie was drowned out.

'If you find something and it comes out, then that's how it is!' He bent forward. 'What did she tell you?' Her face suddenly in shade as he stood over her.

'You should be going to the cops,' Chrissie stayed firm. She didn't trust him yet. Remi loomed in further. Chrissie froze, held her breath.

'It's your job. I know she said something to you. If she didn't, then someone musta thought she was gonna.' The words slapped her face and dug at her self-hate. *I put her at risk.* Her worst fears realised. *My fault.* Remi looked around the crowd. 'You put her in danger. You and your big interview, parading her all over the wharf. This is on you now.'

Your job. On you now.

CHAPTER 13

It was always Chrissie and Dave. As if they were one person. They had been a couple since her seventeenth birthday. The merger of two well-known families in the small prosperous New Zealand farming community was expected.

'Love local,' Dave's father, Tony, had urged his son with a wink to Chrissie. 'Too many kids marry outside the district. Look at the Jordans. Only ever see their kids on birthdays and Christmas or when they drag some city slicker home for a weekend.'

For Dave, that was never going to be the case. He set his cap at Chrissie and nothing could persuade him otherwise. Eventually he would inherit his parents' dairy farm and raise his family there. A new Watford generation to experience classic Kiwi childhoods: roaming safe and free, rafting on freezing rivers, school holidays on the beach, bonfires and surfing. Always a dog or two in tow.

They married in a tiny timber church, the oldest in the district. Chrissie's father walked her down the narrow aisle, between six handmade pews of golden kauri pine. Behind the timber altar a clear window opened to a view across the sparkling lake, hills in the distance, more reverent than any stained-glass saints. The party afterwards was huge. No invitations required, everyone in the district was welcome and everyone came.

As beautiful as the country was, Chrissie's journalism often took her to the city, despite working for a regional paper, and she liked that.

'It's the cities where the decisions are made about country lives,' her dad always said.

Auckland was a jewel box to Chrissie. She would often go out with workmates as they celebrated their achievements. Nightclubs, trendy new people, lots of reasons to be out and about. A whole new world. Dave, however, was a homebody. But he didn't think twice about her independence. 'That's just Chrissie. I love her for the whole package, not just bits,' he explained to those who raised an eyebrow.

—

Melbourne was different but Chrissie had yet to feel a fresh start. On a good morning she would wake with her sorrow sitting heavy on her chest, staring up at the elaborate ceiling. On a bad day, too alert after not enough sleeping pills or wine the night before, it would be memories of Dave that woke her. Those mornings she was forced to swim herself to the surface only to sip the air, unworthy, until she found the strength to push him away so she could cope. Some days now, Skinny would be there, curled against the back of her knees having snuck in during the night. But this morning as she sat up with a heavy chest, her grief and guilt mixed in with the fog of alcohol, Chrissie's mind jumped to work.

Today she had a meeting with Grange Industries. A fishing trip that she had hastily arranged as she went over and over Mas's death. She tried to convince herself that there was nothing she could do with Remi's allegations. Her clenching gut told her otherwise. It might not be as sinister as Remi suggested but she had to check it out. *Dead because of me?* And, like Remi, Chrissie knew the police would blunder in and tell their families. She'd keep his secret. Who was she to judge? After everything she had done, what was one more secret?

Up now and moving around her sparse kitchen, Chrissie was also convinced the wharf had all the right ingredients for a great story, a chance for a strong feature, prove herself. *The new wharves. Why Australia's first female crane driver died.* The docks were crying out for a feature. The other media were covering it piecemeal, just like *The Argus.* No one could afford the time to do a proper job. She could see it: big business, a female, the shocking accident rates, new computerised wharves, blue collar replaced by white.

But first she had to get something more concrete, not just the suspicion of a workmate, a guilt-ridden boyfriend. The company had quickly agreed despite the PR lockdown after Mas's death. Chrissie knew Grange would want to neutralise her as soon as possible and put an end to Mas's profile story. The human face of Grange, the death of the woman pioneer, now had the potential to be a public relations horror story for the company.

Grange's office was on the waterfront, just outside the fenced security zone. The company leased several storeys in one of the area's newest office buildings, built on reclaimed land that was once part of the old port. It had a view across the bay to Williamstown with its postcard pier and dainty harbour, a stark contrast to the brutal industrial concrete wharves at the Grange docks. Security at the building was all about electronic surveillance. Cameras everywhere and not a security guard to be seen. She had been sent a code to use in the foyer to get to the lifts. Then the same code for the lift.

Her phone pinged with a text as she stood in the elevator. Graham Parenta, at last, the transport union boss:

Grange won't help. You're looking in the wrong place.

How the hell did he know? Instinctively she looked around the lift. She had only told James and Harry that she was seeing Grange today. There must be a leak inside Grange, she realised. But why would Grange leak to the transport union? Perhaps someone wanted to stir trouble between the unions. She remembered the gauntlet note; the warring unions. Annoyed at the potential manipulation, she quickly typed back just as the lift doors opened. A young receptionist was directly in front of her, the clear glass table exposing chubby legs, a panorama of crisp blue sky behind her. No clouds today.

Give me something to poke at Grange. I'm there now, she quickly typed.

—

There were hundreds of 'pale, stale, male' PR bosses in the corporate world. They dominated the lunch scene, lived off their connections. Hired guns, they manipulated and cajoled as required. Their contact lists reached up to the highest levels of government and delved into the deepest networks of their industries. They did an unparalleled job of destroying any whiff of bad publicity for their companies and expertly dished the dirt on their rivals. Charlie Thurst was one of the best.

He appeared to glide across the top floor lobby. A measured grin on his putty face. He shook with a firm grip; a good start, Chrissie thought. She hated limp handshakes from men: evidence of latent sexism, she had decided. Thurst patted his hair, preening. *Vanity.* He smelled of freshly ironed shirt. *A dedicated wife?* Unlikely. *Laundry service.*

'Let's head to the boardroom, it's got a great view. And it's extra pretty today – we've got all docks pumping again after the safety shutdown.' He winked at the receptionist, who gave him a reluctant smile as he placed one hand behind Chrissie's elbow and steered her across the foyer.

Chrissie could feel him look her up and down as he ushered her in the room ahead of him. Predictable. She regretted wearing a skirt but at least she had flat shoes on. She went straight to the wall of windows on the other side of the marble board table. Black leather chairs were arranged evenly, except for two pulled out at the far end, expectantly.

'This fatality, Masina Weber. Tragic. As you know, she'd been with us for a long time,' Thurst said from behind her. 'Must have been a shock for you too? To hear it was her.'

'Yeah.' Chrissie glanced at him but couldn't help gazing back out the window.

'Bloody union's using it in another push against installing the new equipment. Mercenary bastards. Never let a chance go by.

The picket's about twice as big outside today but at least we're back in action.'

Looking out from Grange's boardroom, fifteen storeys up, seagulls above and below, Chrissie was immediately back to her childhood, her doting grandfather Jack taking her and her brother William to visit Auckland or across to Tauranga. They would walk the wharves to see which ships were in. William was always surprised at how big the mooring lines were. He'd compare their thickness to either an arm or a leg or two limbs twisted together. The old man would make up stories about the cargo, the route the ships had travelled and the type of men who lived on board. When they had finished inspecting the hulls and debating their new destinations, Jack would drive further around the bay for fish and chips. They'd sit with their newspaper wrappers and food on the opposite waterfront, looking back at the activity. The tug boats, the long crane arms loading and unloading. Chrissie's grandfather had been a truck driver all his life, hauling cargo to and from the wharves. One day he would travel as a passenger on a cargo boat and Chrissie and William would stow away with him, he told them, and they believed him.

Now Chrissie was mesmerised all over again by this new clinical version of an old world. The Grange docks were already the most high-tech in the country. Massive four-limbed monsters lifted metal babies out of the mothership. They passed them to others who sucked them up in new arms and carried them to their families. Wharves poked into the oily, watery calm. Huge ships were tethered by fat umbilical cords. Further out past the channel more mothers lined up at anchor, waiting to deliver.

She heard the air hiss from a leather chair behind her and then a tapping on the table top. Charlie Thurst wanted her attention. Who was worse – him or her? They both had their mission. Chrissie wanted to get Grange's take on Mas's death. The pickets, the impact of the new technology. Despite the activity outside the window, she knew the union's work-to-rule and snap walk-offs must be taking a toll on the company's finances. Were too many corners being cut? People hurt, killed because of cost cutting? A cover-up?

Chrissie set a wide smile in place and took her seat. The chair at equal height to his, she noted, unlike some interviews when her chair was set deliberately lower. To her surprise, Thurst was way ahead of her.

'Here's a little something to get us off to a good start.' He tapped one of the cardboard folders in front of him, spun it around and pushed it towards her. 'It's an early draft of the Safety Bureau report, Masina Weber's death.' He beamed, pleased with her surprise. 'You can read it, off the record.'

'You must like what it says,' Chrissie countered, deadpan. Despite her need to keep him on side, Charlie Thurst made her skin prickle.

'Things aren't always as straightforward as people want them to be. Take a look. But phone on the table, of course.' He directed a bleached white smile at her.

Chrissie turned off her phone and placed it in view. Thurst reached over and pressed the home button, checking the screen was blank, the power off. She flicked through a few pages of the report, then reread several sections. The wording was riddled with jargon, designed to obscure, not enlighten. Even the conclusion, which could usually provide some understanding, was garbled.

'I don't get it.' Chrissie stared straight into Thurst's face. 'No witnesses, no footage.'

'Got it in one,' Thurst said. 'Although it does go on to say there was no evidence of mechanical or safety breaches.' A manicured hand preened his thinning hair.

'How could she have fallen? The report states . . .' she flicked back to find the passage, 'there was no evidence of failure, breakage or damage to the railing.' Chrissie searched Thurst's eyes for an insight. How could Mas have fallen, despite the safety railings, a harness, the end of shift protocol in the cabin? 'Will the police investigate?'

'There was some detective, Bannister, who has been in touch,' he said. Chrissie immediately pictured the tall detective from the wharf, his confidence, his brushoff. Her sudden weakness. 'But we don't expect much from the cops. Of course, the coroner will have a look but that's months away. Technically nothing to ring alarm bells. Basically, nothing to see, folks, move along.'

'What about the CCTV? It's like Fort Knox around here.' Even Thurst must see that the report was wrong.

'Port Authority is in charge of the site coverage,' Thurst said. 'We have some internal warehouse surveillance but the yard is under the port. Federal security, border control, you know?'

'How can a fully crewed shift not see? Must have been twenty people in the area.'

'I agree. This blindness is impossible.'

'Why isn't that in the report then?' Chrissie pushed.

'Not up to the bureau to say at this stage. I'm telling you these union guys are tight. They are trying to use this fatality against us. But it's dangerous – one of the reasons we're trying to automate, make it safer. We've tried for years to break up the brotherhood.' He gave her a quick dry smile. 'But we can't get through. Which brings me to you.'

Chrissie bristled but kept her expression set to neutral.

'You don't have a history with anyone in this town. No axe to grind. I read that piece you did on the rugby rorts in New Zealand. Took some guts to break that code. Took some digging, too.' He smiled. *Ah, flattery, now; currying favour.* 'Anyway, thought you might appreciate something meaty to get your teeth into. But before we get to that, you know it would upset the family terribly if you ran Masina's profile story now.' *Upset Grange, more like it.*

'Cultural sensitivities and all, she was Samoan . . .' Thurst seemed to be waiting for an answer, her agreement to hold off on the story, but she stayed silent, facing him down.

'Well,' he sat back in his chair, 'seems to me you'd be a natural to dig around, yes? And I reckon you might just be able to find something. If you know where to look . . .'

'And you're going to tell me where, right?'

'If you want. And if I've heard right, you do. Got a bit of your own shit to prove over there at *The Argus*.'

Thurst had done his homework. But was he playing her for a patsy? Did he think she would lap up anything just to make a name for herself? *Let him think it.*

'Grange can't be involved,' he continued. 'I need complete assurance this is off the record. And I need you to agree to our timeline.' Chrissie stayed silent. 'We're only talking to you because we need this to stay under wraps, for now. If you agree you can read this.' Thurst pushed the second folder towards her. She opened it immediately, without agreeing to the condition.

Despite her scepticism, what Charlie Thurst had in the second folder shocked Chrissie. It included the final report about Hank Timmons's death five months ago. Mas's friend. The same problems: no witness, no video footage. Official cause of death from the coroner was workplace misadventure.

'But there's photographs of the accident scene, it looks like it happened near the forecourt.' Chrissie examined the prints one by one. 'There must have been witnesses.' Thurst shook his head slowly. She shuffled through more photos and documents about other accidents, other workers. She recognised a few of the names from the list of injuries she had researched last week.

'People are being hurt, killed even,' Thurst said flatly as she continued to turn the pages. Then she heard him take a slow deep breath. 'The union's staging accidents.' She looked up, his eyes focused on her. 'Workers being set up for compo claims.' His voice steely. 'To get a payout, early retirement, insurance claim, as well as reinforce the union's dispute against us. Make us look bad.'

Chrissie stayed deadpan but she was shocked at the suggestion, reaching for the glass in front of her and taking a slow drink. Thurst topped up her water, his hand steady. 'Grange doesn't run these docks, the union does,' he said. 'An increase in accidents and safety breaches is just what they need to get the upper hand in negotiations – so they think.'

Grange's internal analysis, detailed in the folder, showed a jump in safety breaches. It had appeared to start over a year ago.

Now the Grange docks were running at four incidents a week, mostly minor, but still more than double the national average. And the common denominator? No CCTV, no independent witnesses.

'These accidents just happen invisibly,' Thurst said softly, watching her carefully. 'No security, customs officer or supervisor anywhere near. Just the victim – if they live.'

Mas's whisper: *Something's wrong. It's dangerous*. Remi's grief-stricken words: *Mas's death wasn't an accident*.

Chrissie left the folder on the table and walked back to the window.

There was nothing to lose, she thought. Despite Thurst's implication, she would not owe him a favour. She put her eye to an antique telescope, set on a timber tripod. A boardroom showpiece. Her tension washed away, she could watch the view for hours. Mas's world, her grandad's world. The ships had such exotic names – *Ebba*, *Axl*, *Riffa*, *Alameda*, *Taymar*, *Hercules*. The containers, too, faded red, blue, battleship grey, tied this port to the rest of the world.

'What's the timeframe you mentioned?' She turned.

'Embargoed for two weeks. We've got financial negotiations with US head office. We were planning to give the info more widely in a couple of weeks but this new fatality, your profile piece, well it's pulled it forward.' He shuffled on his chair. 'We're being crucified, internationally, the US unions have started raising a stink now because of the pickets here. This is the second dispute in three years, and we can't afford our investors to be deterred. But as soon as those negotiations are in the bag, we need to end the strike, show it up for what it is.' Thurst pushed his chair back even further, widening his knees as he shifted in his chair.

Chrissie stayed standing at the window. *Stay silent, make him talk.*

'These are new stats from the Safety Bureau, they're available but won't be published until next financial year,' he continued. Chrissie already knew some of it but kept quiet. 'No one is going to put these numbers together anytime soon without our input. What we need is a third party, with "confidential sources", to expose it.' He nodded to the folder. 'You want a good story; we want the story to get out.'

'Why would this end the dispute?'

'You think CCTV footage goes missing like that? Conveniently? You think no one saw her die? Bullshit! Look, I don't know what these witnesses would have to say but the fact that they're not saying anything, that's the smoking gun.'

Why did people think journalists have special powers? Some way to compel the truth. See through walls. Their faith was misplaced. She looked out the window. Thurst was tapping again. He wanted her full attention. He was smarmy, gave her the creeps, but she knew how to handle creeps.

'Agreed.'

CHAPTER 14

Chrissie left Grange's building almost two hours later with a pile of photocopies, footage and data files. The information was dynamite. But it was a time bomb. She hurried back to the office, already forming a list of follow-ups. She made a beeline for her desk, her steps fast and excited. But as she crossed the news floor she could feel lots of eyes on her. She slowed her walk, bent her shoulders slightly forward, head down.

'What's up?' she muttered to James as she slid into her chair. Her eyes, however, were drawn to a message on her keyboard: Detective Bannister, fobbing her off again to the police liaison team to make a fuller statement. James didn't reply. 'What's up?' she asked again, 'something wrong?' But before he could answer, Maria Douglas, the flamboyant sixty-something opinion editor was standing beside her desk. She was a woman who demanded to be seen. Tall and striking. Maria's shoes were another attention-grabber. No sensible footwear for this woman. Chunky yellow platforms today. An oversized Iris Apfel, the New York fashion doyen, Chrissie had thought the first time they met.

'I've got a whole lot of empty space, so I need you to help me get a few things rolling,' Maria said and rubbed her hands together, an armload of bangles jangling.

'Me?'

'Yes, my girl. You . . .' She stopped suddenly and looked across the newsroom to Harry. Letting out a sigh, she focused back to Chrissie. 'Better read your emails. Looks like I'm the first to let you know.' She shook her spiky red head. 'Well, I'll just come straight out, you've been reassigned to obits – temporarily.'

Chrissie looked in disbelief at James, his nervous expression confirming it. She looked around at her other colleagues, most avoiding her eyes. *The newcomer, sidelined again.* Harry, however, was standing tall, seeming pleased with himself.

'Come and see me when you get yourself sorted,' Maria said in a softer voice, pulling Chrissie's eyes away from Harry. 'But if I can give you one piece of advice: don't make a scene – not yet anyway.' She winked at Chrissie. 'And right now I need you on your toes. Busy day!'

Chrissie was winded. She watched Maria walk back to her desk. Her slow progress across the room was difficult but Maria never let her head drop. She kept her gaze forward, her shoulders back. The cane always caught Chrissie's attention. Its green and blue duck's-head handle stared at Chrissie, its black eye full of sparkle and dread. Just then Chrissie's phone pinged with another text from Parenta.

Ask Grange about missing boxes. Portainer lifts too high. No one shouting about it.

Too late, she thought. Whatever Parenta and the transport union thought was interesting about crane lifts was minor compared with what she'd just found out. Parenta's feud with Hel Carter and the maritime union had slipped in priority. Her investigation had the potential to blow the strike and the maritime union apart but more than that it would expose the fake accidents, the injuries and deaths. Stop people getting hurt. But now this! Assigned to obituaries. She looked towards Maria. *Be strategic.* It would be her new mantra. Work out a game plan, firm up the information from Grange. Then she would take it to Harry. But the embargo clock was ticking.

—

Maria was grateful for the help and proved easy to work for. She immediately sent Chrissie to a memorial service for a twelve-year-old cancer hero. The boy had broken the internet when he livestreamed his death. It was his final act in an eighteen-month selfie documentary of his cancer and treatment. The boy's death was only two months ago yet his family and friends had seemed so healed. When would she heal? Could she ever heal? A cold shiver ran across her chest. It was another reminder she had failed everyone close to her.

'Last thing I needed was a reluctant conscript doing a bad job,' Maria said after Chrissie filed the story, 'so, thanks for not being her. There are worse rounds than obits. Just let the dust settle. In the meantime, you're all mine.'

'Thanks, Maria. But I don't think I can help for long. I've got a story I'm working on, about the crane driver killed at the wharf last week. I need to investigate it.'

Maria looked over the top of her thick black square glasses. Chrissie met her gaze, matter-of-fact as she stood beside Maria's desk.

'There's always a story to work on, Chrissie,' Maria finally broke the silence. 'But that could still work. No need to throw the baby out with the bathwater, eh? Let's call it an extended obituary, for now, shall we? And I can let you have a bit of flexi time.'

'It's a bit more than that,' Chrissie began.

'Well get yourself a chair and tell me about it. God knows there's plenty spare these days.' Maria waved her hand towards the vacant desks.

Chrissie ran through her visit with Grange and the trove of documents, photos, and data files she'd returned with, her voice getting faster as she spoke.

'The timelines, the reports, the growing hostility between the company and the union. It paints a picture of sabotage.' Chrissie pulled out a photograph or an accident report, here and there, to demonstrate. 'As reluctant as I am to be fed something from someone like Charlie Thurst, there are just too many coincidences. People always looking the other way. Accidents happening, cameras offline.'

'So are you saying this woman's death is one of these fake accidents gone too far?' Maria leaned forward.

'Could be. Or maybe she'd seen something she shouldn't have. Knew too much . . . She called me, left a message, day before she was killed.' Chrissie shuffled. 'Said she was worried, said things were dangerous.'

Maria pushed her glasses back on top of her head, checked the time. Chrissie's palms itched but she willed herself to sit still. Maria raised a knowing eyebrow.

'Anything else?

Chrissie let out a breath.

'I met up with one of Mas's workmates. He thinks, he thinks her death is suspicious.'

'You have been busy. Well, that could be some bloody good yarn you've got cooking there. Blow the lid off that dock pressure cooker. I agree, it doesn't add up and that usually means a good story.'

Chrissie beamed, her shoulders instantly relaxed as she sat back in the chair. She had braced for a squabble.

It was Maria who was talking fast, now. She'd forgotten the page proofs she'd been working on, firing off questions and looking through some of the paperwork. 'How secure is this embargo? You'll need the full two weeks to get this up to scratch and through the lawyers.' She stopped suddenly. They both knew, two weeks was not enough. Investigations like this took months, one of the reasons there were so few. Newsrooms could no longer afford someone off the roster, even for a couple of weeks.

Chrissie looked towards Jefferies' office. The editorial director, Harry's boss. Maria's eyes followed. Jefferies' door was open, light on. 'Ah let's not go there just yet,' Maria volunteered. 'Give me some thinking time, okay? Do us both a favour,' Maria continued, 'keep this on the quiet, for now, let me see what I can rustle up.'

Strategic. She liked this spiky woman.

Chrissie looked back at the open door. Jefferies knew everything about her. He had arranged the job as soon as Chrissie's old boss had asked for help, hiring her over Harry's head. The two men were already combative, she learned after arriving at *The Argus*. Her employment had made it worse. Jefferies had stuck his neck out for her once already. If she went directly to Jefferies, it could infuriate Harry and likely stir up more resentment towards her. She already felt weighed down.

—

The hate had started so slowly, she wasn't even sure it was real. A glance. A hesitation. A sigh. At first Chrissie thought it was her guilt or grief or the medication. Everything was fuddled. She still couldn't recall the car crash but she knew it was her fault. Were people avoiding her?

It was only later, much later, that she pinned it to the funeral service. As if people had been waiting to get through it. Holding their breath on their anger until the ritual was over. As soon as it was done, they let out their hatred.

Bound to a wheelchair, braced and medicated, she sat through the service in silence, her head nodding occasionally in a drug and grief haze. Chrissie's father had tried to bundle her up and whisk her back to hospital but she'd insisted on staying. As he wheeled her around, she thought people looked away. Conversations stalled. No one made eye contact. Or did she imagine it?

When she was finally discharged from hospital almost a week after the funeral, Chrissie moved in with her father. On the way she made a stop, at their place, hers and Dave's.

'Not yet,' her dad had tried to suggest. As if 'yet' offered some magical promise.

But Chrissie had insisted. The flat had seemed so normal, at first, as if Dave was just at work or out playing footy. A few clean dishes on the draining board, his sports bag dumped at the bottom of the stairs. It smelled like Dave and like home. She hobbled around. Folded up the two-week-old newspaper on the kitchen island. Checked the fridge. Then she saw them. The packing boxes in the spare room. Some already labelled, ready for the move into their new home in a few months. Those harmless brown cardboard boxes contained a new hell that broke through the fog of painkillers and sedatives.

'We can do it bit by bit, avoid the last-minute moving panic,' Dave had encouraged her, just a few weeks earlier. He was always so organised.

They had planned it for years, the old Chauncer house, next to his parents' dairy farm near Cambridge. It would be perfect for when Dave eventually took over the running. The white timber house had been empty for a few years while the Chauncer children decided what to do. But there was never any likelihood that they'd sell it to anyone else. It was always going to be Dave and Chrissie's. They had been working on it for about five months, painting, scraping, cleaning. New kitchen.

At the sight of those boxes she had crumpled against the wall, understanding then about 'yet'. She let her dad steer her away.

Dave's parents, Denise and Tony Watford, didn't visit Chrissie again after the funeral. They also didn't ask if they could go around to the flat, but they removed Dave's things one by one. When Chrissie found out she was happy for them to take what they wanted. Happy they were keeping an eye on the place. But when she finally moved back she realised that they had stripped Dave away. Clothes, sports trophies, even his tools. She had hobbled out to the garage to find the shelves almost bare.

Chrissie had taken Dave from their lives. Now they had taken what was left. Almost everything. A framed photo of them, left smashed on the back path. She had rescued it, removing the glass and propping it back on the bookcase. Dave's big grin outshone everything. Her arms wrapped around his waist as she looked up with pride. *Happy. She could never be that girl again.*

'It's your fault that he's dead! I could . . . I could . . . hate you!' Denise had said before slamming the phone down when Chrissie, drunk and sedated, had phoned a few days later.

That night, surrounded by their invisible debris, was the first time she thought about suicide. A month later she made her first attempt.

It had been easy to reject people after that. The depression was unending. Medication was never enough. She stopped answering the door and the phone. She shut herself away from her brother, her friends – Dave's friends – ashamed. It was the same shame and regret she saw every time she looked at her father. He had lost his son-in-law as well as his daughter, the old version, his funny, unstoppable, fierce daughter. It was so hard even to speak to him.

But at work on the local paper she was as thorough and focused as before. She collapsed at night, burnt out from the effort of trying to be normal. She had nothing left, no conversation, no facial movements, no strength except to drive home. Soon her workmates started to avoid her too. She welcomed the isolation, fewer fake smiles to force. But she needed her job. She needed a purpose, a goal. A reason.

Michael Plumb, the owner of the *Waikato Daily*, had other ideas. He had known the Watford family for decades and he saw how the blame had divided the small town. He asked his editor Malcolm Chisel to get rid of her. On the quiet, he didn't want any blowback.

'Plumb said you can't stay,' Chrissie's father George had told it to her straight, word for word, just as her editor Malcolm had told him. 'At first Mal resisted,' her dad continued, his voice starting to jag, 'but I told him it was probably the right thing.' They sat at his kitchen table, the pot of tea between them.

Mal eventually told Chrissie himself, in the same tough straight-talking rural style.

'It would help everyone heal, especially you,' he had said to her. 'The Watfords wouldn't have to read your name in their paper every day. You wouldn't have to avoid them at the supermarket. The town can stop taking sides.' He paced behind his desk as Chrissie sat with her back to the small newsroom. The team at the *Daily* tried not to watch through the glass but most couldn't help nervously glancing. 'I've found you a job, a good job, in Melbourne,' Malcom had said. 'A favour from an old mate. A fresh start.'

Chrissie knew he was right. Some people wished she had died, not Dave. Not the footy hero, the only child, the future of farming, the future of the small town. She agreed. Leaving was the next best thing.

CHAPTER 15

The task ahead of Chrissie was almost overwhelming. Despite Maria's willingness, the last thing she wanted was to work the investigation part-time in between obits. Grange had given her two weeks head start but she could easily fail. Charlie Thurst said he would drop the documents on Channel Two if she missed the deadline. But at least her rivals wouldn't be looking in the same direction. It was Grange who had put together the dossier, Grange who had set the embargo.

Propped up on her sofa, Skinny curled at her feet, she focused.

Data: Third-party corroboration of draft Safety Bureau report. Check Grange's information and photos against actual locations. View official accident or insurance records. Draw up injury timeline.

People: Interview injured staff; families of deceased. Ask to see medical records, insurance payouts. Interview other workers, why do they think accident rate is high?

Grange: Financial pressure. What are the negotiations in the US? Implication of not renewing terminal leases. What other automation and union action in other countries?

Maritime union: Get to the core of the automation dispute. What will the automation mean for workers, careers, numbers? Will automation be safer? Impact of foreign workforce? Union merger speculation?

Legal: Go for broke, write inhouse draft, provide lawyers with documents. See what they throw back. Cover all legal queries.

Round two: Re-interview Grange on the record. Confrontation interview with maritime union (one day before publication?)

Final story: Front page splash. Fake accidents. Full story inside. Case studies: Mas, Hank? Wharf family – four generations?

Graphics: Injury statistics. Accident timeline. Best versus worst ports in Australia/world. Tear-outs of original documents.

Fallback story: If the fake accident evidence falls short. The changing docks. The human toll: Families destroyed, inter-generational impacts. Industrial warfare: The depths of animosity between white- and blue-collar. Dangerous docks: Automation. Foreign workers. Longer shifts. Human error. Cost cutting versus shareholder profits. Bad management versus bad work practices. The 'blue economy' – the world's oldest form of global trade changing forever.

Two weeks!

—

She was slipping away. Fingers too weak to grab hold. *Falling through clouds*. She could smell the ocean, feel the sun. Floating, now. She hung in the sky. Hands lifting her. False hands. Hurt, betrayed. Falling again, through fear and pain and regret.

Chrissie woke with a fright, gasping for air. Slapping her hands down either side of the mattress, desperate to feel grounded, solid. Not falling. Just a dream, she soothed herself. *Masina. Was that Mas's horrible death?* More guilt. Or her own fate? Was she still falling? Still not at rock bottom yet?

—

That morning at work she went straight to Maria to suggest they talk to Jefferies, get her off obits. But Maria had her own agenda.

'I can't tell you everything but nobody's going to like it. One of the reasons I had to defer yesterday. I had a busy evening last night,' Maria started, then stopped. Chrissie didn't need to glance around to know Harry was on his way over. 'Ah, good timing, Harry,' Maria said. Harry had come to a sudden halt beside Chrissie, his prim white collar buttoned tightly behind a navy tie. Grey hair, tightly cropped.

'I'm just telling Chrissie she'll be with me a while longer. The "powers that be" have approved her move, next three months.'

Chrissie felt the air rush out of her. She dared not look at Harry or Maria. It was the last thing she wanted to hear.

'First I've heard of it!' Harry snapped.

First I've heard of it, too!

'Who approved that?' His voice too loud, his face tight. 'Or another one of your little secrets?' Harry spat at Chrissie.

Secrets! What does he know? Chrissie braced herself against the desk.

'HR signed off late yesterday afternoon,' Maria drew him back to her, 'but it's been in the works for months. You know I've been shorthanded, Haz. I thought maybe that's why you suggested Chrissie in the first place.' She softened her voice, gave him an out from his embarrassment but Harry just stormed off.

'Maria, what's going on?' Chrissie half-croaked.

'Not here. Let's go for a cuppa, give me ten.' And she squeezed Chrissie's hand.

Maria stood equal height to most men. With her dyed red hair and trademark red lipstick, she was not your typical section head. Chrissie doubted she had been typical at any stage of her forty years in journalism. She had heard about Maria's reputation for being a rule breaker but apparently there wasn't a single editor who didn't sing her praises. James had once told Chrissie that, before the multiple sclerosis, Maria was Harry's biggest rival for editor.

—

Chrissie and Maria headed for the Junction, the closest place to *The Argus*. Despite the short walk, it seemed to take forever, as Chrissie scratched her palms anxiously.

'My MS is having a "slow and steady" day,' Maria said. But when Chrissie asked if she could carry her bag, Maria barked a harsh refusal. 'I'm good,' she added almost immediately, as a way of an apology. 'Bit touchy about it.'

Being stuck on obits for the next few months was a huge setback. Chrissie had to get to the truth of Mas's death and soon.

If Charlie Thurst got wind that she had been reassigned, he might also look elsewhere. For now, however, he'd given his word, plus he knew she still had Mas's interview up her sleeve, as leverage.

'You get us a table. What about over there, away from the others? Tea?'

Chrissie nodded. She looked around the room, crowded with shelves of European trinkets and photos. She saw a few staffers lined up for takeaways or sitting at the nearby tables.

'You've been reassigned to op-ed; that was finalised last night. Sorry I had to be a bit cagey. Nothing you can do about it,' Maria offered as Chrissie sat forward, 'and I suspect you won't want to do anything, once you know the whole story.'

'But I have to get back on news. Get this story written.'

'Chrissie, it's nothing personal, I've been on the campaign trail for an extra person since January, and when I campaign, believe me, I'm tireless.' She smiled as she lifted her cup of hot chocolate and gave herself a toast. 'When Harry handed you over yesterday, I pretty much knew he'd played my best hand for me. Evidence the news desk could manage one down and, well, nagging had already done the rest.'

'Sorry, Maria, but this is not what I want!' Chrissie's voice was loaded with frustration.

'It will be, my girl, believe me. Given your level of popularity around here.' Maria nodded towards their colleagues. 'There's a new round of staff cuts coming. Harry's not just going to be one down; he's going to lose *several* people.'

Chrissie sat, stunned. How can they? *Another hurdle.*

'No need to say it.' Maria held up both hands. 'I know. No staff, no news, no readers! And no use complaining to me.'

She shifted in her chair, its hollow back uncomfortable, its seat too narrow. 'We're all on tight budgets, no commitments beyond three months. You won't be leaving. Unless you choose to. As of now, you're locked in with me for the next three months – someone must have been looking out for you.'

'But Maria –'

'I know how good your story is shaping up. I haven't got MS of my news judgement! And I'll help you get it over the line.'

Chrissie looked down, embarrassed by her outburst in the face of Maria's courage. She looked around the café. Her colleagues were going to resent her even more, she knew. Chrissie could always quit or ask for help, but there was no way she would hand the story over. It was her chance to make her name in Melbourne. A name she had already earned back home but had to leave behind. Along with the other names she once had; wife, friend, daughter. *Breathe.* More importantly, she had to get to the truth, for Mas's sake – and stop more people being hurt or killed.

'It could get a bit tricky for you,' Maria continued, finishing the last of her drink. 'Harry will put up a fight. And so he should, I wouldn't expect anything less. And what I've said about the cuts stays under wraps. Even Haz doesn't know yet. They only told me because of your transfer. But, listen, I can loosen the reins, time to work on the story.'

At least, something positive.

'But keep it low-key, it has to remain between us.' Maria leaned closer. 'Don't mention anything about this story to anyone, not even your buddy James, but especially not Jefferies or Harry, for now. You're supposed to be strictly on my pages, my budget.

I don't want Harry using my own argument against me – that I can spare you. He'll certainly be on the warpath. Looking for heads to roll. And you know how much he likes the look of yours.'

—

The gym that night was crowded and steamy.

Left, left, right.

Chrissie pivoted on her back foot, weight on her front, hands back in position, curled in front of her face, left shoulder rounded, chin slightly tucked. *Again!*

Jab, jab, cross, hook, cross. *Again!*

Left, left, right, left, right. *Again!*

She wiped the back of her glove across her shiny face. *Still falling. Still not at rock bottom.* The tears easily mixed with her sweat, hidden in plain sight. Hands automatically back in position.

Again!

Again!

The thumping bass of the music drove her on: 'Lose Yourself', Eminem.

She had found the gym a week after arriving in Richmond. At first, she couldn't even budge the bag, not even a shudder from her puny arms. It was a real boxing gym. Not the gushy girl-power version at her mirrored gym back home. Here, Ken, the manager, had kept his distance but still pushed her. Set her a program, tried to get her to come more regularly, put her in the circuit class where she wouldn't have to talk to anyone.

'Getting strong, Chrissie. Getting strong,' Ken shouted from across the room. She knew he didn't just mean the boxing. But boxing was now one of the few times she stopped worrying, stopped grieving. She realised she needed the headspace to be violent. To get some of the hate out.

CHAPTER 16

Chrissie could smell chocolate and sunshine. She could hear Dave in the kitchen making breakfast. Sunday morning, the best morning of the week. Soon he would be standing beside her, holding the tray with their tea and chocolate chip pancakes.

'Chrissie?' she heard Dave call. 'Chrissie? Chrissie?'

She sat bolt up, waking in a sweat just as she tried to call back, to let him know she was there. Skinny sprang to the other side of the room in fright and then just sat looking back. The cat had almost become used to her.

Another dream. At first she had thought of them as nightmares but then she came to welcome them – those few more seconds with Dave.

Chrissie checked her phone, it showed three missed calls. All from Remi. And now as she held the phone, he was calling again.

Her head was clear despite being dragged awake, less wine and pills last night. She let the call ring out, she still hadn't decided what, if anything, to tell Remi or if she trusted him.

She jumped out of bed, there was no time to spare doing two jobs, but the phone started immediately buzzing again. She couldn't keep avoiding him.

'Remi, hi,' she croaked, her mouth still dry from sleep. 'It's early.'

'Can we meet? I was doing some digging.'

Her head slumped. The last thing she needed to hear. If he was blundering around upsetting people, it could tip someone off and make her job harder. She needed him to keep his eyes open and his mouth shut. She'd have to rein him in.

'Yes, okay. After work. The Newmarket. I finish at 8, is that too late?

'At the pokies, see you about 8.20.' He hung up.

Skinny followed her down the stairs on her way to work, she left him meowing at Mike's door.

—

Maria handed her a scruffy stack of letters the minute she walked past her desk.

'Have a look through these please and check the emails. I've also got three obits – can you whip them into shape? One's been written by a PR firm, the guy who ran that big financial advice company. Rip-off bastard, if you ask me.' She looked over her glasses at Chrissie, thin blue half-moon frames today, matching earrings. 'Tone that one down,' she tapped the paper on the top, 'but not too much or they'll want a refund. The other two just need a bit of a tickle.'

Chrissie's eyes widened. *A refund?*

'Ha! Sorry to be the one to tell you, my girl. Even the obits have been "commercialised."' Maria said the last word with an exaggerated, luscious TV presenter's voice. 'We've cashed in on having a nearest and dearest immortalised on the public record.' Maria scoffed as she waved a bunch of printouts in the air. 'And bloody lucrative, too. Price no barrier when it comes to rewriting history. Scandals, public embarrassments completely erased.' She hunted for a space on her desk for a small vase of rosemary. 'From my garden.' She lifted the sprigs for Chrissie to smell. 'Keeps me alert, blocks out some of the stink about this place too.' She flashed a grin. 'Oh, and when I said you could work on your wharf story yesterday, that was before I realised today was going to be so crappy.' She nestled the vase next to her phone. 'Which means all the calls from readers have also been diverted to your extension. I won't even have time to fart today, so you're it.' Maria winced as she stood.

'You okay?' Chrissie ventured.

'Yes, yes,' Maria bristled, her chin up momentarily, then she leaned on the desk. 'Some days it just slows me down.' She shook her head softly. 'Others it's pain up and down my legs like an electric railway track. Or today,' Maria lifted her hands off the desk and flexed her fingers, 'hands and feet feel like they're slowly freezing solid. Plays havoc with my fashion choices!' She turned out a pointed foot to flash her silver patent lace-ups.

—

How does anyone think in this place? The hotel gaming room was a living nightmare. Beeps, rings, whistles, jackpots jumped out at Chrissie. She braced herself against the wall and scrambled in her bag for her earbuds, pushing them in to help block the sounds. The lights flashed every colour of the spectrum. Nothing was in sync; the wallpaper pattern was too bold, the images on the machines changed too often. The music at its own tempo. *Breathe; one, two, three.* Her nerves were already on edge. She had agreed to Maria's plan, despite her reservations. She would keep on the investigation but stay writing for Maria. She still had Jefferies, tucked up her sleeve, as a potential get-out-of-obit card. But he would be her one and only card.

Chrissie shuffled her feet but they kept sticking to the Newmarket's filthy carpet, half the light tubes needed replacing, yet the bar was two-deep with patrons. *Must spot Remi when he arrives.* She made her way to one of the poker machines at the beginning of a row, sat down on a red and chrome stool and fed in a twenty note. *Breathe.*

'Looks like you're ahead.' Remi had come up beside her at the pokies machine. She jumped.

'How can you tell? I've no idea, I just keep pressing.' Chrissie pulled her earbuds out.

'Thought you must have been a player, to wanna come here. This isn't your neck of the woods is it?'

'Nah, other side of town. Remi, I'm not sure where I'm at yet with the investigation.' She shifted off the stool to stand, still unsure about how much to tell him.

'It's almost a week since she died.' Remi's face twisted, his chin collapsed. His pain looked even worse in the grotesque lighting show. 'Mas, she was a bossy thing. Shy but with seven brothers, she would have stuck up for herself. She was a Grange girl, through and through –'

'I thought she'd only been there a few years?'

'Three in Melbourne, but she'd worked for them for years. They trained her over in Guam, then San Diego. She was a bit of a female protégé. Family worked at a seafood factory in Samoa, that's where they first hired her, part of Grange's seafood . . .'

The bells and alarms on the machines were screeching. Chrissie tried to watch his face more closely, keep up with his lips, but the flashing lights were changing too quickly. She steadied herself against a machine.

'Let's get out of here. I can't hear what you're saying.' She waved to the lounge bar.

'Not yet.' He grabbed her arm. 'I want you to meet someone. He's here, Kingi. But he's scared.' Chrissie hesitated. 'He's unofficial, okay?' Remi continued. 'You can't name him or tell anyone.' He steered Chrissie around the next line of pokies to a big Maori guy, floral shirt. He was pressing buttons over and over. His hands shook.

'They were making us sign off on dodgy lift tallies,' Kingi said after Remi's prompting. His neck tattoos moved as he spoke.

'Who told you? Who made you sign?' *Crane lift.* Chrissie's mind jumped to Charlie Thurst at Grange's office and Parenta's text: the crane lifts were wrong. *Fake accidents, fake lift tallies?*

Kingi slumped on his stool, shook his head but his eyes stayed glued to the screen, his hands still busy at the buttons. 'I don't know who. Just had to. No skin off my nose. We knew not to arc up. Except Mas. Not in the stupid boys' club, she said. She stayed quiet but told me no one was going to tell her what to do.'

'Do you know how Mas died? I mean, was it an accident?'

'I don't know nothing. I'm only here because . . .' He lifted his hands off the machine for the first time and buried his face in them. 'I'm done, bro,' he said looking to Remi. 'I've done what you wanted. That's it, mate. That's all, everything.'

He stood, looming over Chrissie. 'Don't quote me,' he said in her face. 'Don't contact me and don't put the cops on me because, if you do, I'm gonna say you're a liar.'

'Can you get me copies of the tallies?' Chrissie tried not to flinch as he pushed past her. But Kingi just kept walking.

'I'm getting them,' Remi replied instead as Kingi disappeared in the crowded room. 'The tallies.' Chrissie's head was thumping. She had to leave.

'I'm seeing the union tomorrow, anything I should know?'

'No, no. Don't tell the union.' Remi grabbed her arm.

'Hey, I'm not going to tell anyone anything.' Chrissie shook him off. 'I'm going there to listen,' she said more calmly. 'But I don't want you to tip anyone off either, if you ask around too much. How did you find Kingi? Or did he come to you?'

'He, he found her that day . . . after, you know. He went to give back her parking permit. There she was, on the ground.'

Chrissie rubbed Remi's arm, a rare touch from her.

'Just keep everything low-key, okay?'

—

She was first to the train door as usual, after leaving Remi at the hotel. On the North Richmond platform three people stood near the exit ramp. One was Toothless. *Not tonight*. But they weren't interested. Already high and feeling good, judging from their posture. The shorter, dirtiest one, leered and feinted a move at her, which made Toothless laugh. The girl, Demi, helpless to their moods, offered a half-smile but Chrissie kept on.

The walk from the station to her flat offered a rare sight. *Mammatus* clouds. The bubble shapes hung low in the cooling air, the long last strands of orange sun highlighted their roundness. Dave had taught her to cloud watch, the only thing she could still share with him. Every day she looked.

CHAPTER 17

Into the lion's den. The Maritime Workers' Association had its name embossed on the front of a stocky building nestled on the edge of the CBD, its red brick facade out of place now among the showy thin skyscrapers. The office had once been much closer to the port, more than a century and a half ago. Since then land reclamation and expansions had pushed it away from the wharves, another metaphor for the union's fate.

The MWA also had a smaller 'tin box' office next to the port, but the grand head office was still the historic show of strength. Tradition oozed from every brick, its foyer crowded with photographs confirming its place in history. In every picture, some so grainy they could barely be made out, proud men posed across the decades; from dirty suit jackets, belted pants and cloth hats, to the drooping moustaches of the 1970s and the fierce faces of the 1998 lockout. Chrissie was drawn to one famous picture, a news photo of a young child screaming in her father's arms as black-booted security approached. That twenty-plus-year-old image was the turning point in the great waterfront dispute, capturing world attention, worth more than a million words. Chrissie wondered how many news photographers would soon be left. Phone images taken by fame-seekers and multi-tasking reporters now often did the job for cheap instead.

Today she was meeting Hel Carter.

On her list of questions, now, was Parenta's text about crane lifts and missing containers.

Lift tallies, she'd discovered, were an indication of how many containers were being handled and productivity. If crane movements didn't match the cargo, it pointed to theft or fraud. Or bad record-keeping. The issue played perfectly into the future of the wharves. The next round of technology was here. Robo vehicles and automated equipment. The new portainers no longer needed to be manned. *Mas's job redundant.* Even the straddles that shuttled the containers around the site would be driverless. In the new world everything would be controlled from high up looking down. A bit like an airport control tower. A bit like Grange's office.

The technology brought with it a new white-collar workforce to push buttons and program machines. Automated terminals posed another big threat to the maritime union. Fewer members and less power. Merger talks between the unions were already in the air. Today she planned to skirt around the allegations Grange had raised, the time for confrontation would come later. Otherwise the storyline and reason for being there was the same:

background about the picket, the safety issues, the workers, their families and the automation.

Carter's bouncing grey curls greeted Chrissie as the union boss crossed the mosaic tiles in the old foyer. 'Let's go out and get some coffees,' she rasped. 'These offices are a bit cramped – not as bad as your joint, probably, but not much better.'

Chrissie was intrigued when Carter led her past several cafés and they jumped on a rattling old tram. *Haven't got all day*, she thought, but kept her mouth shut.

'Just a short trip,' Carter said with a sheepish grin. 'Thought we might go to one of my favourite cafés. First, got a little detour to pick something up. Then we head up to Parli, I've got a meeting straight after. Two birds, ya know?'

The historic tram rattled its way to the Docklands. Apartment towers, exotic cruising boats, the marina and the restaurants of Waterfront City had erased Melbourne's original wharves and wooden sheds. Carter led the way into a shiny French patisserie. Millimetre-precise pastries and cakes sat on display, bright red cherries on tiny circles of coloured sponge, chocolate twirls atop pink fancies enclosed by corrugated walls. Carter ignored the fare, nodding at a suited young man sitting at one of the small marble tables, busy on his laptop, talking through a bluetooth earpiece.

'He's not one for chatting much,' she offered as warning. 'Blair! Blair Johnston, this is Chris O'Brian, from *The Argus*. She's doing a piece about the waterfront.'

'So, the strike finally got someone's attention at *The Argus*? Taken a while.' Johnston stood to shake hands with Chrissie. 'Anyone'd think the port wasn't part of this city.'

'Yeah, well. Our industry's going through a lot of change too,' Chrissie offered.

'And don't we all suffer for it,' Carter butted in. 'We're not stopping, Blair, just need those photos. How was it down there this morning?' Turning to Chrissie, she went on. 'First picket, six months ago, just a couple of hours, once a week. Now we're fully manned every day. Beautiful, just beautiful!'

'Always fires me up,' Blair said. 'Fucking Grange. Pics should be good. Here.' He handed Carter a memory card. Chrissie tensed with anticipation. What would that card reveal?

'Not what you'd expect is he, eh?' Carter said when they were outside again. 'He's a bloody trooper that one, been down on the line, doing a stint since early. Family not so keen on his career choice, but them's the breaks. Now,' she took a deep breath, stretching her navy striped shirt to full capacity, 'fancy a look at the old guard? We'll need to jump in a cab.'

They drove into the heart of the port area. Yard after yard of containers, stacked beside and on top of each other, six high. Orange dominated among the bright blue and green. The draft from the huge trucks shook the taxi, their cargo trays full and looming high above them. The cab drove past the main gates and the noisy picket.

'Toot your horn, mate,' Carter said to the driver as she wound down her window. The taxi slowed and gave a long loud beep as Carter stuck her head out. 'Good on ya, fellas.' The picketers instantly recognised her, hoorayed and blew their whistles in response.

'The picket's big today,' Chrissie noted but Carter didn't respond. She was busy giving careful instructions to the cabby. But she'd heard, all right.

'Damn right, this death's hit hard,' she said.

Under Carter's instructions, the taxi ducked under a free-way overpass, down a ramp and then suddenly veered left. They'd arrived at a rundown truckie café. White painted rocks embedded in the garden welcomed the hungry and stopped vehicles from getting too close. No fancy smoked salmon on sourdough bread in this roadhouse. Sandwiches made with thick white bread. Bacon and egg rolls, bowls of steaming porridge and plates of sausage and mash sat in the glass-fronted bain-marie. Next to it was a hot-box full of pies and sausage rolls. Potato cakes. The café had a 24-hour menu to cater for all shifts. But its glory days were long gone. The neon sign said open every day but a small printed laminated page next to the front door read 'Closed Saturday arvo and all-day Sunday'. On this Thursday, the car park was full of trucks, most with their trailers loaded with containers, others skeletal and waiting for their pick-up slot.

'What'll you have, Chris? My treat. Big spender, eh?' She motioned around the shabby diner with its wooden tables. Relics from the past, both the men and the furniture, Chrissie thought as they slipped into a seat with a car park view.

It had an uneasy feel. She expected back-slapping and male bonding after a hard-worked shift, workmates refuelling on carbohydrates and meat for a new day. Instead the atmosphere was gloomy and it wasn't just the smoky grill. Hunched shoulders, the workers all seemed so tired. The layers of clothes and safety vests homogenised the men but also their expressions. Talkback radio crackled near the counter.

'Tea thanks, black.' Chrissie said.

'You're a cheap date. No sarnie? What about a scone – jam and cream? No? I'll be back in a tick, just seen an old mate. Friend of my uncle's, been here for almost 50 years. Now he could tell you some stories.' Carter signalled to a wrinkled bald head across the room.

As she watched Carter talking to her friend, it dawned on Chrissie what was bugging her. There were no young men here. Everyone looked over fifty, sixty even. Where were the young men?

Carter returned with Chrissie's tea. She sat heavily, hitching her belt, and slurped a diet soft drink through a paper straw.

'This is the old world,' she said quietly, as though reading Chrissie's mind. 'Young Blair, that's the new world. This is where we've come from though, where our membership grew up.'

'What's this I hear about union infighting? Down at Trades Hall? Is that a new-guard-old-guard situation?' Chrissie recalled the gauntlet note.

'Always some bitching going on. Politics. Keep my nose out of that shit as much as possible but, then, I've been known to make a move or two.' Carter gave her a wink. 'Why?'

'Just getting the lie of the land.'

'Sounds like you've been reading the business pages too much. Corporates always want to make out we're dysfunctional. Crush the unions, keep wages low. Old news,' Carter bristled.

Chrissie looked around the diner; nothing much had changed in these places since her grandfather's day. But now, instead of being a welcome guest of her grandfather and his mates, she realised she was an intruder. A dangerous intruder. She was soon going to inflict a mortal wound on this world.

Carter surprised her again with the next destination. Weaving back through the city, they arrived at a small city park caged in by an elaborate Victorian wrought-iron fence. Inside, a fountain of sorts, a triangular framework of stainless steel sprayed water down into a shallow pool. A young Asian couple to one side were having their wedding photos taken, the shifting fountain spray adding beauty and light. The noise of the water drowned out the traffic and the pedestrians. It created a sound capsule. A cone of silence.

Chrissie felt she had moved into another dimension. The small park with its tall fence now seemed like a prison, cutting her off from the rest of the city. A tram jolted around the corner on its dusty track, she imagined the noisy squeal it was making but could barely hear it. On the other side of Spring Street hundreds of lightbulbs flashed in time to a silent tempo around the awning of a theatre.

'There's major fraud on Grange's docks and nobody, I mean nobody, is shouting the odds.' Carter was straight to business. Union business. She leaned towards Chrissie as they sat on the park bench. 'We've got too many lifts and not enough containers to match. Truck movements that don't match.' Her face hung frozen for a moment then quickly moved back to action. 'Whatever's going on, you can bloody well bet it's designed to make us look bad.'

Chrissie's strategy had backfired. Carter was raising the issue before she'd even had a chance.

'It's not pilfering. It's organised,' Carter said, jabbing a hand angrily in the air. 'We're talking tonnes of cargo, multiple boxes. Don't know what's in them or who they're from or who's picking them off. And don't let anyone bullshit you it's our blokes fudging productivity.' Both hands were doing the talking now. Jab, swing, jab. Her grey hair ducking and weaving around her face. 'That's fucking nonsense, excuse my French. Invented by some pen-pusher with an economics slash dick-counter degree.' Carter leaned back, her face red, eyes barely slits. She took a few breaths as she calmed herself, lowered her voice and focused on Chrissie again. 'We also know that Grange doesn't want the cops or anyone involved.'

The wedding photographs reached new heights as the photographer made the groom leap in the air beside his stock-still bride.

'Grange is worried they'd lose millions in contract withdrawals if their shippers found out. We also know they've slipped in extra security to keep it in-house, under wraps. No cops. No insurance claims. No publicity. As if it's not even happening.'

'Can they do that?' Chrissie asked. 'I mean if stuff's going missing, someone's got to pay.'

'We assume Grange is coughing up for it. They've also got a lot of extra foreign workers. Spanish speaking, most. Temporary bloody visa crap.' Carter threw her hands in the air again. 'These new guys stick out like sore thumbs, don't know shit, don't take breaks, twelve-hour shifts, makes it bloody dangerous for everyone.'

Chrissie sat silently. This was not what she'd expected. She only had ten days left on Grange's embargo. Her palms itched at the thought of failing. Not just fear of missing a story but failing. Failing the truth and now failing Maria's trust, too.

'How the hell am I supposed to know what all that means?' she blurted to Carter. 'Just spit it out. Give it to me straight.'

'Ha!' Carter slapped her on the arm and gave a matey laugh. 'I'll give you what I've got although there's still holes. But there's something you need to be aware of.' She leaned forward again. 'Might be another problem, closer to home.'

Carter paused, searching Chrissie's face.

'Some of the bad news about certain people or companies doesn't always get ink at *The Argus*.'

Chrissie stared back, unsure what she meant.

'There's a little too much picking and choosing what gets published,' Carter said more slowly. 'You might have a bit of internal work to get this story printed. Being short-staffed is one thing but avoiding stories, well, that's a different kettle of fish.'

Chrissie's face stayed still but her ears popped as she clenched her jaw. Surely, she would have noticed something like that. Stories were mis-reported by accident or slashed for space reasons or no staff. But as a strategy?

'No. You've got that wrong,' Chrissie said. 'I've never seen evidence of *The Argus* avoiding a story.'

Like her counterpart at Grange, Hel Carter was an old hand at manipulation.

'I'm not making this up. I've been in this business more than twenty years. You journos don't have the monopoly on the fucking fallout from this digital shakeout.' Her colour rising again, she scuffed her feet. 'Social media? Yeah, fantastic, no gatekeepers. Win-fucking-win.' She was in full flight, hair bobbing. 'But it opened the door to Gomorrah. You think it's easier for us to get the spin across? Now no one believes anything. Nothing fact-checked. Too much noise, nothing cuts through anymore.'

It gave Chrissie comfort to know the likes of Carter recognised the problems.

Carter stood, shook her stiff leg and hobbled a few paces. 'Netballer's knee,' she said as an explanation. The bride and groom had packed up.

'Anyway, got to head off.'

'Yeah, thanks. Let's set up that briefing. By phone?' Chrissie stood too.

'No problem. Stick to the old landline, eh, switchboard to switchboard,' she said. 'I'm going to send you a few tidbits. Nothing electronic. Envelope will be on your desk tomorrow.'

Chrissie took the tram back to the office. It dinged its bell almost the whole way as the driver warned wayward pedestrians to keep out of the way. What had shaped up as a scoop about the union faking accidents, causing a death, had turned full circle. Now Grange was accused of being involved in large scale fraud, hiring heavies, foreigners, keeping it under wraps and making the workplace even more dangerous. *How the hell am I going to pull this off? Ten days.*

—

'Hey James, fancy a drink after work?' Chrissie pounced as soon as she got back to the newsroom. No matter her promise to Maria to stay quiet, she had to tell him about the new redundancies. Several times she had leaned over to whisper, only to be sidetracked by a phone call or someone walking too close. Or she just froze. Not that being laid off would bother him financially, but she liked having him there.

'Can't, sorry. I've got to run, dinner with Gina and my parents. We're finalising the seating plan for the wedding. I'm already late. You do know how big this wedding is going to be, don't you?' he teased.

'I can only imagine the politics involved in that seating plan. Wouldn't want to be AWOL when they decide to put great Aunty Joan from St Georges Road next to one of the Californian hoi polloi.' She sounded more distracted than she meant.

'What's really up?' He gave her a look. 'Come on, spit it out, Chrissie.'

'Just trouble getting my head around a few things on this wharf story.'

'You're still on that? You must be working 24/7.'

'What else have I got to do?' She smiled bleakly. 'But strictly under wraps, especially from Harry – budget wars between the sections. I heard a whisper about more redundancies. You heard anything?'

'Nothing. But I didn't hear the other times either.' James grinned. 'Besides, they're not going to cut anymore. They hired you.'

'And look how well that worked out.'

CHAPTER 18

'O'Brian, you're wanted: Jefferies' office,' Harry shouted from across the room. Chrissie was startled, still struggling to wake properly after too many sleeping pills last night. What now?

She had intended to get stuck into the material she had received from the union. The envelope was on her desk when she'd arrived this morning. Inside was a list of foreign workers and non-union casuals, their shifts and their job allocations. Carter had also included a letter from the union to Grange dated almost six months ago, notifying it about disputed exit checks and malfunctions in the container location system as well as an increase in restows as ships had to be unstacked and restacked because of stuff-ups, the cargo put aside temporarily.

Standing slowly, Chrissie searched her desk for a notebook and walked towards the office. She could hear Harry whistling, pleased with himself.

Tom Jefferies was early fifties, handsome and about six or seven years younger than Harry. The simmering resentment between the two men went deep. It was Jefferies who had taken the job from Harry just over three years ago. The board was convinced that Harry was a dinosaur in the modern newsroom and they wanted someone switched on to new media. Digital was the way to go and Jefferies convinced them that he was the future.

In contrast to Harry's aloof, demanding style, Jefferies was friendly, talkative. A smooth operator. His greatest skill was his mouth, not his writing or his news judgement, and it was a skill he had honed since his first job as a cadet. Even if Harry had changed his ways, and kept his job, Jefferies – or the next one – would have been waiting to pounce.

'Jefferies has a knack for getting people on side,' Maria had told her.

It was a skill that worked well at *The Argus*. Jefferies had schmoozed himself into the top job, because he talked the part. He had told the board that news wasn't news anymore. It was entertainment. And the board of accountants, afraid because they didn't understand this new media puzzle, believed the handsome confidence he offered them.

The paper's current crisis was its worst since the 1950s when it almost closed. Back then, the owner was saved at the last minute when he married the flamboyant Patricia Templeton, the wayward heiress to a Bendigo gold family. Already twice married, Party Patty, as she was known (even by herself), outlived her husband, inherited the newspaper and partied on as sole proprietor until her nineties. After her death her many heirs, including a dozen great-grandchildren, had other plans for their time and inheritance. They had agreed, like all good committees, to pass the buck and had installed a team of accountants who ran the business on a shoestring, unable to understand its true value: trust and truth.

The shareholders, mostly Templeton descendants, soon realised there was a lot more to the industry than counting costs and they, too, were eagerly convinced by the confidence and style of Jefferies. Yet, during the past three years that he had been in the top job, revenue and readership numbers continued to fall.

Chrissie was unsure which way this chat would go. She took some comfort that Jefferies was the one who had hired her. He and her old boss, Malcolm Chisel, had been cadets on the tear together, back in the day. Only Jefferies had interviewed Chrissie, which Jefferies knew would piss off Harry.

As she crossed the news floor she felt all eyes on her. Despite attempts to keep the new sackings under wraps, the word was out. A visit to the ed director's office was usually to get the sack.

Jefferies' door was partly open. His famous open-door philosophy, part of his image. One of his talents was finding out what people wanted. And telling them what they wanted to hear. Despite knowing him only a year she could see how smoothly he manipulated those around him.

She knocked lightly.

'Come in. Just finishing this email.' He waved towards a couch.

Chrissie picked up a dummy of this week's fashion section from the coffee table, covered in red ink. That wouldn't be Jefferies' proofing, she knew – someone else was drawing it to his attention. An example of all the mistakes getting through, she thought.

Chrissie pictured Lou, the fashion editor, with her perfect make-up and blonde ponytail. She was sometimes stereotyped as ditzy; exactly the impression Lou wanted. But Lou was the first person that fashion players and rivals called with tip-offs, the highest currency in the media. She knew that the fashion industry didn't want someone who challenged or pried too deep. Fashion was about fun, desire and aspiration. Lou might have trod lightly but she never missed a trick. She knew how to get information without alienating her contacts, she was both hard and soft whenever required. She was the best fashion editor the paper had ever had. And Jefferies knew it.

Now, here was someone doing a hatchet job on her section. Chrissie bristled. With more staff cuts in the air, story counts and scoops were suddenly calculated. Comparisons made, reputations sabotaged to protect their own. Someone had it in for Lou. Chrissie made a note to mention it to her after the meeting.

'Right.' Jefferies rubbed his hands together. 'What's going on with this wharf story?'

Chrissie slumped in her seat. So much for keeping it low key.

'Harry tells me you're skipping out on Maria and snooping around the docks. I've only just approved her new budget.'

'I've got something on the hook and I want to follow it through.' She locked on his eyes. 'This is just Harry trying to squeeze me out. It was his idea to cast me off to obits. Now he wants me back, so he can chop my head off in the next cuts and keep one of the others.' She put it out there, nothing to lose.

'Are you skipping out on Maria?'

'No, absolutely not.' Chrissie didn't want to implicate Maria. *We're all just chess pieces.* 'But the story has potential. Could be massive.'

'Details? And don't leave anything out. I haven't got time to have this conversation twice.'

'It started a week ago. I interviewed that woman crane driver and then almost the next day she turned up dead.'

Jefferies got up from his desk. Tie-less, shirt sleeves rolled up, short and compact, his arms and chest fit and strong.

'So?'

'I think it's my fault.' It was hard to speak those words. *The guilt. More guilt.* 'She called me but I didn't hear the phone; left a message which I didn't get for a few hours. She seemed afraid about work. If only I'd spoken to her . . . maybe she got killed because of me.'

'So you're God now? What do you mean, killed because of you?'

She swallowed. *Count.*

'I figured I'd have a crack at a bigger story. Hers was the second death in a year, and there was another guy got hurt last week, almost died, accident rate sky high.' She met his eyes, took a breath. 'I talked to a workmate of the woman's, he reckoned her death wasn't an accident. Reckoned the other death might have been suspicious too. Maybe someone didn't like me interviewing her. Worried about what she might have told me. Then Grange comes straight out and alleges the union's setting up fake accidents to ruin the safety record. Whole folder of data, scene photos, injury reports, including a draft from the Safety Bureau about the woman's death. It's not even official – and Grange had the report.'

'A lot of "ifs" in all that.' Jefferies looked at his mobile vibrating on his desk.

'These fake accidents for compo claims, well, they think a couple went wrong, went too far. Manslaughter, murder even. Masina Weber and maybe this driver, Hank –'

'Jesus!' Jefferies interrupted. He pushed his phone away. 'Murder? Step me back. Why is the union setting up these accidents?'

'Not deliberately killed but manslaughter. Accidents staged to ruin Grange's reputation. The bad safety record reinforces the pickets and industrial action, which holds up workflow, more pressure on Grange. But there's more,' Chrissie said.

'Steak knives?' he quipped.

Chrissie rolled her eyes. 'The wharf union has now dumped on Grange,' she continued, 'told me there are problems with fraud on the container terminals. Grange has installed extra security, new workers – thugs possibly – put them in with the casuals. They want to keep it under wraps. Avoid the cops and publicity. They think these casuals are making it dangerous, causing these accidents. That's where I'm at, so far.'

'Can of worms,' Jefferies shot back, as he sat back behind his desk. 'Okay. Good story. How do you think it's going to play out?'

'It's a story no matter which way it falls. Human element, increased accident rate – whether its fake set-ups or these foreign workers, either way, industrial warfare, foreign employees, automated machines. But if we firm up the fake accidents, it's huge. But I think there could be something else.'

'Spit it out.'

'Grange is pretty keen to dish the dirt on the union. They're saying it's to save lives, of course, but I reckon they've got other motives. They don't just want to break the strike, they want to bust the union. But Grange is also in financial trouble. I searched the financial records, losses for the past two years. It's a private company so there's a limit to what I can get; registered in the US, makes it even harder.'

Chrissie paused. Jefferies was nodding. Then raised his eyebrows at her, guessing there was still more. 'And . . . I agreed an embargo.'

'Grange set an embargo? Why? Wouldn't they want it out soon as?'

'They're doing some big investment deal, new leases overseas, and don't want any ripples until it's done. Maybe the new money is conditional on these leases being renewed? They can't make money if they don't have any wharves to work.' Chrissie's chest was thumping. *Breathe.*

Jefferies sat quietly. 'Good work, Chrissie. Really good,' he said. 'Okay, stick with it but keep Maria in the loop. And get the lawyers to look over everything.'

Chrissie tried not to beam. He was on her side. She got up to leave.

'Now . . . Harry.'

She slumped back again.

'I don't want Harry or anyone back in here with another beef about you. Understand?'

'Yeah.'

'And sounds like I won't be telling you anything but we're losing another three or four. You're not one of them. Maria's budget is safe.'

Chrissie's stomach lurched. She shifted on the hard sofa, not sure whether to relax or sit up straight.

'I think Harry's also got wind of . . .' Chrissie rubbed her palms over her thighs and let out a breath. 'About me, back home, you know. Maybe that's why he's, um, difficult. Been digging around.'

'Ah, he's just difficult, full stop.' Jefferies moved back around to the front of his desk. 'But you know it'll come out sooner or later.' He held her gaze. 'It is what it is. People will react, some good, some bad. Just be prepared.'

CHAPTER 19

No no no. Can't do this can't do this.

Again and again she bashed the letters out on her keyboard, then slammed her hand beside it and pushed the laptop away. She was angry and frustrated, hunched over her small kitchen table, papers and reports spread out. *No progress despite working at home all day.*

The wharf story didn't add up. *Something's missing.*

Scraping her chair back, Chrissie tossed her notebook to the floor and scuffed to the fridge in her pink wool slippers, a rare touch of comfort. Her grandmother had knitted them for her years ago and she couldn't part with them. They made walking on the floorboards a hazard, but she persisted.

The wine bottle was almost empty, she upended it into her mouth then screwed the lid off a new sav blanc and poured and poured.

The colour was beautiful, the barest hint of yellow, a crunchy grass smell. She crossed the room and sank heavily into the leather sofa.

Everything in the flat, except the old timber floors, was painted white, as if someone had gone in with a spray gun, blanking out the past. She loved the white ceiling, its centre rose still intact, even though the chandelier of past times was now a huge white paper shade lit by a soft bulb.

Bit by bit Chrissie had bought furniture, her sideboard shipped at stupid expense from the farmhouse, two sofas. One was dark blue modular, in case she ever had an overnight visitor (she hadn't yet). The other was the tan leather Danish she was sitting on. She'd found it online at half the original price. Her eyes fell on her biggest indulgence, a 1960s Arco floor lamp. It had been one of the first things that made her feel a little bit happy. She didn't even look at the price. The cost was still on her credit card. Soft grey veins flowed through its cold white marble block, warming it up like blood through a body. The huge steel arc reached high over the sofa, its white globe shining above the indentation in the leather that marked her favourite spot. She burrowed into the cushions.

To an outsider she hoped the room looked like it was put together by a woman in control. A woman with good taste and style. It was part of Chrissie's recovery, her subterfuge: an attempt to force herself to be better than she felt.

But tonight, the more she drank, the more frustrated she became with the story. She pushed her thumbnails into her finger-pads, permanent rotation. What had she missed? The accident information and other documents that Grange had sent checked out. The problem was there was nothing linking anything to the union. The fake lift tallies, Grange's secrecy about the missing freight, the foreign workers. *I need to bounce this off someone.*

The *Argus* lawyers had given her the go-ahead with what she had shown them, so far. But she knew their only focus was defamation. Even if a news story was defamatory, it could still run. The decision came down to how likely the person was to sue. The legal committee sat around and weighed up the person's financial worth, their connections and social standing. But even if they were likely to sue and could afford to sue, the story could still run. The focus then switched to the cost versus the benefit. A private settlement versus the readership boost and the advertising pull. Or if they wouldn't settle and the case went to court and the paper lost, it could still be worth the risk, depending on the payout. But big companies like Grange just had to roll with the punches. They might have the money and the ability to sue but they weren't human, so couldn't be defamed. A free shot. Unions, however, were a different type of legal beast. They could be defamed and they would definitely sue.

Despite getting the green light, Chrissie still wasn't happy. She wanted to get the whole story, not just what she had been fed. Was Mas murdered? Who by? Why? *My fault.* More wine. Why were there extra crane movements – what were they lifting? Whose freight was it? Why wasn't someone complaining? And Mas's workmates – how could they have turned a blind eye? How does Parenta at the transport union seem to know so much? Another drink.

She needed a reason for the police to investigate Mas's death. A reason that would not involve exposing the affair with Remi. She owed her, her family. Part of the truth had to come out.

Walking to the bay window, Chrissie shuddered. The faded sky was filled with large black fruit bats returning to the botanical gardens from their daytime sleep. She still hadn't got used to their nightly pilgrimage. The chill didn't last long; the real problem was her story block. Her anxiety had never touched her writing before. The realisation made her panic more. And the redundancies! More hate. More wine.

'Those involved will be told on Monday,' Maria had whispered yesterday.

She strode across the lounge room and grabbed her notebook. She'd draw the story connections, see if that threw up the missing links. She sketched the main boxes. Mas; Grange; maritime union, workers. Then the satellite boxes. Remi; transport union; *The Argus*; fake accidents; fake crane records; missing cargo; medical industry; insurance; foreign workers; financial trouble; lease renewals; union mergers.

Within each box she scrawled events, dates, times, anything relating to each topic. Then she looked for the crossovers, the duplicates that made a direct connection. But there was nothing she hadn't already considered. Except maybe for the transport union, the odd one out. Graham Parenta knew things; he saw connections.

Her thoughts jumped elsewhere. She should have told James about the sackings. What if he was one of them? She had to tell him before work on Monday.

She reached for another bottle to dull her hunger. Food was always scarce, she hated to shop or plan ahead. She usually bought food from the all-night store or picked up a takeaway. She peered in the freezer. No frozen meal packs. She took a few slices of frozen bread from a loaf that had been tossed in weeks ago and put them in the toaster. She spied a container of fried rice – jackpot! She had ordered home delivery a couple of days ago but by the time it arrived she had drunk so much she was no longer hungry. It was a windfall meal tonight. She prised off the plastic lid; yellow rice, corn, egg and pink-edged meat looked back at her in the eerie blue glow of the fridge. It passed the sniff test. With her bread and rice, she plopped back on the sofa, eating quickly, using torn pieces of the toast as a scoop.

Redundancies! She would phone James. Now. No more hints. She would say it quickly, not give him a chance for too many questions. The phone rang out and switched through to voicemail. She froze. She didn't have the words prepared for a message. She ended the call. More prepared, she rang again but as the voicemail clicked in again, she hung up a second time. Surely, she couldn't leave a message about something like that? Her thoughts were getting too muddled. She walked to the window, draining her wine. No matter day or night there was always noise and activity in her street, unlike life in the country. Even when everything was supposed to be quiet, the trees of Richmond had a permanent rustle, the traffic a constant hum, the trams a rumble and piercing screech. But tonight, as usual, the old windows in Chrissie's flat vibrated from the music from a nearby bar, cars revved then squealed away. She could just see the neon Skipping Girl sign in the distance above the rooftops. She was once a carefree young girl, skipping rope.

Across the road, two men held up a mate, too drunk to walk. The three stumbled between parked cars, as they tried to cross the road. Another couple walked quickly past them, hugging. Happy. She felt Dave creep closer. *Don't go there. Refocus.* But he kept coming. She flung the sheer curtains across, they wafted slowly from the draught through the leaky old window frames. She sat heavily on the sofa, leaned back and stared up at the ceiling.

The next thing she knew, Chrissie groaned, her neck awkward, twisted against the sofa arm. She must have fallen asleep. Her arm heavy as she tried to look at her watch. The black numbers were a blur on the white face. That watch was one of the few possessions she had from her old life. She lifted the bottle from the floor and poured herself the last of it.

She squished herself over on the sofa and pulled out the diagrams from under her, wrinkled and crushed. She smoothed them out against her legs. She tried to sit up but her stomach cramped. Her head began to spin as her stomach heaved. *The rice!* Her feet knocked over her glass and bottle as she rushed to the kitchen. Sweat sprang up across her face and chest and, shaking, she leaned over the sink and spewed.

Blindly she reached across the bench for a glass or cup. *Water.* The taste in her mouth was sour and salty. Still slumped over the sink, she struggled to turn on the tap. Her hands were too tender, her fingertips raw. Finally, the tap turned. Exhausted from trying to keep standing, she pushed the glass under the flow and lifted it to her mouth. She sucked the water down. She finished another and forced herself to stand straight. Sounds started to come in waves, the running water wafted in and out of her consciousness. She braced her arms against the bench but not for long. Vomit rushed, unstoppable, into the sink. Her head was being squeezed tight but finally her nausea eased. Shaking uncontrollably, she dragged herself to the bathroom and searched among the packets and bottles in the cabinet looking for something to help.

Chrissie tipped out a handful of anti-inflammatories and swallowed them. She searched again, something for her headache, Panadeine Forte. Couple of those. Diarrhoea! Please no, don't let that happen. She dug around for some Imodium and swallowed those too. A couple more, just in case. She reached for the Ambien and shook the bottle. Almost empty! She always kept them topped up. She tipped out what was left, three purple tablets. Aren't they red? Her vision blurred again. She needed to sleep this scourge away, she quickly swallowed two of the pills. As she closed the cabinet door, she saw her face splattered with vomit, her damp and disgusting t-shirt reflected in the mirror. Chrissie piled her clothes in the corner and rinsed herself off under the shower. Finally starting to calm, she ran a bath. The light glowed gently from the hallway. *Warm, safe, relaxed.*

She remembered the first time she'd had too much to drink. It was back in high school. Dave, the tallest and oldest-looking of their group, had bought the drinks. Pre-mixed cans of rum and coke. To this day Chrissie still could not stand the smell of rum. Luckily her father only glanced up as she came inside, he was perched on the edge of the sofa watching a loud replay of the rugby, the Chiefs versus the Hurricanes.

Chrissie had stumbled up the stairs to her teenage bedroom, a homage to the colour purple. Aiming for her single bed, with its blue and white striped sheets. Fully clothed, she fell into a heavy sleep. But the brown cola vomit wouldn't stop.

Chrissie dismissed the pressure behind her eyes, the pills would kick in soon. Her stomach calm, at last. She slipped her shoulders under the water and took a deep slow breath. Another and another. Her arms floated, gently lifting her hands, she let the water run through her damaged fingers. Of all the leftovers she'd taken a chance on, it had to be tonight. The water felt cold. How long had she been in? Shivering, she reached for the plug to lower the tide, then turned on the hot tap. A slow hot dribble began to warm her up.

Her phone rang in the distance. How strange, she thought, she didn't have that phone at high school. She remembered being surrounded by banging and shouting. Her dad's team was getting thumped. He was yelling at the referees. She was weightless, flying, it felt good. She squeezed her eyes tight. She didn't want her dad to know she had been drinking. Someone forced something in her throat, she couldn't breathe, she tried to fight. Her arms and legs were pinned, a face hovered above. She was in pain, someone was pushing her, she pushed them back. She blanked out. Voices called her. She was in the underground loop. The train kept stopping at the same stop, Flagstaff, over and over. But no one noticed. They were looking at their phones, ignoring her panic. Finally, she was out but someone was following her. It made her furious, she wasn't going to let them rob her. Then – *Dave's voice?*

'Chrissie, that's amazing. I love you so much. So great.' He was here, with her. She began to cry.

But it wasn't Dave. She had been tricked, she tried to run but it hurt to breathe. Now on the ground, they must have beaten her up, robbed her again. She tried to lift herself but her arms wouldn't work. She couldn't shout. Her teeth were stuck dry to her cheeks and lips.

'Water!' she finally burst out. 'Water!'

But she couldn't hear anything, not even her own voice. The rest of the world was silent, except for the whoosh-whoosh, whoosh-whoosh of her pulse. She forced her eyes open. Her vision focused on a drip bag above her head. She followed the liquid down the plastic tube under the strip of white tape stuck to her arm but she knew it went into her vein. Something had happened but she was safe now. Was she in the car crash again?

A woman appeared and put a straw in her mouth. Chrissie sucked greedily.

'More,' she croaked as the straw was taken away.

'Not just yet, honey. Let that go down. I'll bring you some ice instead.'

She closed her eyes again. *I'll think about it all later.*

'Don't steal my water.' She faded out again.

—

'Chrissie? Chrissie? It's me, James. Chrissie? You're okay. You're in hospital.'

She drifted back. James? Why was he at the crash? She opened her eyes and turned towards his voice. His face was all screwed up. Where was his smile? Where was his floppy hair?

'You're okay. You're in the hospital. Gina found you. You're okay.'

'Gina found me? Where was I . . . the car? Where's my bag?' Something stopped her from saying Dave's name.

'Lord, I'm glad you're awake. We've been here all night. It's Sunday. Sunday morning. You're in hospital.' He gave her a close look and through the haze she wondered what else she'd said. 'In Melbourne, Chrissie.'

'How did I get here? Jesus, what happened?'

'I had two missed calls from you, then you didn't answer. We stopped at your place. This guy came out, shouting about water coming through the ceiling, said your spare key was missing.

We all freaked out. Gina said we should bust down your door but when we went up, it was unlocked.'

'I can't . . .' Chrissie struggled.

'You were in the bath, unconscious, floating. The water over the edge, the tap was running. You took a lot of pills. There was this cat sitting outside the bathroom, glaring at us. Wouldn't budge until Gina shooed it away then she quickly pulled the plug.'

'I must have passed out. Yeah, I remember. I was sick . . . food poisoning.'

James broke eye contact and looked under the bed. The hydraulics, the wheels, levers, angled struts were suddenly of great interest to him.

'They want to keep you a while.' He looked back at her. 'I saw your note. While we waited for the ambulance.'

'What note?'

'On your laptop: "I can't do it. I can't do it. Life's too hard."'

'That wasn't a note. That was frustration with the bloody story.'

She tried to sit up but winced at the pain in her chest. She tried to push herself up again. James put a hand on her shoulder.

'Hey, no need to get up,' he said. 'You'll be sore, they had to resuscitate you. You'd sucked in a bit of water.'

'I want to leave. Hate hospitals.' The smell of the ward, the pillow, the room. She'd been here before. Her anxiety was rising. *Got to get out.* She planted her elbows on the mattress and pushed. But James tried to keep her lying down. She looked him straight in the eyes but he looked away.

'What is it? Tell me!'

CHAPTER 20

The morning sun squeezed through the venetian blinds and striped across the floor to Chrissie's hospital bed. *Prison bars.* Through the window, across the parkland treetops, the city skyline sparkled. *A view to die for.*

'They think you tried to kill yourself,' James said. Chrissie avoided looking at him. 'I'm sorry, they said you have to get a psych assessment.' He looked down. 'We could all do with a mental finetune now and then, well I could, anyway. What do you say?'

Chrissie held her stare out the window. A clear sky, again. No clouds to share with Dave today. 'A shrink? I was sick, I had food poisoning. It wasn't suicide.' *James knows. He must have found the clock.* Was it different this time? Had she meant to do it without even realising?

'I collected up all the bottles, from the cabinet, the kitchen, they always tell you to do stuff like that. I gave them to the paramedics.'

'Those pills were nothing. Just the usual.'

'I'm sorry, seemed like a lot to me. Is it because of your past? I know you don't like to talk about it.'

'No. Don't.' Chrissie had told James and anyone else who had asked that she was once married – the truth but only part of it. She couldn't pretend otherwise, the indent on her finger from her ring was still evident. She still shuddered every time at the thought of her little gold band alone in the memory box stored at her dad's place. Her in-laws took Dave's ring along with everything else.

'Sorry. Sorry. I'm sorry, Chrissie.' James reached for her hand. But she slid it under the bedcover. 'They also wanted to know your next of kin for your admission.' James switched the subject. 'I couldn't unlock your phone, so I got Harry to authorise HR to pass on the details.'

'Harry knows? Oh god. This just keeps getting better and better.'

'No, no. Just that you were brought in,' James tried to reassure, 'not the reason.'

Despite the drip feeding her arm, it was of little relief. She started to work her hand under the sheet. Methodically, her thumbnail sought out each finger. *Count the pain. Time will pass. Here and now.* Concentrate. She could feel the pulse in her head start to slow. 'Ah, and,' James stumbled, 'they rang your father, I think.'

'Oh god! You and your stupid assumptions,' she croaked, her throat on fire. Poor Dad! She couldn't believe the mess she was in. 'Now what? My father comes and commits me and everyone just goes about their merry life. I fell asleep in the bath. I left the tap on, stupid but that's property damage not fucking suicide.'

'I panicked. Sorry, Chrissie. I'll ring him – I'll ring him now and tell him it was a mistake.'

Chrissie's mouth twisted, her eyes slipped behind a wall of tears. Everything she had fought against was beating her. A lung-emptying sob surged out of her mouth. She tried to bury her face but she was laid bare. A rattle sounded as she sucked in air, followed by another louder sob. Her distress spread around the room and crawled into the hallway. James's face was twisted in misery. He was trying to help, she knew, but Chrissie couldn't stand the kindness. She wanted to disappear into the mattress to be nobody. It was almost two years since she had let her defences down. She had been too busy pretending to be okay.

A nurse rushed to see what the commotion was and glared at James. She pushed a fat arm under Chrissie's shoulders and stood with her wide hip propped against the bed.

'Time for visitors to go,' the nurse said firmly. Chrissie nodded and James reluctantly said his goodbyes, still in his dinner clothes from last night.

Sprung, accidentally, she thought as she lay in the hospital bed. Her secrets, one of them, discovered. Her suicide roulette. Exposed because of fried rice! She began to laugh. It hurt her chest but she couldn't stop for a few more seconds.

There had been no hospital, no paramedic, no psychiatrist, no friend to pull her through before. She had just got up and gone to work.

'He didn't upset me.' She indicated James's departure. 'I just don't want my family coming,' Chrissie said to the nurse. 'Someone phoned my father. Can you call him, let him know I'm fine? I want to leave as soon as possible.'

The nurse tilted her head back and looked down the full length of her nose.

'In my experience this is exactly when you need family.' She bent and whipped the sheet tight across Chrissie, then pushed it energetically under the mattress. 'One thing I know and that's that dads are usually pretty good when it comes to the crunch.' She marched around to the other side and pulled and tucked.

'This isn't a crunch,' Chrissie shot back, lifting her knees and loosening the claustrophobic covers. 'This is a mistake, someone jumped to the wrong conclusion.'

'Well, why not give him a quick call yourself, yeah?' The nurse ignored Chrissie's aggression. 'Your friend brought these in with you.' The nurse showed Chrissie her satchel and passed her the mobile phone. 'Besides, hospital protocol is that you need an assessment from the senior emergency doctor and a psychiatrist. In the meantime, you're staying here with me.' She tucked and fussed and pulled the sheets even tighter as she redid the bed.

Chrissie smiled weakly. *I'll never get out of here.*

She looked at her phone. Five missed calls. Two from James last night, one from Mike, one from her dad, she cringed when she saw it, and one from Remi that morning.

She pictured again her father's face, his expression as they said goodbye at the airport a year ago. It still haunted her. She had seen relief in his watery blue eyes.

The phone picked up on the first ring.

'Oh sweetheart,' his voice broke almost immediately as she heard him trying to gag his anguish.

'Dad. Dad.' The words came out as croaks, despite trying to put on a good show. She knew what he had been thinking all these hours. 'I'm okay, it was all just a mistake, a misunderstanding. I'm going home soon and straight back to work.'

'You've made the same mistake before, bub,' he replied but she cut him off, blurting out her version of events in a stream of croaks and swallows.

'Chrissie, I'm worried. Please let me visit,' he begged now, his voice trying to be strong. 'I checked the flights, I can be there about 9 your time, we can have a late dinner.'

'Don't come,' Chrissie's resolve finally broke. 'Please, Dad, let me do it my way,' crying now. 'I don't want you to come. Dad?' She slipped further under the sheets, glad now to feel tightly held. She curled to one side, the phone pressed hard against her ear as she listened to his silent misery. 'Not yet, Dad,' she whispered. 'I'm okay. I promised you, remember. I promised you.'

'I know . . . I trust you, Chrissie. You do it your way,' George O'Brian finally said. The same thing he'd been saying to her after each challenge. The thought of breaking his trust was one of the few things that cut through to her. He knew that. They eventually said goodbye with George agreeing not to fly over, on the condition she phone every day for the next two weeks. 'We'll speak tomorrow, then,' he said slowly. 'But your brother and me . . . we were hoping you might come home for Christmas. Just for a few days, eh bub? William and I, we . . . don't want to be without you, it would be the first time.'

'No. I can't . . . I can't say. Not yet.' *Not yet. Ever?*

As soon as she said goodbye, she realised how good it had been to hear his voice. She had switched to emailing and texting him since being in Melbourne, to hide her frailty. Bravado was easy in writing.

The story began to click back into her thoughts. She had work to do. She started an internet search – casual labour hire firms to check what the union had said – but she was soon drawn to look up as a murmuring shuffle grew louder.

The man looked more like a nightclub bouncer than a doctor. Chrissie put her laptop aside as he walked in the room. Aggressive, short, stocky. Even his blue hospital scrubs didn't soften the impression he was up for a fight. Too tight around the arms and chest. He was obviously important judging from the entourage that flowed in his wake, students or interns, she guessed, in their flapping crisp white coats.

'I'm head of emergency today. You're looking better,' the bouncer said. 'I'd like to keep you a bit longer. Do you know what happened?' Chrissie didn't catch his name but she certainly caught his tone. She could be stuck there all day.

'I had food poisoning, leftovers. I took a few painkillers, something for my stomach and to knock me out so I'd sleep through it.'

The bouncer picked up the chart from the end of her bed and started to read the latest information to the entourage.

'Anything else?' He kept his eyes on the chart.

'I had vomit on my clothes. I was taking a bath. I wasn't trying to kill myself, if that's what you're getting at. That was a mistake, my friend –'

'I saw you on admission, you were unconscious,' the doctor interrupted. 'Your breathing was compromised. There was evidence of medication abuse and you'd consumed a large quantity of alcohol. To avoid further absorption, we did a gastric lavage. Your stomach, chest might be tender, bruised a little.'

Chrissie nodded, watching him carefully. This man had power over her.

'We've taken another lot of bloods. I'll start you on antibiotics. Although we're still waiting for full toxicology. In the meantime, your hospital records have arrived.'

'Records! What records?'

'From New Zealand.' He guessed her next question. 'We data share, through the MyHealth system. Given the situation last night and your history, I've organised for a psychiatric assessment, it'll –'

'That's not necessary. I want to leave. Now! I was unwell, that's all.' He didn't look convinced but stayed silent. 'Yes, I'd been drinking, I was working on a project and I'd been drinking since the afternoon. I had leftovers in the fridge, they must have been off, I took the pills to stop the vomiting and to sleep. Nothing else.'

He'd heard enough. 'If you were conscious and weren't drug affected when you were admitted, you could determine your treatment. That wasn't the case. I have a legal duty of care.'

His voice had switched to automatic. A cold shiver ran across her chest.

'If you are pushing me to decide right now, I could put in place a temporary treatment order. Temporary means up to twenty-eight days. That would result in you being transferred to a psychiatric facility.' His tone softened slightly. 'But I'm willing to let everything settle. Got to cover my arse, first.' His eyes looked slightly less stern. 'The assessment will be early afternoon and I'll discuss it again with you after that.'

'I understand,' she said and kept her mouth shut. She had to get smart. *Be who they want.*

Her hospital records from home would show not one but two suicide attempts. They would also show her injuries, the car accident report, her blood alcohol level and the police statements taken in the hospital. Everything she had tried to keep hidden.

—

One of the car crash doctors had mentioned it in passing, as if she should already have known.

'Of course, your pelvic injuries caused you to miscarry.'

A baby! Chrissie's hand flew to her stomach as she lay there, alone. Empty. She winced at the pain from her broken bones but also this new grief.

It was a few more hours before she could bring herself to ask for more details. She had been thirteen weeks pregnant. It was the last thing she had expected. She had been feeling tired for weeks but she assumed it was her work schedule, the extra travel, renovating the old house. Pregnancy was the last thing on her mind. She hadn't even missed a period.

That short offhand comment was the last heart-breaking straw. The last part of Dave, his DNA, his being, gone forever. She didn't, couldn't, tell anyone. Later, she thought. Later. But the longer she held the secret, the harder it became. Wait until after the funeral. Wait until their pain eases. Spare them. And finally, better if no one knows.

The decision, however, was soon taken out of her hands, by the same doctor or one just like him. Dave's mother, Denise

Watford, had come to sit with her in the hospital. It would be her last visit. Perhaps the doctor thought she was Chrissie's mother. Perhaps the doctor didn't think.

'There hasn't been any permanent damage, which means you can always have another baby,' he had told Chrissie as he smiled tentatively back and forth between the two women.

'Another baby?' Denise had said. 'What do you mean, *another* baby?'

Chrissie could not bear to tell the truth or make a denial.

Four months after the crash, Chrissie was convicted of drink-driving causing death. The sentence was one hundred hours community service, two years on probation, five years loss of licence. She had suffered, too, the judge said, and would for the rest of her life. The sentence wasn't harsh enough. She wanted prison. Her second suicide attempt soon followed.

CHAPTER 21

The Melbourne sun felt good on her face. Brilliant white cushions made the sky almost perfect. *Cumulus*. Chrissie stepped into the taxi, having knocked back James's offer to drive her home from hospital. She was perfectly capable, she had said, although she was secretly wobbly; but she wanted to be on her own. To push away those hospital triggers.

Just as well James wasn't there because the paperwork proved a nightmare. She had to sign an agreement to attend at least three sessions with a psychiatrist, or the bouncer doctor wouldn't sign the discharge plan. But she was willing to agree to anything. Worry about it later. There was work to do. She had contacted Parenta about containers taken off the dock by road. He said he would get back to her. She had researched the foreign labour hire statistics. Next, she needed to make a contact at the rail network, which was the only other way for containers to be transported off the dock.

She got out of the taxi at the 24-hour corner store near her flat. Demi, baggy track top and jeans, swayed against the shop's side wall, a sad grin on her face. *Just hit up*. Chrissie stocked up on a few basics and on her way out swung Demi a bag – muesli bars, tampons, water.

'Thangs, Chrizzie.' Demi could barely hold her head up.

Chrissie stopped, turned back and took both of Demi's hands. 'Sit down, eh Demi?' She helped her slide down the wall, tucking the bag of goodies in close beside her.

—

As Chrissie checked her letterbox she heard a familiar noise. Skinny Cat came running across the tiled floor. He purred loud and strong as he pushed against her legs. She felt the tension fade, her muscles relax.

'Hey, mate. What a lovely welcome.' She bent and scratched behind his ears. 'Come on up. Let's find something to eat.'

The pain in Chrissie's chest from the stomach pump had eased but her throat still burned from the tube they had shoved in. Despite her insistence at the hospital, she had begun to have doubts about her motives on Saturday night. Was James right? Was it deliberate? One thing she was aware of – she'd have to cut back on the booze.

A mushy microwaved packet curry later, half for her, half for Skinny, she felt relieved to be home. Her notes and wrinkled diagrams were piled on the coffee table. The bathroom looked tidy too, wet towels dumped in the bath – someone had cleaned up. She opened the cabinet to unload the bag of pills the hospital had returned to her with a blow by blow caution about each one from the bouncer. She made a mental note to get her Ambien refilled but when she shook the bottle it was more than half full. She twisted the cap, neat pale red tabs. *What did I take last night?* She shakily screwed the lids off other bottles, checked blister packs, even searched old packets for anything purple. Nothing. *Must have been the fluorescent light, red-purple.* She headed to the bedroom and carefully opened the bedside cupboard, nothing disturbed. *Phew.* Not that anyone would know what the timer signalled, she reasoned as she pulled it out: eleven days, seventeen hours, eighteen minutes since her last spin of the wheel. Skinny jumped up and stared at the numbers, too. He batted the white digits as they changed. The cat stretched and meowed before heading for the kitchen window, to visit one of his other worlds, she accepted. Chrissie gently put the timer back in the cupboard, unchanged.

—

'Come in. Wow, you look good, lady,' Mike said, relief in his voice. 'Better than the last time I saw you.' He beamed.

After a nap, Chrissie had knocked on Mike's door to apologise for the damage, but she also wanted to reinforce it was an accident and that James had made the wrong assumption. Yes, she might have played suicide roulette in private – but this hadn't been one of those times. She still couldn't understand how it had happened. Two sleeping pills often wasn't enough for her to even doze off, never mind put her out cold.

'Yeah, all good, except for my throat,' Chrissie explained. 'They must have shoved a cheese grater down there.'

Mike bowed and ushered her through the door. As she stepped in she instantly felt something was different. She looked around, trying to place it. It was only about 6 pm but Mike appeared to be dressed in pyjamas. 'Oh, were you in bed?'

'No, I'm having a pyjama day.'

She laughed and at the same time realised what was different. Mike had set up an oil burner, the fragrance fresh and crisp, calming. He had taken her remarks about airing his flat to heart. She liked him even more, again.

'I just wanted to apologise for flooding you out. I'll pay for the damage or the excess or make up any shortfall, the landlord . . .' She paused, her arms fell to her sides. 'Sorry, Mike.'

'Hey.' He took hold of her shoulders. 'I'm glad you're okay. I trust you, I know where you live, remember. I'll let you know about the insurance but it's nothing. Come on, sit down. What's a bit of water between friends, eh? You were in a bad way. Wasn't sure if I was going to see you again.' He gave her a huge smile.

Skinny Cat walked up from behind him. 'Food poisoning,' Chrissie continued. 'Some rice I had left over in the fridge.'

'OMG. It could have been me. What if I'd eaten it!'

'Ah, well, maybe that's a sign you shouldn't be helping yourself to my fridge.'

'You know your door wasn't locked last night, don't you?' he asked, suddenly serious. 'Not wise around here.'

'Did you do a tidy? The towels and stuff?'

'Yeah, a quick mop, after they took you. Those two mates of yours didn't look like the practical type. Hey, I saw those boxing gloves of yours hanging up. Didn't know you were into that.'

'Yeah, well, I can look after myself.' She immediately hung her head, aware of the out of place bravado.

'You know, if there's ever a time . . . if you need help, I'll be up those stairs quick as I can. You know that, don't you?' Mike's voice soft and gentle.

'Funny you should ask,' she deliberately misunderstood. 'How about a bit of brainstorming? I'm stuck on my story. Doesn't have to be now, just sometime.'

'Now's good. You want to join the pyjama party?'

'I'll stick to my tracky dacks, thanks.' She raced upstairs to get her satchel.

Chrissie showed Mike the photographs of the wharf accident scenes, Safety Bureau reports with no witness accounts, the new draft about Mas's death, the analysis by Grange, the casual worker shifts from the union, the incorrect container counts.

'They're blaming each other but neither of them knows what's going on. Yes, it looks like fraud or theft and Grange doesn't want that to get out. And yes, the accident and death rates are spiking and that plays to the union's dispute against Grange. But causing deaths? Even accidental? Doesn't gel for me,' Chrissie said.

'When I'm cracking, I always start by looking for the weakest point. These wharves are your weak point, too hard to control. But what about a third element? Smuggling, either in or out. Maybe involving union guys, maybe Grange,' Mike offered. 'Would whoever's doing it kill to keep from being exposed?'

A shiver raced across Chrissie's arms and shoulders as she stood beside Mike's front windows. The sky was again filled with black-winged bat silhouettes.

'I think both the company and the union are afraid of what's going on,' she finally said. 'I don't think either of them really knows but I'm going to find out.'

'But is this your job? You're not a cop,' Mike said. 'Not that I would rely on a cop!'

That's for real, Chrissie thought as she recalled Detective Bannister's lack of help the day of Mas's death.

'Can't you just write about the suspicions?' Mike continued. 'You know, what they're saying about each other. The publicity does the rest.' He spun around on his chair. 'It's the authorities, the cops that are supposed to find the answers.'

But Chrissie was already thinking about who to talk to next. Investigations were what she did best. And she wanted to prove it. Mas was counting on her, she needed to get back in control. She was counting on herself, too.

CHAPTER 22

Chrissie filled her lungs with the energy of the newsroom. It was Monday morning. The usual symphony of noises was in full concert. It was her first day back after the hospital stay. Her colleagues would all have heard about her weekend. Hopefully the suicide speculation hadn't got out. She kept her gaze forward, shoulders relaxed, head slightly down. *Don't look at anyone.* But as she walked the floor she felt a change in the atmosphere. The crackle of tension wasn't as intense, heads were bowed – the redundancies!

It happened like this every time. The cost cutting throughout the industry had been relentless for more than a decade. The stress built before each announcement, like the build-up before a monsoon. When the names and numbers were finally known, the worst was over. Relief for most. Chrissie spied James at his desk. And she, too, felt relief. She would have to do something special for him, make up for everything she'd put him and Gina through.

She lifted a hand to indicate the empty desks. 'The redundancies. I'm sorry. I knew they were coming. That's what I was ringing you about before, before you came over . . . From now on: everything I know, you know.'

'Gosh. No denial? No but this or but that, Ms O'Brian?'

Chrissie shrugged and looked down. 'You probably know all the "buts".'

'Anything else?'

She looked away, instantly alert. Had he heard about New Zealand? Had someone let slip at the hospital? Maybe Harry had finally found out. Chrissie cast her eyes down and stood in shame. What did he know? Should she confess, try to explain?

She looked up again to see James with his arms out wide, Christ-like, as he waited for a hug, for all the newsroom to see. He was showing them all she was worthy of staying, of being accepted. She reached one arm around him, then pulled quickly back.

'Thanks for . . . everything, you know, since . . . and before. Sorry for flying off the handle at you in the hospital, too.'

'Moving on,' he said, 'just don't ask me over for dinner anytime soon.' They were back to normal. She glanced around, expecting angry stares but kinder faces looked back. *That's what pity looks like.*

'Did you tell anyone about your, your first thoughts?' She kept her eyes down.

'No, no. Just that you had food poisoning, had to have your stomach pumped.'

Her desk phone was blinking a message, she was relieved to break her conversation with James.

'Chrissie, where the hell are ya?' Remi's voice. 'I got two tally sheets. We just need to match them to the manifests. My cousin's wife is gonna get them for me.' *Yes!* As she listened to the message she saw Maria slowly walk towards her, the stick taking the weight of each step today. Chrissie braced herself.

'Now that's a face I'm pleased to see,' Maria said. 'Come on, let's have a chat while it's still quiet. You want to go somewhere? Cuppa?'

'Let's see if the kitchen's empty,' Chrissie said, 'no need to go out.' She noticed the glances as they walked through the newsroom.

'Well, my girl,' Maria began when they had got to the kitchen, 'you gave me a fright, when I heard. Glad to see you're looking well. But I'm worried about you. I want the truth.' Maria took off her glasses, black and tan shell frames today, and gave her a firm stare.

'It was an accident. It was food poisoning. That's the truth.' Chrissie kept her gaze direct into Maria's eyes.

'What about all those pills and the booze? How come you had so much, then?'

Chrissie's heart started to race. Her palms itched. She felt her face getting red. Who told her? James? No. *Breathe.* No journo would be worth their salt if they didn't have a source at the hospital or the paramedics. Private and medical lives were big business for the media. *The Argus* had contacts like every other outlet and Maria wouldn't be squeamish about finding out.

How could she say that she needed those drugs to try to feel normal? That each time she closed her eyes at night her thoughts accused her. She needed pills to go to bed each night, to get up each morning, to get through each day.

'I have insomnia, prescribed medication. And I like my wine. But neither is an issue. I'm fit, I need to work. Not as if this place is full of teetotallers, anyway. You only have to look at the news desk any bloody day of the week.'

Maria matched her gaze. 'Humph. Feisty enough. You must be feeling okay. I've got every confidence but I want a promise. If you feel like shit, I want to know. If you're not up to the work, I want to know. Got it?'

Chrissie nodded. She put a cup in front of Maria, black coffee, no sugar.

'Which brings me to the not-so-good news,' Maria said. 'I can't give you as much time for the wharf story.' She held up her hands before Chrissie could protest. 'We've just lost six – more than we thought; three reporters from the floor, three from production. Things have got to give. Your story is one of them . . . for now. You can pick back up again when things settle down.'

Chrissie's mouth opened before she could stop it. 'So we just rewrite press releases? Let everything else go unwritten, untold . . . Because a bunch of arses decided to cut the budget again. The same stupid arses in league with all these shit-awful advertisers and poli-ticians we're not reporting on. You're going to let that happen?'

'Enough! I'm not letting anything happen. Strewth. Think you got double your plucker back. It's happened already, to everyone, to the whole bloody industry, the world. It's the new friggin' economy. That's how it is.' Maria was firm.

'I was warned about this! That *The Argus* wouldn't publish. And if I don't keep at it Grange will give it to someone else.'

'Nonsense! You're not going to lose it, no one else has got what you've got. If worst comes to worst, the fallback story is still really good, everything can run except the allegation about the union setting up these accidents. Look,' Maria lowered her voice, 'people around here are a bit touchy. They're resentful and tired. Just for now, keep an extra low profile on it, eh? Regardless of how much further you get, we'll plan to run something as soon as the embargo is done.'

Chrissie was exhausted. She wanted to tell Maria how important the story was. How this time it wasn't a suicide attempt but many times it had been. The story kept her going. She wanted to say that she hated herself. How the hospital was making her see a psychiatrist. That she was terrified of what they would see in her. Instead, she just nodded.

—

'Maria wants me to go with what I've got on the wharf story,' she said to James, when she sat back at her desk.

He leaned over in his chair. 'That doesn't surprise me, given we're so shorthanded. You're supposed to be on op-ed and obits, anyway. So where are you at with it? We seemed to have been a bit side-tracked by your hospital stint.'

'Is that what we're calling it? My "hospital stint"?' She smiled. 'I have to nail it soon or I'll lose my head start. I want to get the truth out. For Mas. For god knows how many others – all those injuries. Shit, only a week left! But maybe I'm being sidelined because they think I'm crazy, a flake, can't hack it – Maria knew enough to ask about my medication . . .'

'Chrissie, I didn't mention it to her.'

'She could find out for herself, I know, but what if someone's had a word, sabotaged me and the story?'

James leaned towards her. 'Don't start seeing conspiracies where there aren't any. There's nothing stopping you working on it in your own time. I can help you, you know that.'

'And that's how it sucks, even more. Sack everyone and we do the stories in our own time. There's no way I'm letting this story go.'

CHAPTER 23

'There's been another death at the wharf. I want you on it.' Harry loomed in front of Chrissie's desk. *Another death? Harry wants me on it?* The world had changed again.

'Jesus. When?' *Jesus!* 'Was it at a Grange dock?' She stood up suddenly, to remind herself it was real. *Another one.*

'Are you okay to do it? After the weekend, you fit to be here?'

'Yes! Of course.'

'Sounds like it's at Grange,' Harry confirmed. Chrissie glanced at her screen, 5.30 pm. An hour max until she would need to have a first draft, two hours before final deadline. The pages had already been allocated. Chrissie's story would have to bump some other piece. *Another death!* In the meantime she needed to file something immediately for online. She rang Remi back. No answer.

Charlie Thurst wouldn't take her call. She rang Helen Carter.

'Fucking Grange again,' Carter said. 'You'd think they'd be playing things double safe at the moment, eh?'

'Who was it? What happened?'

'Can't give you the name, Chris. Still dealing with next of kin. But we'll have it soon, they've had a positive ID, probably ready in half an hour or so. Our safety reps have been there since it happened.'

'Jesus, Hel, that's three deaths – all at Grange. You know what the rumours are, don't you? About the accidents?'

'Whaddya mean, rumours?' Carter snapped back. Despite her denial, a moment's hesitation indicated she might already know what Chrissie was talking about.

'That your guys are staging accidents, trying to make Grange look bad.'

'Don't-start-any-crap-like-that,' Carter's fury melted her words together. The hangdog had turned attack dog.

'To put them under financial pressure,' Chrissie pushed on, 'political leverage. But some must have gone wrong. Fatal.' *There, it's out.*

'That's dead-shit wrong. I see a fucking hint of anything like that in the fucking *Argus* tomorrow and the lawyers are coming! Where the shit did you get this? Political? This government's doing too many favours for Grange. No, don't tell me, Fucking Grange. Right?' Chrissie held the phone away from her ear as Carter shouted. 'More mud to sling our way and away from them! How fucking convenient and you're soaking it all up. Doing their dirty work.'

Keep her calm. 'Hel, I'm not writing anything like that tonight. I'm just letting you know what I've heard.' She scrambled to recover but could not lie outright. 'But we do have some material that I need to put to you – but, no, no, not tonight. Just giving you the heads up.' Chrissie looked around, had anyone heard? She shouldn't have tipped Carter off.

'I'll email our statement about this casualty within the hour,' Carter grunted. 'And between us, things are going to ramp up. For you, too, if you're not straight down the line.' Chrissie held her breath. 'Don't think Grange can sling mud like that while our members are getting killed. This'll cost 'em. Bout time we raised the roof on what's really going on down there: the missing boxes, fraud. I still have doubts about the fucking *Argus* putting its spin on this feature you're writing, but, yes, let's have that briefing. In fact, I'll be looking forward to it.' She hung up.

Chrissie could see Harry standing at the news desk looking towards her. She stood and gave him the thumbs up to signal she was making progress; a rare moment between them.

'Three hundred,' Harry mouthed at her. Oh, god, just another mid, she thought. *Been here before.* He held up three fingers. Page three. She smiled back, another rare moment. *At least it's getting a prime spot.*

—

Chrissie looked through the incident room windows, *Stratocumulus*. Bunches of dark clouds had formed, forewarning of rain, the last of the day's sun made large patches of blue and pink sky which tinged the edges of the lumpy white masses. It would be dark soon.

She checked her watch: 6.05 pm, just over an hour before deadline.

Like the last time, Chrissie had gone straight to the port to get a first-hand account. The picket outside the perimeter was loud and angry. The union had started livestreaming, interviewing its people. At least a hundred workers had gathered, banners had been set up: Teachers Federation, Nurses Association, Transport Workers. The Port Authority and Grange were more prepared for the surge of media this time. An incident and press room had been set up immediately.

Outside the window she could see the frantic efforts across the concrete forecourt. Emergency vehicle lights swirled, throwing the scene and its people into repetitions of red, pink, blue, purple. The fluoro strips on safety jackets bounced the light back angrily at each rotation. Police tape, people, vehicles everywhere. The crew of a towering ship stood lined up against the railings, a front row seat to the sad chaos. The ship's hull bleeding rust, its tie rope tethered to the wharf. Containers still piled high, uneven, frozen in time. Everyone, every machine was at a standstill but Chrissie's mind was in overdrive. There were more than thirty people in the makeshift incident room by now. She pushed her earbuds into her ears. They weren't connected to anything, just helped to muffle the sounds. *Breathe.* Journalists, safety consultants, Grange staff, no sign of Thurst, union reps, police, Port Authority staff, everyone glaring, ready to accuse.

She plugged the earbuds into her phone and pressed redial. Remi.

She could barely hear the phone ringing, the room was filled with so much talk: instructions, camera crews, photographers. She shook her head. *Simultaneous ringing?* She looked up. The other journos had hushed, clustering to one side of the small incident office. There, behind a glass partition, were the safety team and police. Among them she recognised one. *Him again!* Bannister. Just then Remi answered his phone.

'Hello.'

'Oh, Remi!' Chrissie replied quickly, relieved, lifting the microphone on the cord closer to her mouth. 'Thank god! For a minute there . . . You've heard the news. Hope it wasn't anyone you know,' she kept talking, 'I'm at the port now, waiting. They're about to hold a press conference. Where are you?'

'Who is this please?' the voice came back. Chrissie tried to suck in air but her throat had suddenly closed. The voice wasn't Remi, but it also had a strange echo about it.

'Who is this please?' the voice said again. Was it familiar? She looked up, directly at the office with the glass partitions. But now others were looking back at her.

'This is Senior Detective Jason Bannister.'

Bannister!

'I've answered Remi Bassill's phone.' She saw him stand up and held her stare. Chrissie couldn't speak. 'The phone's caller ID says Chris,' he said into her ear as he looked across the room straight at her. He recognised her immediately. 'Chris?' He saw her holding her microphone to her mouth, listening through her earbuds, her eyes locked on him. 'Chris O'Brian? From *The Argus*?' She gave no response and looked down, steadying herself against a table.

Chrissie could hear his warm voice through the phone and in the room. Her hand shaking as Bannister walked slowly towards her. Taking small careful steps, despite his large brown boots and long legs. The noise in the incident room surged again.

Can't breathe. Remi. She looked around at the other journos as they watched the detective cross the floor. She tried to sit but her legs shook too much. Bannister was almost in front of her, his pale blue shirt filled her vision. She closed her eyes, ashamed all over again of her reaction when they first met. *Get a hold.* She held up her hand to him.

'You knew the victim?' He had lowered the phone and now spoke to her directly, still puzzled. 'It's okay, the family knows,' he offered as permission for him to tell her. His voice calm and soft. A rare calmness in her dawning misery.

'Wait. Just wait, give me a minute,' she almost shouted. She pulled the earbuds out and pressed the app for her emails. Refresh. She didn't want Bannister's words. Refresh. She turned her back to him and fiercely jabbed the icon. Refresh. Refresh.

'It's okay, the family knows,' Bannister again, even gentler. She slumped back in a chair. *Mas, now Remi. My fault. Remi.* She had to tell Maria, Jefferies, that this victim was also one of her contacts. No coincidence. She was connected to these murders. She waved the phone in front of Bannister to silence him, as the email finally landed.

'Our colleague Remi Albert Basill, father of three, fourth-generation dock worker, has become the third fatality within a year of the dangerous working conditions at Grange Industries in the Port of Melbourne . . .

'The MWA has immediately called on its Australian affiliated organisations and the International Maritime Council of Unions to black ban Grange terminals around the world until their safety practices are investigated. This callous disregard for human lives is intolerable. The MWA calls on the Safety Bureau to immediately shut down Grange operations in Australia and stand down our members on full pay, pending an independent safety audit.'

Hel Carter had kept her word. *War.*

Chrissie felt the heat of Bannister, now, as he stood too close, again. Amid the chaos and sadness, it was his safe smell that threatened to derail her. But then a gasp went through the room. They both looked up. An eerie silence settled as everyone stared out the window. Chrissie followed their gaze. A lumpy body bag slumped on a metal trolley was being wheeled across the smooth dark concrete yard, disobeying the yellow safety lines. The coloured emergency lights bounced off the shiny black plastic bag and the trolley's crisscrossed under-frame. The trolley collided into the back of a long low dark car, its frame automatically folding under itself as the escort of men pushed the tray with its plastic cargo into the back of the hearse.

CHAPTER 24

Where was Skinny, the little scoundrel? Chrissie paced her lounge room. She needed a bit of calming down. Some purring to relax her. *Remi and Mas both dead.*

'Listen, Chris, things are stirred up. You're on your own with that story angle we talked about.' Charlie Thurst had surfaced at last.

'What do you mean, on my own? You're the data source,' she barked back down the phone at him.

'Yes, yes, of course. You can still work from it, all of it, but I've got to focus elsewhere at the moment.' She heard him sigh, as he smoothed out his voice. She pictured him preening. 'Got to settle things here, with the bloody union, before it all goes haywire. But if you can get the story written, as we agreed. The embargo still stands for everyone else but you, you go as early as you can now, okay?' Chrissie gasped but he kept talking. 'I need it out, so Sunday, Monday, or a couple days earlier would be good. I can't hold your hand, got bigger fish to fry.'

'What do you mean, "everyone else" but me? How many others are you stringing along?' Chrissie's voice was hard and loud.

'No one. No one,' Thurst tried to calm her. He clearly didn't want Chrissie to turn on him. She knew too much. 'Slip of the tongue. It's yours as agreed but if it doesn't come off as planned, I told you, I'll put it elsewhere.' Chrissie knew the game. He had probably already part-briefed one or two rivals, most likely a chosen TV station and at least one radio. That way the broadcasters could be prepped and ready to go, with file footage and background, as soon as *The Argus* published.

'Just tell me: Remi Basill,' she choked on his name. 'Any witnesses, CCTV?'

'Course not,' he said, and hung up.

—

The knock on the door made Chrissie jump. It could only be Mike.

'Jeepers. You got yourself mixed up in some bad shit, lady. That's two murders. You could be next.'

'Oh, great, thanks for the reassurance.'

'No, I'm serious. Gotta watch yourself, okay? Keep your door locked. You want me to put up a camera or two?' He looked around the room for a likely spot. 'Did you ever find that spare key?'

'Come on, help me with this,' she said, ushering him to her laptop, avoiding his questions. They were too hard to answer, she had to focus. 'I need to know what type of cargo is missing.'

'Let's have a trawl,' he said, rubbing his hands together, 'see if we can find the ships in and around the time of the others.'

'Nothing illegal,' Chrissie interrupted. 'I can't be involved in hacking or anything.'

'Nah, nah, all public records, just got to know how to look deep.' Mike shook his head. But she had her doubts. 'Well, no need for anything too fancy this time, but better if we don't use your device.' He gave her a wink before he raced downstairs to get one of his laptops.

'How'd you learn all this anyway?' Chrissie said when he returned.

'Misspent youth. Got a scholarship to a posh school, well, my mum did, she was determined, you know for hardups. Then another to Melbourne Uni.' He found a spot on the coffee table to set up. 'I ticked all the right diversity boxes. Computer sciences. Then a masters. It was easy. The other students used to pay me to do their coding, I was rich.' Mike inserted a USB. 'I'm using a private network to block our location,' he added as he typed in a long address. 'But I was thinking, from the other night. You should break it down more. The safety side is one aspect, the missing freight is a second. That's what my brain says,' Mike continued. 'They don't have to be connected, do they?'

Chrissie looked back through her notes.

'Yeah, okay. Let's look for expensive cargoes, maybe. Something exotic, unusual,' she said. 'There should be a list of cargo for each vessel. Maybe regular arrivals? Anything like that, I'm just fishing really, not sure where to start. And can we go back to the earlier death, Hank? Here, I'll get the date. Double-check the time of day, the ships tied up, those departing,' she continued.

'This isn't going to work,' Mike said after about thirty minutes. 'I've got some of that info but what you really need is someone on the inside. To narrow it down. A whistleblower.'

'I'll work on that.'

—

Chrissie poured another glass of wine. Mike had left her to it. Slow down, she thought, skolling the glass. She had promised herself to go easy. A text landed on her phone.

Hear you've got hurdles at work. The screen said Parenta, the transport union boss.

How could he know? Only a handful of people knew she had been sidelined to obits, asked to spend less time on the story. There must be a leak at *The Argus*. Harry. She recalled Parenta's text to her when she was in Grange's elevator. But this was the second warning about the paper. She raced through the possibilities of where the leak could come from.

Her glass froze midway to her mouth. Gina? She knew Parenta's daughter. Could James have spilled something to Gina, pillow talk, who passed it on to Parenta? She shook her head, dismissed the thought. Lawyers don't make mistakes like that.

Let's meet tomorrow. Dome room. Chrissie replied by text.

She suddenly felt exhausted. Fighting on all sides. *Remi!* The details of the accident were still preliminary but a container had dislodged during a restow and Remi had been underneath it. *Or pushed under it.* Skinny had let himself in and sat on the small table surveying her.

'Enough for tonight?' she asked him. He meowed and stood up, arching his back. 'Yeah, I agree.' His head pushed hard against her hand and the purring began instantly.

She got into bed, pulled her quilt high, the smell of her mother still in it. She had made it for Chrissie's twelfth birthday and another for her brother William, finishing them, Chrissie later realised, just a few months before she died. Chrissie gave it another tug higher, careful not to disturb Skinny. Only one pill tonight.

—

It was as if Chrissie could see through the lens as it twisted and whirred. Perched high on its girder, the CCTV camera saw everything. The man's breath was gone in an instant, his legs and chest crushed flat. The camera zoomed in to inspect his face. Brown hair. Hard hat askew. Remi! His face filled with pain. He took 16 seconds to die as the electronic eye watched. The lens whirred again. Fuzzy white letters sharpened to show the side of a hulking red container. Yellow lane markings on the cold concrete floor made a safe path through the warehouse maze. The lens went wider, showing the backs of four men as they walked away. Adrenalin breath huffing in the warehouse air until they disappeared through gigantic sliding doors. Identical heavy boots, collars up, hoodies pulled low, the four men walked away strong and sure, unseen.

CHAPTER 25

The enormous glass dome was mesmerising. It was lunchtime and Chrissie was surrounded by city workers taking time out in the serene octagonal reading room in the State Library. The skylight in the dome lit the bookshelves and balconies with a soft diffused glow. She could sit there for hours and often did. This grand room, built with gold rush money, was one of the few places in the city Chrissie felt calm. She leaned even further back and gazed up.

It was her idea to meet Graham Parenta at the library, a large open space with lots of people – hidden in plain sight.

From her vantage spot on a balcony, she spotted him as he walked confidently through the double doors. She had looked up a couple of photos from the archives. Neat black hair, brown skin. Shorter and slighter than she had assumed or that the search images implied but he was once a truck driver, just like her grandfather. His pale grey shirt and charcoal pants belied his working-class roots. Today he blended seamlessly into the city office crowd. Almost the complete opposite of Hel Carter's angry, rumpled image. Chrissie blended in too, easily overlooked, just as she liked it. She watched Parenta stop to examine the 'ribbon of words' sculpture that ran around the room. He took his time, before picking up a book from the biography section. Cautious, she thought. He sat at one of the big reading tables and flicked through the opening pages. This man could hold the key to her story. She wanted him to trust her. To fill in some of the missing pieces. Relax, she told herself. He's the head of one of the oldest, toughest unions in the country. He's already decided to play.

'I'm Chris,' she said softly, sitting down on the opposite side of the antique reading table.

'I haven't been to this place in years, decades even,' he said, a half-smile warming his face. 'Nice to meet you, finally. Looks like you've got yourself a good story. If what I've got gets out, it's going to be very interesting.' His voice was smooth and controlled, almost lyrical – another contrast to his rival Carter's high-pitched gravel rash of shouts and exclamations.

He pulled out a single folded page from his inside pocket and pushed it across the table, composed, business-like.

'It's not on letterhead but keep it to yourself. There's a black hole at Grange's terminals, sucking up tonnes of cargo. They're all pulling out their hair, blaming everyone, our blokes, too. Grange is even investigating itself.' He paused while a couple of people walked by. Chrissie already knew this but she let him go on. 'There's only two ways in and out of that place, land and sea.

And we've got everything landside covered. No way our guys are turning a blind eye to this much racket.'

'Surely some theft goes on?' Chrissie probed.

'Nothing like this.' He pointed to the paper he had handed her. 'If you ask me, it's organised. No petty theft or insurance job. Too big, too often. But you might have a bit more luck.' *That's what the maritime union said.* He fixed his gaze on her.

'If you need someone with luck, that isn't me,' Chrissie returned. 'But this will help. Thanks.' She finished reading his note. It was estimates of missing containers during the past six months. Boxes off-loaded at Grange terminals, transported offsite by rail and by road and those on-loaded to other ships. The gap was about fifteen containers. No mention of the accidents or deaths. *Clinical.*

'How did you tumble to this, anyway?' Parenta asked.

Could she trust herself? Her instincts? Was this guy on the level?

Chrissie took the leap. Her heart sped up. Maybe whoever was leaking at the paper had also told him she was unreliable, suicidal, a pill-popper. She rubbed her palms against the wool upholstery of the chair. But he had already risked a lot to talk to her, she reasoned. He had shown trust in her. *Trust yourself.* She told him about the fake accident theory. The lack of camera footage.

Chrissie watched Parenta's face as closely as he watched her. He didn't move a muscle.

'There's been a surge in workplace deaths. Not just at Grange but everywhere, construction, agriculture, mining,' Parenta finally responded. 'But it's far worse on the docks. The tech on the ships doesn't match the tech at the terminals. Millions of dollars wasted on trying to cope with the mismatch. Jesus, there's still vessels almost fifty years old. It's just good business sense to keep investing, keep changing. That's what's going to save this industry,' he said.

'Sounds like you know better than the maritime how things should run down there.'

Parenta sat up slightly.

'Not my area.' He leaned back and eyed her off. 'Just keeping myself in the know. My workers rely on these docks just as much as MWA.'

'The missing freight, is it all the same cargo? Same shippers?'

'Don't know, can't tell from those stats . . . But assume Grange knows, and has known, from day dot. They must be running crazy. If this comes out it would hurt them bad.'

'What did you mean when you said it wasn't an insurance job?'

'An exporter wants a shipment lost or damaged; sometimes it's the receiver.'

'Like what. What's an example?'

'Tanker recently hit a reef in the South China Sea. Soy bean oil, worth tens of millions. But it got contaminated, only good for fuel, not even worth the transport cost.' Parenta looked around, leaned a little closer. 'The exporter knew but tanked it up regardless. And what do you know? Ship runs aground. Captain makes sure nobody hits the black box, the data saver, so just the captain's report about how it happened. Insurance pays out millions as if it was the premium grade. Simple really.'

'If you had to guess, then, what do you think is going on? Up to three people dead; two of them within weeks. Workmates not saying anything. Cargo missing. What sort of cargo would someone kill for?' Chrissie could feel her pulse in her fingertips, her breathing just that bit faster.

He casually surveyed his surroundings. Habit, Chrissie realised. A man used to holding secrets.

'One of our guys had a theory. Sounded like nothing a few months ago. He was waiting to enter the port but was told to stand off. These drivers all have pre-booked timeslots, so he was pretty pissed off. The port's ten times more complicated than any airport with its slots. Someone was given priority over him. Anyways, he knew the other driver.'

Parenta leaned forward across the desk. This time Chrissie looked around.

'They had a chat at the old diner afterwards,' Parenta continued. 'This driver told our guy he'd been contracted by a new lot. Never has to book a slot now, just told to turn up in the standby queue, gets shuttled through almost immediately. Some mining outfit up country. Special clearance. Carries the boxes all the way to the Alice. Same thing, every time.'

'Mining? Okay, I haven't heard anything like that. Thanks, I'll see if it leads anywhere. Also what's the hurdle you mentioned at *The Argus*?'

Parenta leaned forward even more, a different light in his eyes now. 'I heard one of your guys is in tight with Grange. He might have passed on some info that you had. Something you might have got from those big fat loose lips at the maritime union, maybe?'

Chrissie didn't react to the reference to Hel Carter. But Harry's face quickly sprang to mind about the leak. Did he move me to obits because he didn't like me or to protect Grange? Or could it be Neil? The business writer. He sometimes seemed to hover too closely. He would have contacts in several boardrooms. Neil had also downplayed her story about the vacant city stores, recommending it be used to fill up space at the bottom of his piece on the day, instead of running as a standalone story.

'From your silence, I assume you might know who it is,' Parenta said with the slightest of nods.

'More of a shortlist,' Chrissie said.

'I'd play it a bit closer to your chest with everyone, until you know for sure.'

—

So who was it? Back in the newsroom, Chrissie watched Harry closely that afternoon. Each time she saw him cross the newsroom she wanted to confront him, but she had to be smart, wait for more ammo. The media was the only safe place for whistle-blowers; if it became corrupt, there was nowhere for people to go.

'He's not the person he used to be,' James said quietly when he saw her watching Harry. 'This place has been his life. Career going backwards. Short-staffed, cutting corners. That's hard for a stickler, a perfectionist, like him. You know his wife left him, not that long ago? Gloria. He's trying to get her back.' James swivelled back to his screen.

Chrissie shifted sideways to look towards the business section. Neil was there, red-grey hair, balding, paunchy, pushy. He was frequently lunching only to rush back late to the newsroom and loudly swear his way through writing and filing a story. She'd also pay closer attention to Neil from now on.

Lately, more people at work seemed to smile at her, or was she just imagining it? Small talk in the kitchen was easier. People didn't stop talking when she was near; some even included her. Sympathy after the hospital stint, perhaps, had softened the edge of their resentment. Could it be more than that? Perhaps they had stopped seeing her just as the interloper who took someone's job.

Maria, however, was more demanding. Subeditors, the picture desk, producers; everyone was short of staff.

'Chrissie. What's going on with that page? You're pushing it! And there are two others to get over the line.' Even Maria, cool-headed Maria, was under the pump. Chrissie didn't want to be the cause of this woman being under more strain.

'I'll get it in on time,' she assured Maria.

'Good on ya, my girl. I've had enough hold-ups today. I swear I'm going to spike the water jug next time, give them all a case of the squirts. That'll speed up these endless meetings about "commercial opportunities". Why they can't just leave us to write?'

Chrissie had been on edge since meeting Parenta. Should she tell Maria or James her suspicions about a leak? She knew that despite Harry's faults, James still had a soft spot for him. A soft spot for everyone.

'Harry set up the first dedicated investigation team in Australia, a trail blazer,' James had said, not long after Chrissie had arrived at the paper. 'But he changed, you know, as newspapers changed . . .'

Traditional skills were no longer valued, Chrissie knew. Instincts, logic, writing ability, even Harry's golden contacts list had become almost obsolete in the clickbait world of new journalism.

If she told James about her suspicion of Harry, he'd know she'd been in contact with Graham Parenta. What if he blurted it out to Gina, or someone else? She'd have to watch what she said to him.

Chrissie finished her pages and filed them to Maria then typed in an archive search: mining companies, importers. One hundred and thirty hits.

She wouldn't tackle Harry yet, she had to be strategic. If he knew her suspicions it might encourage him to dig into her past. To shame her, to lessen her credibility. She couldn't deal with everyone knowing what she had done. If Harry knew she was getting too close to exposing him as the leak that might spur him on. It could also prompt Grange to ruin her feature by putting out a soft spoiler, with only a few details, to a rival publication. Thurst had already threatened as much. Or Harry could delay her story. Cut it to shreds, blame it on no space. But one thing she knew, once she exposed him, he would never be accepted in the media again. He had a lot at stake, and he would be more determined than ever to ruin her.

By the time she left the office, she was exhausted. A red rash was spreading up her neck. Her nerves sparking, her palms itching. But her day wasn't over. Now she had to front up to her first appointment with the hospital psychiatrist. Part of her discharge plan from the hospital but also a promise to her dad.

Dr Darcy White, 'call me Dr Darcy', welcomed her with warm forty-something-year-old hands and a sympathetic face but Chrissie refused to look at her. Darcy was just a puff of smoke, transparent and annoying, as she breathed out her questions and swirled her suggestions and prompts around the room.

'Is there a history of mental illness in the family?'

'Thinking back, what would that suggest?'

'How does that make you feel now?'

Chrissie strained to keep her arms unfolded, hands glued to the arm rests of the chair as she batted the questions away, giving the answers she knew the doctor wanted to hear. She had been through the routine before, in New Zealand.

One visit down, two to go.

CHAPTER 26

'Hi, Chrissie, this came for you. Where do you want it?'

The editorial assistant held a small package towards her the next morning. He was looking for somewhere to put it, every spot on her desk littered with papers and documents.

'Who from? Here,' Chrissie pointed. 'Thanks.'

'Must have come by courier.' He handed it over.

The Argus received an endless stream of press releases with samples, elaborate invitations, gimmicky PR attention-grabbers. It was one way companies hoped to get a press release read. Chrissie turned the package over but there was no sender. Inside, a small white box. No press release or envelope under the lid. The wrapping was haphazard too, messy. Inside the box was something glass, covered in bubble wrap. She couldn't make it out but it looked like a small jar. As she pulled the bubble wrap off she felt uneasy. Her unwrapping slowed to a stop. 'What the hell?'

James leaned over. Chrissie used her fingertips to remove the last of the bubble wrap.

'Chrissie, stop!' He grabbed the back of her chair and pulled it away from her desk. The momentum spun Chrissie and the chair around 180 degrees. She turned back to see James standing, peering at the package, not wanting to step too close. She joined him.

It was a clear glass jar, complete with a red and white checked lid. Inside was a grey thing, half soaked in what looked like blood. *Ugh, a rat or a mouse.* Some bastard had sent her a dead mouse. She leaned over a bit more, unwilling to move too close. It was rounded at one end and bloody at the other. Her hand flew up to her mouth, acid surging up and burning her throat. It wasn't a mouse. It was a cat's paw! Chrissie's mind skidded immediately, horrifically, to Skinny. She couldn't take her eyes off it. *Oh god, please don't let it be Skinny!* She made herself look more closely than she wanted to. Examined the colouring as she pictured the cat prowling across her floor, meowing at her from the sofa. Was it Skinny? She couldn't tell. She gagged again.

'I think that's, that's Skinny. His foot . . . The cat from my place,' she whispered.

'Jesus H. Christ.' James reared back a few steps. 'Someone knows where you live. They probably think that cat is yours . . .' He leaned slightly forward to take a cautious peek but quickly looked away again. 'Jesus, we've got to report this one. It's not some random. It's someone who's stalking you.'

James didn't wait for a reply. He called security.

The security chief, Jonathan, arrived within minutes and bustled around as he assessed the situation. Was an evacuation required? Was there any substance released? Any spillage from the jar? Was it an incendiary device? Everyone knew the drill.

Security at the paper was tight. As more interest groups decided intimidation was the fastest way to get attention, the number of threats had increased every year. Threatening letters, phone calls and death threats were old hat. Now it could be asbestos dust in the mail, messages left in their children's schoolbags. Most journalists were hardened to it.

Jonathan asked for a ten-metre clearance. People at nearby desks obeyed. He leaned into his mobile phone and gave a whispered message. Within seconds the security alert sounded.

'Alert, Alert. This is a security alert. It is not a fire alert. This is a security alert. Do not attempt to leave the building. Step away from the windows. Move to the central core of the building. Do not use the elevators. This is a security alert.'

Nobody on the news floor panicked. There was a security event every few months. They had been taught to congregate near the stairwells, toilets and kitchen, near the lift well. Some didn't bother, especially if it was close to deadline.

Today was no exception. A few people even walked towards Jonathan to see what was up. Powders and liquids were the most dangerous, but the jar's lid was tightly screwed on. No immediate danger, Jonathan knew, and so did most of the journos. They soon drifted back to their desks.

A uniformed security worker arrived, carrying a contamination kit. Gloves, masks, specimen bags, tongs. He took photos of the jar and the packaging on Chrissie's desk. Then he gloved up and used the tongs to lift the jar into one of the clear plastic bags and passed it to Jonathan. Another bag was used for the bubble wrap and a third for the outside packaging.

'That's it, peeps,' Jonathan told them, tapping a code into his mobile phone.

The loudspeaker crackled back into action: 'Stand down. The security alert is over. Stand down. The security alert is over. You may go back to your desks. The security alert is over.'

'Chris, can we get a description of what happened, please?' Jonathan asked as he found a clear space on her desk and propped up the contamination kits.

'I've got to get home. Check,' Chrissie ventured.

'Sorry, best done straight away.' He grabbed a chair and sat next to her. The chair gave an exhausted sigh, Jonathan's knees too high, his bulk overhanging both sides. She explained about Skinny Cat, and Jonathan shuddered.

'Poor defenceless cat,' he muttered. 'I have to report this to the police, you realise,' he said, still shaking his head. 'Anything with a direct link to a staff member's home must be reported. Someone knows your address and went there. Sorry, Chris, there'll be follow-up. I'd say the cops will want to take a look around your place.' He pulled his chair even closer. 'Come on then, just type it in an email to me now, I'll read as you go, maybe ask some extra questions.'

Eventually Jonathan got up to go, finally taking the parcel away from her.

'Too friendly for its own good, that bloody cat.' She turned to James. Despite her harsh words, Chrissie burst into tears. Skinny had been her comforter. James scooted his chair towards her but

Chrissie motioned for him to keep his distance, wiping her eyes and shaking her head. She had to get control of herself.

'It's got to be something to do with the wharf,' he said quietly. 'You've been stirring things up; it probably means you've got someone worried. They're trying to scare you, derail you.'

'Yeah. Well, I reckon I can do that pretty much on my own. But Skinny?' She stifled another sob.

'You do know what a cat's paw means, don't you?'

Chrissie looked blank.

'I never thought I'd be more streetwise than you, O'Brian. I came across it in a bikie story. If you're a cat's paw it means someone is using you to do their bidding. Their dirty work.'

'Perfect. Well, that's right. I'm being used by everyone to do their dirty work. Grange is using me. Hel Carter and the maritime union. Probably Parenta and the transport union. Poor Mas, poor Remi tried but I wouldn't listen. That's me all right. A little grey useless cat's paw doing everyone's dirty work.' She felt the rage bubbling, frustration and fear. And then it just came out.

'What about you, James? Did you leak anything about my story?'

'Whoa, Chrissie. Where did that come from?' James looked genuinely shocked. *But he would, wouldn't he, if he'd just been sprung?*

'What are you doing here? Really?' she demanded, waving her hand around the newsroom.

'Chrissie, you're upset.' James looked around. 'Keep your voice down.' He gestured to calm her, leaned in. 'I'm only telling you because I, well, I don't know why. To shut you up, I suppose.' He dipped his head closer. 'Nobody knows, not even Jefferies, well

Harry found out somehow, he's been here so long. But he's kept dead schtum all this time.'

Chrissie sat back. *Found out what?* She started to gently sip the air. She didn't really know why she was accusing him. It had been in the heat of the moment but he looked truly troubled now. *What have I stumbled on?*

'My mother, she's related to the Templetons. You know. Party Patty. A bit far down in the pecking order of the family line, but related.'

'What's that got to do with anything?' Chrissie asked. *Breathe.* She was still in shock about the parcel, never mind whatever this confession of James's was going to reveal.

'As to why I'm here, it's what rich families do – they give positions to their water-treading, do-gooder relatives.' He gave Chrissie a half-smile and a shrug. 'Geens and I are heading to the States next year, so I'm just sitting it out for a bit longer.' Chrissie started to relax. *Nothing to do with the leak.* 'But it didn't start that way. I really wanted to be a journalist, use those lawyer skills for good instead of evil.' He gave her one of his hapless shrugs. 'Besides, there's still a bit of kudos in this game. Opens a few doors. People still think you've got some gravitas. Best of all, it stops people asking when I'm going to get my act together. Apparently it's okay to earn nothing and have no prospects if you're a journalist – a calling, as they say. Well, that's what my parents choose to say.'

Chrissie controlled herself. Skinny's paw had devastated her but she felt bad attacking James. He had his secrets too; perhaps that was why he'd always let her keep hers. He'd never pried and she had often wondered why. *Explains a lot.*

'But what does that mean? You have to spy on us or something?' she asked.

'Goodness, no. Although I like the sound of that: international man of mystery, people might suck up to me a bit more.' He gave her his old smile, though a little faded. 'No. Certainly not. The board, the owners, honestly, they have no interest in what goes on with the journos. All they care about is revenue. The socials, the platforms, suck up all the advertising dollars now, leaving the old media facing a slow death.'

'Oh great, thanks for the good news.'

But her shoulders started to relax. She watched Jonathan, who was still making his way out of the newsroom, stopping constantly to show off his bloody haul. Journos were a gory lot.

Now she was responsible for Skinny's death, too. Another small life gone. *Death all around. Me next?*

CHAPTER 27

Glimpses of the city flashed by as the police car sped its way to North Richmond. The tall brown silos topped by the Nylex clock read 11.33; the traffic on the Swan Street bridge forced the car to slow as it drove over the brown ribbon, the Yarra River, that twisted through the city. They drove through the back streets, past the old knitting mill, the meat packers' hall, both now swish apartment blocks. Up and over toff hill, the tall steeple of St Ignatius almost reaching the low cloud, *stratocumulus*. As they drove, Chrissie felt more and more disconnected, it was as if the car was stationary but the landscape was moving.

Two detectives had arrived at *The Argus* about an hour after the paw was reported. Maria had insisted Chrissie stay until the cops arrived. She didn't want her going home by herself. The jar and its contents would be sent to the lab and then the three of them had piled into an impossibly small car for the drive. They had run out of small talk in the first few minutes. She faced away from the window and stared at the head of the police driver in front of her. Short blond hair cut high enough to show a tattoo on the back of his neck, dipping down into his collar. *Tribal.*

What would she find when she got home? Skinny's body strung across her doorway? His blood over the floor? She couldn't think about that yet. But not knowing soon proved worse.

'Puss, puss, puss,' Chrissie called as they walked around the foyer, her voice catching. There was nothing obvious. The entrance hall was its usual jumble. Out the back door, the cops followed her into the small yard. 'Kitty cat, Skinny Cat.' She didn't care if they heard her 'cat voice' she just needed to find him. 'Puss, puss, puss.'

There was no meow but that wasn't unusual, she explained to them, trying to hold out hope. Another car of cops arrived, detectives, and they all went up to her apartment. No signs of a break-in, although she had to tell them she had lost her spare key recently. One of the detectives started to take photos, the other dusted for fingerprints. They were there about an hour when Chrissie heard a familiar voice.

'They probably just wanted to scare you.' He had just walked straight into the room, no knock or hesitation. Already fully briefed by the sound of it. Senior Detective Bannister. 'To let you know they know where you live. Nothing to gain from breaking in.' He looked around the room. Chrissie felt exposed as he took in her life in one swoop. 'What about this cat, then?' He shook his head slightly. Kindly. His brown hair partly fell across his eyes.

She swallowed. She still hadn't got back to him after her statement about Remi's death. Not that she'd told him everything about her contact with Remi. 'It also visits downstairs: unit one, directly below,' Chrissie said.

She could hear Bannister on the wooden stairs as he clomped his way down. He was more like an athlete than a policeman stuck behind a desk, working all hours. The sort of guy you'd want on your side in a brawl. There was something about a police knock. She could hear it from inside her flat and then Bannister again on the stairs as he made his way back, taking two steps at a time.

'Not home. How about we take a look around the rest of the building, knock on a couple of doors? Who else do you know here?'

'No one.' She paused. 'I mean, I'm pretty busy at work.' Too defensive. 'I get home late and everyone keeps to themselves.' Chrissie was surprised to discover that she didn't want Bannister to think she had no friends.

'It's a rough neighbourhood, I'd keep to myself too,' he offered, half-smiling.

'It's close to work,' she said, cutting him off. Then her tone softened: 'Besides, it's cheap. Journos get crap pay. A bit like cops.'

'You're not wrong there.' He nodded. 'Look, my officers will check if anyone saw anything. They're finished inside your flat, you might as well head back to work. If they find your moggie skulking under a bush, they'll let me know.'

'Oh god! I hadn't thought.' Chrissie slammed a hand on the table. 'What if he's lying in an alley, bleeding to death? I've got to go look.' The panic was back, bubbling up. 'Can you help me look?' Chrissie was in full flight to the door before Bannister grabbed her arm.

'That's not likely. Listen. Chris, listen.' Bannister gently turned her to face him, dark serious eyes. His grip unbreakable but soft. *Used to dealing with people in stress.* 'I'm sorry, the cat . . . if it's yours or another one, they probably would have killed it first. They wouldn't want any noise, scratches, you know? Quick and quiet. I'm sorry.'

No. Chrissie shivered the image away. Yet she had to face it: the thought that Skinny died quickly was better than worrying he was curled up behind some rubbish bin dying slowly. *Another life.*

'We'll need to talk with you again, more formally, later,' Bannister said, bending his head towards her. 'And this story you're working on – and, before you say it, I'm not going to need names and sources. Just a general chat. Unless you suspect someone. If it's something criminal, then you could be out of your depth. This type of threat is usually well targeted,' he said gently.

Should she tell him about Mas and Remi?

'The story's about the wharf. The death of Remi Basill, which you know about, and another.'

'And you're connected to both, right?' He already had the answer. Her interview with Mas was no secret. 'Come on, I'll drive you back.'

As they drove off in the police car, she glanced up to the house just in time to catch a flash of Mike behind his curtain.

—

'Chrissie, over here. Here,' Maria called as soon as she walked back onto the floor. 'You all right?' she said, holding Chrissie by both shoulders. 'If anyone did anything like that to one of my cats, I'd string 'em up.'

'It wasn't actually my cat, it just visited me.'

'Ha! You can say that about every one of them.' Maria adjusted today's large circular white glasses. *So Iris.*

'I was a bit shaken,' Chrissie admitted, swallowing. 'But I'll be okay. I'm back and ready to get stuck in.'

'Not so quick, my girl. Jefferies wants us both in his office. You ready now?'

'Just give me a minute.' Chrissie dashed to the bathroom. She rubbed her palms together to stop the itching. Usually just being in the newsroom helped dial down her anxiety. Her stabbing thumbnail was usually the only tell-tale sign.

The car crash had left her fingers crisscrossed with deep scars. One of the police officers at her flat had noticed today as he took her prints. He didn't say anything but when the images popped up on the screen, the scars were clearly visible.

She scrambled in her bag and found some Zoloft. Scooping water up from the tap, she swallowed one. *Breathe in, one two three. Out, one two three.* She had to find a black market for her anti-depressant; constant shortages around the country played on her mind. What if she ran out?

Chrissie stared in the mirror; sunken eyes, grim mouth. A ghost-white face stared back at her. She put her mask back on and strode out as confidently as she could, head up. *Play for time while the med settles in.* She checked her emails. Leaning over her desk phone, she was surprised to see a little bunch of flowers to the side of her screen. Three pink hyacinths tied with a white ribbon and a note. *So sorry to hear about your cat. Lou.*

Chrissie was touched. That Lou, the fashion editor, had bothered struck her hard.

'Thought you might need something good on such a shitty day.' Lou suddenly appeared beside her desk and gave Chrissie a hug, the huge bell sleeves of her silk top flowed around Chrissie like a pink cape.

Time to face Jefferies but, as she headed off, James waved her into the kitchen.

'Watch yourself in this meeting,' he whispered quickly.

Before she could ask anything else, Maria came up behind them and swept Chrissie along to Jefferies' office.

'Come in. Chrissie, Maria. Harry's here; you know Jonathan from security; and I've asked the duty lawyer to sit in.' Jefferies was straight to business. 'We don't know yet if it was a direct threat against you, Chrissie. But until we do, let's be on the safe side and assume it was.'

Chrissie was temporarily mesmerised as he turned his pen over and over in his hand, a cheap transparent biro with a chewed plastic end.

'The police will work through the security footage from the lobby and hopefully get a lead about who dropped it off. For some reason, the parcel didn't go through X-ray screening.'

Jefferies looked at Jonathan, suddenly tapping the pen twice on the blotter which made Chrissie jump. 'But that won't happen again. Jonathan has suggested the mail room not only X-ray but also open all outer layers before putting anything on the trolley. Okay. Now, I want to talk about the wharf story.'

'I'm doing it in my own time,' Chrissie said defensively.

Harry's head made the slightest sideways movement.

'Do you think the cat's paw is related?' Jefferies asked.

'Well, I'm being played by all sides, and the stakes are high. It fits. A cat's paw is supposed to be a warning, a sign that I'm doing someone's dirty work.'

'Don't we all in this business?' Jefferies replied.

She continued cautiously. 'This second death at the wharves has rattled everyone. Maritime union's getting together an international campaign. Grange has battened down the hatches, even with me. I heard Grange was even asking the government for help to break the strike. Just a rumour, so far.' Chrissie watched Harry's face at the mention of Grange. Nothing. She looked around at the others in the room. 'Or it could be one of those financial advice victims getting back for that smarmy obit we ran about the bank executive the other week. Or the restaurant, the one that got firebombed after we exposed the rat shit.'

'I'm not taking any chances, I'm telling you to hold back. The story is on freeze. We can't have you at risk,' Jefferies said.

Great. Grange will be pleased.

Harry gazed out the window. *Not brazen enough to stare me in the face?*

'You sure about this, Tom?' Maria asked, quiet till now. 'It's got all the potential to be a great piece.' She stopped at Jefferies' shaking head. 'But, okay,' she continued. 'If we can't take it further let's print the fallback, it's a good story as is. The second death makes it topical. Good weekend piece.'

'Too speculative just now,' Jefferies said switching his gaze between Chrissie and Maria. 'It's still linked in with this threat, we need to hand it off to the police. That'll tie it up for a few days, then I'll reassess.' Jefferies was looking directly at Maria now. He knew her well.

Keep it together, keep it together. But the morning's events still jangled.

'This is crap.' Chrissie couldn't help herself.

'That's the decision, crap or not,' Jefferies replied coolly.

Maria nudged Chrissie with the toe of her red shoe, a warning not to fire up again. Everyone looked uncomfortable, except Harry. But Jefferies stayed on track.

'I want your notes, the photographs, documents, data, footage – everything – on my desk tomorrow morning latest. The lawyers are going to review everything before we decide what to hand over to the police. And Chrissie?' He got up and walked around to her. Propped himself on the front of his desk. 'I'm sorry about what happened. About the cat.'

Chrissie stood, still angry.

'You okay at home?' Jefferies said. 'You worried about this? Do we need a threat audit on Chrissie's home?' He looked to Jonathan.

'Of course not,' Chrissie interrupted. 'No different to any of the other shit we get around here.'

—

'Chrissie, wait.' Maria was doing her best to catch up after she had stormed out of the room. 'Take it easy.' The older woman grabbed Chrissie's arm to slow her down.

'Seems to me some people around here are determined to flush this story down the drain.'

'You've had a dreadful day,' Maria continued. 'You're upset. I want you to go home. I'll get an extra pair of hands for the rest of the day. This is too much!'

'You think I can't handle it, too?' Chrissie snapped.

'I'm just saying,' Maria grabbed her arm again, 'if you'd stop and listen for one second!'

Chrissie stopped, hip thrust out resentfully.

'I'm just saying if you went home you'd be able to work on whatever you wanted.' Maria had her big grin on. Chrissie's shoulders dropped.

'Oh! Oh. I'm sorry.' She hung her head for doubting Maria. 'Yeah, I'll take the rest of the day, thanks,' Chrissie said. 'Maybe I need a couple of days?' Energised again, she raised a cheeky face to Maria.

'One day at a time. Call me tomoz, bright and early. But get some rest, too. You're all hyped up now but this is serious, these people are not playing games.' Maria looked worried.

'The bastards killed Skinny,' Chrissie shot back. 'It's personal now!'

CHAPTER 28

Richmond on the afternoon train opened her eyes to a new world. Mothers and yia-yias with their children. Men with lunch boxes and workers' vests. Ordinary life. The dealers and druggies mostly absent, but never fully, as the suburb showed its working-class migrant roots. Even the railway station looked welcoming in the afternoon sun. Schoolkids joked around. A different weekday universe.

She didn't take her usual shortcut, instead walking slowly along Victoria Street, Little Saigon, constantly dodging the daytime shoppers. Boxes of vegetables, blood red plums, bananas and bundles of leafy bok choy tied with string. The stacks of boxes added to the pavement chaos. She paused at one of the fish shops, the colours, purple, silver, blue, blush, deep red. Tuna, her favourite. The smell of the French bakeries called to her, pork rolls and escargot pastries.

The light shone through the stained glass around her big front door, issuing a red glow across the foyer tiles, Chrissie checked her letterbox.

'Psst, hey, Chrissie. *Chrissie!*' Mike's face peeked out his door. 'Come in. I've gotta ask something.'

Chrissie dragged herself to his door. Just the thought of having to tell him about Skinny hunched her over. Her appetite replaced with sadness again. *I'll have to console him. I can't even console myself.*

'Those coppers. Why were they here?'

'Oh. Yeah, but why didn't you answer?' *Delay.*

'One thing I've learned: don't open the door to a cop if you don't know what he's there for. And most of my customers don't like other people knowing what's gone missing or what they want me to find . . . Come on, tell me what's up. You had a whole posse here this morning. Guessing it's you who sent them down to me.'

'Yes and no. But first –' she swallowed. 'Did you see Skinny Cat, earlier today?'

'No. Why? Oh my god, what? Something serious!'

'The cops.' *Delay.* 'Yeah, sorry, I suggested they go ask you. It was about Skinny.' Chrissie sat on one of the stools.

Mike pulled two beers from the bar fridge and waved them at her. 'I think I'm gonna need one of these,' he said.

'Not for me, thanks. I've got bad news.'

'Then I insist.' Despite her protest he twisted the cap off and handed her the beer. Chrissie took a long, deep drink. *Delay.* She was not a beer drinker, the flavour was like sour bread, but it allowed her to stall for time. *He'll hate me. I'm responsible.*

She watched Mike's expressions as she told him the morning's events. The shock, the grimace, the sadness: Mike had them all. Chrissie kept her own face deadpan until almost the end when her faced screwed tightly in sudden sadness. She looked away and quickly walked to his desk and busied herself looking at Mike's screens as they switched through pages and calculations.

'Bloody hell. I hope it's not him,' Mike said behind her. 'Oh, I've got some of his treats,' he remembered. 'Chicken dumplings. I'll put 'em out near the back door just in case. He has to be the best-fed, skinniest cat in history. He'll probably turn up soon.'

'I don't think so.' She looked back. Tell him straight. 'Pretty sure it was his foot. Pretty sure he's dead.' She watched his expression darken as the reality sank in.

He sighed. 'Me and him, we didn't chat much. I never gave him a name because animals don't like names. Me and him, we just sort of looked at each other. That's how we knew each other. That's probably too deep.'

'Is that a Buddhist thing?' Chrissie asked. Mike didn't seem religious.

'Partly.' He was silent for a while. 'There's plenty of other strays around here. We can adopt someone else!' He was doing his best to cheer her up and Chrissie almost felt loved by the attempt. She shook it off.

'Are you freaked out? You think someone's trying to frighten you, stop you writing your story? Never picked you as a journalist when you moved in. Wasn't even sure you had a job, such a sad face you've got. Scare too many people away.' He glanced up to check her reaction.

'Actually, I've got a little rush job, today, tonight. If you can help?'

'Of course, I can help. I'd help you anytime, anything, you know that, don't you?' He walked right up to Chrissie and put an arm around her shoulders.

'Ah, don't get mooshy,' she said and started to unload her satchel. 'I have to give some of this stuff to the cops tomorrow but I need to keep access to everything. Private access.'

'Let's have it all, lady. Unload away.'

Chrissie would have to walk a tightrope with her contacts for the next few days. If she didn't come up with anything this week, she'd have to push Jefferies to let the fallback piece run on Monday when the embargo ended. But that still didn't get to the truth of Mas or Remi. Or Skinny.

As Mike scanned the material, Chrissie looked through the search she'd done on Alice Springs mining companies. Just about every exploration and resources company had some sort of presence or consultant or contractor in the area. Copper, tin, zinc, nickel, cobalt, lithium, gold, iron, salt. The Territory had a bit of everything.

'What would a mining company import to Alice Springs?' Chrissie snapped her laptop shut.

'Hmmm. Camping gear, swag stuff for workers – cheap made in China shit? Shovels, drill bits?' Chrissie burst out laughing. 'Jesus, I don't know.' Mike feigned insult but he looked pleased to see her happy.

'We're not in the eighteenth century, you know. Two blokes and a shovel digging for gold. Mining's massive, high tech. Big camps, fly-in fly-out . . . Just something a transport contact said, shipments coming off the wharf going inland, outback. Doesn't make sense. I'm trying to –'

Chrissie's phone rang and she stopped in surprise at the caller's name on the screen. Helen Carter.

The maritime union had immediately gone into battle mode after Remi's death. Carter hadn't responded to her follow-up messages about the fake accident speculation. She hadn't even been drawn to respond after Chrissie had texted that the story might run on Monday.

'Got something juicy for you,' Carter's gravelly voice was excited. 'One of your guys is short-listed for a job with Grange.'

'No! What sort of a job?' Chrissie was shocked.

'Exec level PR, reporting to the board.'

'Can't think who it might be,' she said. 'But we've just lost a bunch more staff; it's probably one of them.'

'Nup, big fish apparently,' Carter came back. 'Thomson . . . Thompkins? Something like that. You know him?'

'Yep, I know him. Thompson. Harry Thompson.' It all started to fall into place. The leak. Her transfer off the news round. The profile assignment instead of a hard news story. 'How did you find out?' Chrissie pressed her hand to her chest to keep the excitement out of her voice.

'It's my job to know who I'm going to be up against.' Chrissie could hear how pleased Carter was from her tone. 'You know their main guy, of course, Charlie Thurst, not sure if it's his job or the one he was supposed to be promoted to in the US.' Carter was enjoying the message. 'Off the record, apparently Thurst has had a few internal issues, involving young women. Latest one recorded him on her phone. But he's a survivor, been pushing those boundaries for years. He'll probably talk his way out of it.'

Was this why Thurst had been giving her the cold shoulder? She had assumed he was hunkering down after Remi's accident; had even worried he'd been lining up other journos. But this fitted with Thurst's strategy to control the story, he needed to curry favour with his bosses, get the timing exactly right and he'd prove his value ten times over and avoid the sack, no matter how serious the indiscretions. The boys' club always looked after its own.

'So Thurst gets his promotion as planned and Harry Thompson takes over. Or Thurst is rapped over the knuckles and Harry gets the gig in the US.'

'About right,' Carter said.

'I bet it pays a fortune.'

'Base is half a fucking mill, plus incentives. The US job easily double that,' Carter muttered. Chrissie could hear her two-finger typing on a keyboard while they spoke. 'Plus, Grange is huge internationally, lots of first-class travel. Pretty cushy, either job, while I fight my guts out to get our guys a pissy three per cent.'

'Who else is short-listed? Like, is Thompson a shoo-in?'

'Don't know. My mate's son is on the list. Not that I want him working for Grange, but he'd be a good hire. The boy cut his teeth with us when he first graduated and he knows exactly how unions think. Grange definitely pays for inside knowledge.' Carter paused, took a deep breath. 'Now, am I going to need my lawyers at hand? What're you doing with that fake accident crap?'

'Look, Hel, thanks. Really, thanks. Nothing'll be written without you getting the chance to respond, you know that,'

Chrissie said. 'But at the moment I'm not sure if it's going to survive the cut.'

—

'So what if this Harry guy at work is spilling the beans to Grange?' Mike demanded from his command position in front of his computers after the call. 'Not a crime, is it? No different to what you're doing. You're poking your little freckle nose into other people's business. Now me, I am special. Very special. But I'm in and out without anyone knowing.'

'Leaking information on a story would be the ultimate betrayal from an old-school journo like Harry. The end of the world as we know it,' Chrissie tried to explain. 'The media is supposed to be the last bastion of truth-telling. Trustworthy, you know?'

'I didn't peg you for an idealist,' said Mike. 'Hate to be the one to tell you, but there is no last bastion. Cops are dirty, government, even bloody priests. No frontier, lady.'

—

Upstairs in her flat, Chrissie took a deep breath and pressed Maria's number.

'You do realise what you are saying?' Maria was furious but kept her voice steady. 'This is a serious accusation. You have to be one hundred bloody per cent about Harry before telling anyone, let alone Jefferies or the board.'

Chrissie paced the lounge room. Not the reaction she'd expected.

'Harry's allowed to interview for a job, just like anyone else,' Maria's voice was rising. 'That doesn't mean he's in cahoots with Grange. Given the state of this place, I'd say that was a pretty smart move. Jobs at his pay scale wouldn't come around too often.'

'I know, it's just hearsay,' Chrissie said, 'but I had to tell you. He seemed consumed with downplaying this story.'

'Because he resents you, not the story,' Maria shot back. 'He's got a problem with you; you were brought in over his head; given a job at a time when he was being forced to sack others. Too many decisions taken out of his hands. You really think he'd sink so low? That he'd risk his career and reputation?'

'It's not just any job. It's a future,' Chrissie persisted. 'Grange is paying half a mill, plus perks.'

'Hold up, hold up.' Chrissie could hear the slight puffing of air as Maria sat. 'He's a good hand, just having a difficult time.' Maria sighed. 'You of all people should understand that.' Oh god! Maria knows about me.

Chrissie felt deflated, she realised she had misjudged her decision and Maria's reaction.

'Do I think he would consider a plum PR job?' Maria continued. 'Be lured by the big bucks? A job where he could big-note himself? Absolutely. But he wouldn't deliberately destroy a story or leak details. If he is on this short list, then that's nothing to do with your story.'

'It can't be just a coincidence.' Chrissie shook her head.

'No. It's not a coincidence,' Maria insisted. 'It's two separate issues. The story and the job.' Maria took another deep breath. 'Look, let me dig around. It doesn't smell right to me.'

As she poured herself a glass of wine, Chrissie wondered how deep Harry and Grange were. Her first story about the accidents had been downgraded, he let the news desk cut the background about the picket; the comments from the union, gone. Could he also have orchestrated it for Grange to feed her the anti-union angle? Still, even if that were the case, there was nothing to be gained by making her allegations against him public – yet. It was even more important now to get to the bottom of the story, find the truth. Then fight to get it published.

CHAPTER 29

Chrissie's next session with the hospital psychiatrist hurt. She had got out of bed heavy and sad this morning but walked into Dr Darcy's office head high, shoulders back, determined to keep the conversation away from Dave, her past, her pills, her roulette, her timer, her miscarriage, everything she kept locked away. She had crafted a story to distract the doctor, about the blood-soaked parcel, the mystery contents, the unspoken threat, Skinny's demise. But Dr Darcy, small and thin, had taken Chrissie's measure at the first visit. This time the doctor was fire, not smoke. She scorched her way past Chrissie's attempted avoidance and burned her with each comment: 'Another loss in your life, Chris, this cat. But let's not delay understanding the past and the others.' *Ugh, too much.*

'What's to understand? I killed my husband. I caused our baby to miscarry. I ruined our lives, destroyed Dave's family.' Chrissie sat forward, annoyed her distraction had not worked.

'I'd like you to take a step away from those words. Look at them from the other side.' Dr Darcy leaned back, allowing Chrissie distance. 'Would you, Chris, say that to someone else who had been through the same situation? Would you tell a grieving widow or a childless mother she had no right to mourn?' The doctor cast her eyes down, relieving Chrissie of her scrutiny while she waited for a reply.

'I want to die.'

'How would that happen? Do you have a plan?'

—

Chrissie's face was numb when she left, her facade in ashes. *Two appointments down, one to go!*

The story of Skinny wasn't just a deflection. Chrissie was surprised at how upset she still was. The psych session had made her acknowledge that Skinny had been her companion, her confidant. His purrs had kept her connected. Now she was angry because she had let her guard down and angry even more about how much she wanted him back. Despite the dumplings that Mike was leaving out, Skinny hadn't turned up. But as she walked home from the psych, picking her way through the dregs of last night's chaos, past the injecting room and its straggle of morning visitors, avoiding the throng of addicts drawn to the area by the surge in dealers, she resolved not to give up on Skinny so readily. She would still keep her kitchen window open.

A text from Maria landed as she got to her front steps: **You'd better have another day 'at home'. But make sure Jefferies gets the docs.**

—

'I just found out unit two used to shoo Skinny out,' Mike said after Chrissie knocked on his door on the way back in. 'Not cat people. But they said he had been here about five, six years. Our relationship was never exclusive; he was obviously multi-timing all of us. Belonged to the building, I guess, and whoever lived here.'

My fault. Mas, Remi, Skinny. Dave.

'They were fascinated about the paw. Wanted to know every detail. You didn't take a photo did you?'

'Of course I didn't take a photo! Jeez, what the hell would anyone want with a photo? Anyway, I haven't paid for scanning my stuff last night,' she said as he ushered her in. 'When's the website you're building going to be ready?' But he just stood there, giving her a sly grin. 'What?'

'You had a visitor when you were out this morning.'

Chrissie leaned against the kitchen bench, openly refusing to ask who or how he knew.

'That big handsome cop,' Mike finally said. 'Your knight in shining armour.' He raised his eyebrows. 'I saw the way he opened the car door for you yesterday, fixed your seatbelt.'

Chrissie, too, had noticed that the detective had appeared to linger over their conversation. Took just a little too long explaining procedure, discussing when they would speak again. She had only seen him twice, no three times, she had tried to wipe out that initial meeting, her reaction still made her face burn. But after Remi's death he had been warm and comforting. Maybe he liked her? And when he arrived at her place yesterday, it flashed through Chrissie's thoughts, amid the sadness and shock, that he had looked at home in her flat. But she had quickly shaken the thought away. She was not ready. She didn't deserve to feel affection again. The dreadful depression had taken a bit of a back seat while she was working on this feature. Bit by bit Mike was helping her back into the world. *Skinny, still connecting her.* But she wasn't going to react to Mike's snooping.

'What do I owe you? And, yeah I heard you mention you get paid a lot.'

'Just a few hours, mate's rates, couple of hundry. Cash, please.'

'Can I give you half now? I'll have to get more cash,' she said.

'If that's gonna make you short, split it across a few weeks.'

'You always this easy with your customers? No, the amount's fine, I just don't carry that much anymore. It got too . . . expensive.'

'Oh, and your copper. He's coming back,' Mike looked at his watch, 'in about ten minutes, 9.30. I told him you were probably just out at the gym or one of those runs of yours, before work. But looks like you were doing something else.' Mike eyed her clothes.

'Yeah, sort of. I'm working from home today. But I forgot about an appointment this morning.' Why hadn't Bannister called instead of just showing up? Chrissie quickly paid Mike and checked her own watch. She rushed up the stairs to tidy up.

—

'I hope you don't mind me just dropping in. I was nearby,' Bannister said when she opened the main front door to him a little later. 'Your neighbour, finally met him, told me you'd probably be back soon. He didn't have anything to add about the cat, obviously.' Bannister stepped into the foyer. 'I was hoping to kill two birds, oh . . . sorry, bad, um, I wanted to discuss your connection with the wharf casualties and the paw. Assess any potential links or risks.'

Chrissie led him up the stairs. She had changed into jeans and a loose white shirt, shrugging off the in-control work clothes that she'd worn to the psychiatrist appointment. She offered to make a pot of tea but he surprised her when he produced a small folded bag – green tea leaves.

'For you. I noticed,' he indicated the packets of tea, piled in a basket on the bench. Did his face turn a little pink? *What else did he notice?* Her hand crossed his as she accepted the cellophane bag, his skin was still warm from his jacket pocket. She felt the heat on her neck.

'We're concerned about your involvement, this story of yours,' Bannister was back to business. 'We'd like to take a look at your research material and see if we can narrow down some, um, coincidences. You seem to be in the middle of things.'

Chrissie noticed he helped himself to a chair at the small round table. He immediately looked through the window, at the fire escape. The sun lit up the dusty pane, filtering a narrow streak across the floor. She half watched him as she poured the hot water, he tested the partially open window, checked the metal fire escape landing outside, and then nodded at his finding: locked.

'Our lawyers have got to check everything first,' Chrissie said, 'but I can talk you through it a bit now. As long as it's a two-way conversation. What will you be able to tell me?'

'Ha. That's not really how it works,' he said. *That smile!* 'But let's see how we go.'

She ran through some of her findings, the allegations from both sides, the fearful message from Mas and Remi's concerns. *Mas,*

Remi, Skinny. My fault. At least now she had connected Mas and Remi, through her involvement, without their affair being exposed.

Some of it would be public soon, anyway, Chrissie thought, if she and Maria got their way and the fallback gets a run. She had only three days left on the embargo. By publishing what she had so far, it would still give *The Argus* the jump and it would take the sting out of anyone else that Thurst passed the information to. Besides, two deaths now. Other journos would be sniffing around. The rival stories, however, would look like rushed follow-ups. *But I want the whole truth. Justice!*

'Have you had any safety worries?' Bannister asked. 'I mean, apart from the cat. Nothing more on that, by the way.' He shook his head in sympathy. 'Has anything unusual happened, approaches, something missing, unexplained, found? Any new faces you've noticed?' Bannister leaned forward, his hand completely surrounding the china cup, the handle too dainty to be useful.

'Nothing, until yesterday, until the parcel.'

'Weren't you in hospital recently? Did we hear that right, from your work?'

Chrissie took a sip, controlled her expression. *We?*

'Yeah. Food poisoning.' Her voice steady.

'Poisoning how?' Bannister sat forward.

'No, nothing like that.' Chrissie let out a breath she'd been holding. 'Leftovers, from the fridge.' *Had someone been in here?* She looked around the room but then focused back to the bench in front of her and poured another cup. Her anxiety was growing by the minute. *Breathe.*

'My boss is pretty keen on me following up. He was on my back last night.' Bannister sat back and closed his notebook.

'Seems like it's raised a few flags with the feds. Probably border control poking around, being the wharf. You have any idea about that? Does *The Argus*, you know, have any connections there?'

'Not that I know of. Speaking of which, I've got to crack on. I'm working from home today. I'll get our guys to forward you my research.' She walked to the door, Bannister was forced to follow. She walked in front of him down the stairs. Before he left, he gave her another business card.

'It's got my private mobile on the back.' Chrissie turned it over and a number had been handwritten in blue ink. *Pre-prepared.* 'Call anytime, okay? If you think of something or anything happens, you know. Or if there's something maybe you want to tell me unofficially . . .' That smile again.

Chrissie shook his hand and she felt the warmth spread up her arm. *Safe hands.*

She knew that Mike would probably be watching behind the curtains of his front window or listening near the door as Bannister left but he stayed out of sight. He'd want to tease her again but she had a lot to do and most of the morning had already gone. She raced back up the stairs.

—

'Mr Basill, I'm sorry to be calling again,' Chrissie said when Remi's father answered the phone. They had spoken on the night of Remi's death. The phone version of the death knock, Chrissie hated those calls but knew they had to be done. On Monday night he had robotically given family details for her story. He had still been in shock, Chrissie thought, as he had just kept talking, he kept asking if she needed more. Today, three days later, the shock had worn off. His voice sad but warm.

'No, no, Chris, no bother. What can I do? Thank you for your story about . . .' Chrissie could hear the agony and rawness in his voice this time. She knew his pain.

An image of her own father's face flashed across her mind. The grief in his eyes as Chrissie had said goodbye at the airport. She pushed it away.

'I'm also working on a feature story about the wharf, but I've still got a few gaps in my research. Remi, he helped a lot, he mentioned a cousin who worked at the port?' She kept her voice low.

'He's got plenty of relatives there but no cousin, love.' Vince's voice steadying. Chrissie continued.

'Maybe not on the dock. Somewhere in the office – schedules, planning, I think?'

'Oh, you mean Janice. She's married to Remi's cousin.'

She could hear Vince moving around. It sounded like he was in the kitchen, a slight echo, lots of voices in the background, dishes, glasses.

'Janice, yeah,' he continued, stronger now, perhaps the phone call was a small distraction. 'She does all the arrivals, decides when each ship can berth. Pretty high up. She knows everyone, not just our lot, but all the shippers, the agents, the planners. Those planners, love, now that's a good job, paid overs, you know, over award. I reckon that's who you mean. Janice.'

Yes!

'She's coming to the wake today. You coming too, aren't you? I left a message at your work. Told everyone you'd be coming.

The burial was yesterday, mainly family, love, you know, quick, too, the coroner understood, got their report done. But we're having Remi's mates, neighbours, everyone, at my place from midday, till, well, till whenever. Open house.'

'Ah . . . I'd be a bit out of place, wouldn't I?' Chrissie was taken aback.

'No! Of course not. You met him, love. Everyone cut out Remi's article, they're stuck on fridges all over the west. We'll keep that story, you know, he's in history now, forever, thanks to you.'

Thanks to me.

CHAPTER 30

Music, voices, laughter. The sounds hit Chrissie as soon as she stepped out of the taxi. Thursday afternoon or not, there was a big shindig going on in Kingsville in Melbourne's inner west, a stone's throw from the docks.

She had watched out the window as the car had driven slowly along the street looking for the address. The 1910 weatherboard house she now stood in front of must have once been part of a whole street of Federation-style homes. At the time they had been built, the modest middle-class homes were not too fancy but not worker's-cottage poor, either. By the 1980s when Remi's father probably bought in, the suburb had long been overlooked. Not Footscray, or Seddon, or Yarraville, but a little bit of all of them. Cheap. Increasingly surrounded by hectic roads and noise. But its location near the port was a drawcard for the wharf families.

Now, it was a haven of inner-city chic, pretty gardens, painted fences, in the midst of the fast-paced industrial pulse. Part of the fancy inner west.

Property prices had overtaken the tiny, triangular suburb nicknamed K'ville. The area had become yuppyville. Several homes in the street had been demolished to make way for fifties brick modern and later nineties townhouses, while others had suffered various renovations over the decades. Two doors down Chrissie noticed that a Californian bungalow veranda with columns had been added to one late Victorian house, while on the corner another had been assaulted with an art deco curved brick front porch.

At the Basill house twin weeping cherry trees decorated the tiny front yard with its short central path to the blue front door. Chrissie smiled as she noticed a faded yellow metal butterfly stuck on the side fence. Her dad had one just the same, a relic he had rescued from a garage sale. It had sat on his work bench for years, to be 'put up' one day. It was probably still there. *When would she see him again?* She hurried up the path.

The front door of the house was propped open with a wedge and a homemade sign: 'Come in'. She hesitantly walked down the hall. *Wish I'd thought to bring James, he's a good mixer.* He could talk his way in and out of any situation but Chrissie knew, sometimes, it was the silences that got the best responses.

Then it really hit her, the last wake she'd been to was Dave's. Her palms instantly on fire, her thumb automatically started working pain across her fingertips. *Breathe. One two three.* She continued straight towards the back of the house until the passage burst onto a McMansion style renovation. Staircase up to a new storey, the biggest flat screen TV Chrissie had ever seen mounted onto the wall on the lounge side of the room, framed by three green sofas. A glass dining table against the wall on the other side was the congregation point for a group of women. Every surface of the marble counter and island bench of the kitchen was covered with plates of colourful food. Sandwiches cut into triangles, cakes sliced in neat segments, sliced meats draped across platters. Cheeses, olives, biscuits, dips, the feast was endless and bottles everywhere, water, soft drink, red wine. She walked through the room, attempting to smile.

The backyard was a postcard of suburban life. Behind the garage was the compost and the wood pile. In the other corner, the veggie garden. The rotary clothesline. An old swing-set for the children. Children with no father now, Chrissie thought.

She had lost her own mother at a similar age to Remi's kids. The cancer, as it was simply called, took Chrissie's mum when she was twelve; just when she thought she didn't need her. But then she had died and Chrissie realised she needed her more than ever.

A loud cheer erupted as a David Bowie track started to play. 'Starman'. Chrissie looked across the yard to the group of men in their uniform of beige work boots, jeans and t-shirts. Arms rested across shoulders, beers in hand. Remi's workmates. The world she was writing about. She scanned the scene for Kingi. He wasn't among them. The men began a loud chorus of the song at the top of their voices and lifted their heads to the sky. Chrissie shaded her eyes and looked up. Waiting in the sky, *altocumulus*. Fluffy white sheep today, Dave's favourites.

'Awww, thanks for coming, love.' Vince greeted her with a hug. After a few minutes' conversation and what seemed like a hundred introductions, Allegra, Remi's wife, said a short hello as Vince slipped an arm around his daughter-in-law. Her jet black hair tumbled out of what would have been a tidy up-do earlier that morning. Big hoop earrings. All carefully put together. Her job was to host this wake and that's what she was doing: pushing through. Chrissie recognised the signs, barely coping. She wondered how much Allegra knew about her husband. Then Vince pointed out Janice, the cousin-in-law, as he gently steered Al away.

'Over there in the green. I told her you were coming, that you'd asked after her. With the blonde curly hair, over there. See?'

Chrissie pinpointed her immediately. The air flurried around Janice's big gestures and loud constant chatter. She was one of those people who over-filled the space around them. A little too large in personality for many.

'I work at the Port Authority, you know I was there that day,' Janice said, after Chrissie eased her to a quiet chat. 'Everyone's devastated. It's a pretty tight community at the port. Poor Remi. Two in a row. It's rocked us all.' Janice's hands worked in tandem with her words.

'I'm writing about the docks.' Chrissie slowed her speech and dropped the volume of her voice, encouraging Janice to copy her. 'I wouldn't have to quote you, so you could feel free to dish the dirt. Everything could be totally off the record.'

'You know there's a lot that goes on down there that nobody seems to want to talk about.' Janice was enthusiastic but now spoke more quietly. 'I've been at the authority for thirteen years, not much I don't know. And I don't owe any of them any favours.' Chrissie could hear the bitterness as Janice tossed a hand over her shoulder, her voice had crept louder again.

'Would you be able to tell me which ships went through Grange's docks that were worked on by the portainer operator, Masina Weber?' Chrissie's voice quiet, as Janice leaned her head in to hear. 'The shippers, the receivers, the type of cargo. Any restows? Anything unusual?'

'Yes, yes. Remi was asking me about all this.' She stopped and used a large scrunched-up serviette to dab the tears in her eyes. 'You know, he told me about you.' Janice was conspiratorial now. 'He gave me the roster and dates and I got the vessels, manifests and stuff for him. No blockchain cyber transactions on these wharves, yet – but they're coming, part of this new system Grange is trying to put in, ehh.' Janice screwed her mouth up in distaste. 'Everything in our office still good old computers. Yeah and who would have thought computers were ever going to be old tech?' Janice's eyebrows shot sky high. 'But it wasn't just for Mas, Remi asked for. It was for another stevedore too, Dan Kingi. Here, I brought them with me.' Janice reached in her shoulder bag and pulled out several sheets of paper, neatly folded. Chrissie slipped the papers into her bag.

'You know the family took her body home? I mean Mas,' Janice added. 'Two of her brothers were already here when she died. They'd just arrived for a holiday, I guess.' Janice shook her head. Remi was right, Mas must have told her family she was leaving. So maybe others also knew she was planning to leave. The brothers had come to take her home, help her pack. Help Remi leave too? But now they were taking Mas's body. Chrissie's hand went to her chest to ease the guilt.

'How awful.' Chrissie tried to bring Janice back on track. 'And for you and all of Remi's family, it must have been a shock.

I'm sorry to ask here but there's also a suggestion that containers are going missing,' Chrissie said. 'Crane lifts not adding up, Remi mentioned it.'

'I told him. It'd be a stuff-up.' Janice shrugged. 'Supposed to be top-notch security down there, you know, with all this terrorist stuff. Drugs. Guns. Jesus, they even smuggle in fancy sports cars.' Janice threw her hands in the air.

Chrissie took a half step forward, despite her discomfort at being so close, to encourage Janice to speak more quietly again.

'But Grange got taken for a ride with their new planning system.' Janice leaned in conspiratorially again. 'Designed to talk directly to the automates, you know, the machines, our new best mates.' She laughed. 'Then the machines are supposed to talk back to the computers which are supposed to get the blockchain thing to check it all and release the payments,' Janice scoffed loudly and rolled her eyes. 'Well, that might be all bloody good and well in the future but problem is the future's not here yet. Nobody's telling nobody nothing.' She slipped a hand inside her neckline and hauled up a bra strap. 'Everyone's in the dark. Had to go back to hand tallies. Timeslots screwed. Warehouse mix-ups. Planners pissed off. Restows, you asked? Constant!'

Chrissie looked around and bowed her head slightly. Hel Carter had told her how vessels were loaded in a specific order so that unloading was done in the right sequence. A restow meant unloading a ship and stacking the containers off to the side temporarily.

'Planners getting the loads wrong,' Janice was on a roll, 'have to deep dive – you know, lift half the bloody cargo out just to find the right boxes. Locations, codes wrong or missing completely. Costing everyone a fortune.'

This time Janice looked around then leaned in and lowered her voice.

'You know, there's talk of a law suit, big losses for Grange, shippers losing money. This new automation system they got, friggin' useless. Stuff-ups all over the place.'

She moved even closer.

'Some big government contract involved too. Helping Grange pay its way out of the shit. Hush hush deal moving environmental waste or something, I heard.'

—

On the ride home Chrissie unfolded the papers she had received from Janice. Printed. She shook her head. That meant there'd be a record of the information going from Janice's computer to the printer she'd used. The taxi drove over the West Gate Bridge, high above container town, the vast tracts of land next to the wharves full of containers, stacked empty and full. The information included the ships Mas and Kingi had unloaded and loaded during the past six months. Remi did good, she thought, asking for both of their rosters. She assumed since Kingi had also signed off on the dodgy lift tallies then they must have worked on some of the ships together. Five thousand containers took about twenty hours of nonstop lifting, they would have tag-teamed on shifts, she reasoned – and so must have Remi.

At home now, Chrissie quickly divided the paperwork into two piles: Mas and Kingi.

The print-outs included the country of origin of each vessel, the shippers, the description of their cargo and the receivers. Chrissie highlighted the ships that they both worked on. As she looked at the lists, she pictured it again, how she had flown between the dock and the ship with Mas in the glass box. As Mas had lifted and lowered the containers. As Mas had hitched her safety rope to the rails.

There were more than thirty ships that they had both worked on during the past six months. She checked for the shippers that had cargo on more than one vessel. Seventeen.

All-Sam, All South American Management, an agent based in Brazil and Peru, was the most regular sender, it had sent cargo on eleven of the seventeen ships. In each case the cargo was listed as dried foods, tea leaves, coffee, acai. Acai berries, even Chrissie had joined the Amazon super-food craze. All-Sam's cargo was received by three agents acting for who knows. But it was a lead. A good lead.

—

Chrissie had seen the envelope under her door when she first got home from the wake. She knew it had to have been from Mike and she'd just thrown it on the kitchen bench, her head too full with the shipping news to concentrate at the time. Now she opened it properly, set up her laptop and followed Mike's instructions. First inserting a flash drive he had wrapped in with it, 'to block any spyware' he'd written and added a smiley face. Then she typed in an address for a private network and then a server in Afghanistan, then a second server. She marvelled at Mike's precautions.

Finally, a set of numbers and a password. Up popped the website he had created for her:

SadFacedGirl.af.

A laugh burst out before she could stop it.

There it was, all her research, page by page. Videos, photos, scanned documents. A search function in which she immediately typed 'Weber': twenty-seven hits. 'Remi': thirteen hits. She tried another, 'Maritime': forty-three. She clicked again, the Safety Bureau report popped up. Mike had also added photos of the port from the air, the dark channel, ships at dock. Mike was a genius. She rang work and organised a courier to pick up the originals. The in-house lawyers still had to sort out what they'd send to Bannister. *Bannister.* She smiled and sat back as she saw the card he'd given her, still on the table where she'd left it this morning. But she shook her head. She would never be enough for anyone again. Chrissie logged off the website and backed her way out of her connections, keeping to Mike's instructions.

Standing at the basin, she tipped two sleeping pills into her hand, then paused as she studied the pale red tablets. She slipped one back in the bottle. Even with only a couple of glasses of wine tonight, she knew she would be quickly to sleep. One tablet would be enough. Chrissie glanced across the hall to the still open kitchen window. Just to get some air circulating, she told herself, as she left the hall light on and headed to bed. She hated the dark and so did Skinny.

CHAPTER 31

'I've got something that's going to surprise you.' Maria had taken Chrissie out of the office as soon as she arrived the next morning. They were in the coffee shop an extra block away, 'the confidential café' as everyone at *The Argus* sarcastically dubbed it. A small Greek restaurant with blue and white checked tablecloths, strings of lights and plastic flowers. Everyone went there when they didn't want to be seen by their colleagues. Friday morning was no exception, at least two other tables had *Argus* staff.

Maria was in 'good walking form' today, she had said. Maria sipped her hot chocolate. Chrissie shifted on her chair, silently strumming under the table.

'It's not Harry who's on the short list for the job at Grange.' Yep, Maria knew how to drop a news bomb.

'How can that be? It all fits. He's been against this story at every turn.'

'Chrissie, it's not Harry.'

'So, who's telling Grange what's going on? I've had two sources say similar things.'

'It's not a Thompson on the short list for the job,' Maria said, quieter now, pausing to make sure Chrissie was concentrating. 'It's Thomas. As in Tom Jefferies.'

'No way!' The words used up the last of Chrissie's breath. She heard a short squeak as she sucked air back in. 'That can't be,' she said helplessly. But she knew too well that Maria wouldn't get something like that wrong.

'Harry loves this industry. He couldn't, even at his worst, do what you thought,' Maria insisted. 'He's a newsman, Chrissie. Oh sure, a pompous overblown git, but what you said didn't make sense to me.' She was slowly shaking her head from side to side. 'There's still life in the old girl yet,' Maria grinned. 'So I phoned Grange's human resources director. We'd met at a media conference last year. I was all set to ask about the vacancy and recommend a couple of those who've just been sacked. But, lucky for me, she was on leave, so I told her secretary I was calling on behalf of Tom Jefferies.'

The words weren't making sense. Chrissie poured water from the jug on the table and drank the whole glass.

'There's one benefit of being an old woman, people stop thinking you might be important,' Maria continued. 'Miss Secretary just came straight out and asked if he needed to reschedule his interview. No, I said, I just wanted to reconfirm for his diary. And she replied, Friday week, 1 pm.'

Chrissie was floored. Betrayed. Jefferies had given her a job, a new start. Kept her secrets. Now he was trying to ruin her.

'Jefferies! Hell, I briefed him on the whole story. He knew everything. Do you think he was with them all along?'

'Don't know, but you telling him – well, it might have given him a foot in the door. Made him very important to them,' Maria replied. 'I also had a word to Caroline, his assistant, yesterday.' Now she gave a slow nod. 'She let me take a peek at the minutes from Wednesday's meeting, after the paw, you know, after you went home. They clearly showed Jefferies argued against you continuing with the story. And, well, he also raised doubt about your hospital admission.'

'The fake bastard.' *Breathe.* Jefferies would have also gone through all her documents and research she had sent to the lawyers yesterday. Everything. *Grange certainly pays for inside knowledge.* Carter's words.

Maria sat back, put both hands flat on the table. 'Chrissie, it wasn't Harry. I went and talked to him, told him his actions looked suspicious, as if he was trying to derail the story –'

'*You told Harry?*' The checked tablecloth seemed to be moving. Chrissie felt her hand slide but stopped herself just in time before she pulled the cloth off. She sat still and slowly sipped the air.

'Most of it. But hold your horses,' Maria warded her off with both palms up. 'He was pissed off. Angry as shit! But that never slows me down. I said he should want to get this story as much as you did. And that's when I knew for sure. He was still angry at me but he was stunned with what you'd found so far, he even argued against Jefferies. But you know him, he's such a stickler for rules.'

Chrissie looked down at her knees, sure they must have been shaking wildly but they were steady.

'It's not Harry we have to worry about,' Maria said.

'I thought Jefferies was on my side.'

'Hey. It's a business decision, for him. Besides, I'm long over being surprised by people.' Maria's eyebrows rose above her pink glasses. 'You learn to accept people as they are . . . Now we know who we're up against, so let's get this story finished.'

The bell tinkled as the café door opened. Chrissie looked up and froze.

'Ah. Right on time,' Maria said, waving an arm. 'Harry, over here.'

Chrissie sucked in a large deep breath. Trusting Harry felt like one shock too many after all the times it seemed he had tried to thwart her. Her doubts were not going to go away so easily. But Maria proved an adept mediator.

'Harry, tell Chrissie what you've heard.'

For once, he sat down. It was the first time Chrissie had talked to him at eye level.

'First I want to say I'm not happy that you were still working on this story. Especially when you were transferred off the news desk.'

'Haz. Haz! That's not what we're here for,' Maria interrupted. 'Besides, Chrissie's my charge now. Let's set a game plan?'

'Wait a minute.' Harry wasn't going to be silenced. He focused on Chrissie. 'I'm sorry for, for . . . well, I'd lost so many staff, plenty of others were owed a job before you. But you've been . . . worthwhile. This wharf story has legs.' He attempted a smile.

'Great, got that sorted.' Maria jumped in, relieved. 'Now, from what I can see you still need to find out how the cargo and crane records are connected. Chrissie's got an insider at the port who's analysing the cargo lists.' Maria drained the last of her hot chocolate.

'I should be able to help on that,' Harry took over.

Chrissie sat back. Okay, she thought, show me what you've got.

'The dead guy's theory, that the woman was bumped off, you need to focus solely on that. That's your key,' he said, his hands still face down on the table. 'You need that or you've got nothing. If that proves suspicious, it indicates the guy was murdered too, if we don't have that proof about the woman we're going to have to leave him out of it. Too speculative.'

'But the whole reason for this story stems from Remi, not Mas. He tipped me off in the first place, put himself at risk. A risk that might have got him killed. We can't just leave it untold.'

'There might already be a police operation at the dock.' Harry said. 'I've got a contact that could put some of these final pieces together. He used to be Federal but he's tied up with the joint Homeland force now.'

She almost shook her head in disbelief. Maybe Harry really was going to help?

—

Back in the office, Chrissie watched Harry on the other side of the newsroom, his hand thumping the air as he stood over two journos at their desks, both wilting under his words. His gestures and body language were aggressive, as if he were going to poke or prod them at any moment. People often took a step back when he talked to them. His voice always seemed liked controlled anger.

In this moment, from across the floor, Harry looked just the same to Chrissie. The same old bully. He's not going to let up on me, not going to support me, she thought, whatever Maria says. But perhaps Harry would switch some of his hostility to Jefferies now. Especially since Maria had told him about the Grange job. He had been furious. Perhaps a little jealous, too. For now, Harry would be distracted by a renewed quest against Jefferies and the possibility that he might even get his old job back. If Jefferies resigned to take the Grange job, *The Argus* board could give him a second chance. Or maybe they would skip straight past him to someone else?

Yet Tom Jefferies hadn't been born with a silver spoon in his mouth. Like Harry, he had worked hard to get ahead. The media was one of those industries where background didn't matter. It was about networking. Every type of networking, community, social, religious or demographic. And Jefferies was a network master.

James had told Chrissie that Harry's fall had been slow at first. The occasional bad decision, then giving in reluctantly to pressure from the board to get rid of the features department. Everyone knew it would never work. The rounds people had to tread carefully, keep a daily working relationship. They worked in a different way to feature writers, who could swoop in, go hard or soft, and swoop out.

That decision was a double failure. It reduced the number of scoops from the rounds and the feature quality was terrible. So was the reader feedback. Harry took the fall.

But the biggest blunder was sending a junior off to a political presser. She missed the angle and *The Argus* was accused of whitewashing the real story. Jefferies was in the right place at the right time, and the two virtually swapped jobs.

But there was never any thought that Harry would resign, everyone knew, Chrissie included, people constantly went up and down the power ladder in the media industry. Snakes and ladders. In one day, out the next, until the dice played their way again.

Chrissie couldn't shake the feeling that Harry's turnaround this morning was too quick. He had given her the number of this cop, Andy Dorn, too readily. If Dorn didn't already know about the suspicious deaths and missing cargo, then Chrissie could be tipping him off, thanks to Harry. That could further risk her getting to the truth about Remi and Mas. And didn't Bannister ask if *The Argus* had any contacts at police headquarters or the feds? Even if it was Jefferies going for the Grange job, Harry could also be a candidate. Either way, it didn't rule him out as the leak or that he still had her in his sights. She sat turning over the handwritten note in her hand. Harry also only used blank paper. Old habit. The back of a business card or even an old envelope could sometimes still make it possible to identify a source.

Chrissie dialled the number from her desk phone. Despite what people might think, most journalists didn't have access to the latest encrypted technology. The old-fashioned landline and a large switchboard was the best way to keep callers confidential.

'Yeah?' an impatient voice answered.

'Hi, it's Chris O'Brian, I'm a journalist from *The Argus* – a colleague gave me your number. I'm working on a story about the port.'

A long silence.

Chrissie continued, 'I got your number from um, Harry Thompson.'

'So?'

'I'm chasing some missing cargo.'

'You and probably twenty others.'

'And there's been an increase in accidents . . .' Silence. 'Harry thought you could help me join the dots.'

'What else?'

'A couple of those accidents might not be accidents,' Chrissie said.

'What do you think is going on?'

'I don't know, but the union and the wharf operator know something. If you can't help, I'll have to go with what I've just told you – raise a bit of public speculation,' Chrissie replied. *See if he bites.*

'I wouldn't do that if I were you. We need to get off the phone.'

Bingo! 'I can meet you anywhere.'

'Nup. Give me your number; I'll be in touch. This is on the understanding nothing will be published until we talk.'

'Depends how long it takes you. I'm not going to hold off unless there's something worth waiting for.' Chrissie had to play hard ball or he could just keep her dangling until it suited him to go public, and that would destroy her scoop. 'People seem to be getting killed. But sure, you take your time, sort out your paperwork.'

'Cut the drama or I'll get a court order, an injunction. Lie back, put your feet up.' The line went dead.

CHAPTER 32

Chrissie stretched full-length on her sofa. The Arco lamp extended over her like her very own moon. Her back muscles ached – journo's hunch, everyone called it at work – and her head throbbed after another hectic day. As she rested on the cushions her thoughts buzzed. Faster and faster they spun, like rogue planets beneath her lamp moon. She had finished two bottles of wine since she got home from work.

Almost two weeks since Mas had been killed yet she wasn't much closer to finding out what had happened. Janice had come through but who were the shipments going to? Poor Mas. And this new cop, Andy Dorn. What sort of injunction could he get? A court order to stop the story or a search warrant? She shivered at the possibility. She should ring *The Argus*'s lawyers. This Dorn cop didn't realise she was bluffing, not ready to go to print for a couple more days. If she told the lawyers, would they then report back to Jefferies or Harry? Harry would know that she still didn't trust him. Jefferies could tip off Grange. Maybe Gina could help her? No. She couldn't tell Gina, just in case.

She took another sip of cool white wine. Alcohol usually settled her but tonight her mind kept racing. The last couple of days had been a rollercoaster of stress and adrenalin and Chrissie had well and truly fallen off her attempted two-drink-a-night limit.

After the surprise meeting with Harry this morning she'd had to squeeze in her final lunchtime appointment with the hospital psychiatrist, Dr Darcy. Privately, she had nicknamed the sessions 'Chirpy Tuesdays'.

Last week's session was gutting. She had left angry and defiant. Again in today's session, Dr Darcy had persisted in asking even more about Dave and her family.

'How do you think the accident affected your father and brother?'

'Look, this is not about the accident,' Chrissie interrupted. 'It's about some rotten leftover takeaway. I keep telling you. The questions about my family, it's like picking a scab. That's what I'm doing in Melbourne. I'm letting things heal. Starting over.'

Chrissie had braced herself before this appointment, but expert that she was at keeping things bottled up, she was no match for Dr Darcy.

'What do you feel, Chrissie, when you remember your family around that time?'

'Yes. Okay, I feel blame,' Chrissie snapped. So much for being prepared. She focused on the window blinds, hoping it would make Dr Darcy think she was contemplating. She needed a good report card, to be done with this woman forever. Chrissie couldn't see out through the blinds, but looking towards the light made her feel as if she could. *Why didn't they have a proper window? What was with all this looking inward?*

'I can see blame in their eyes and I am to blame.' Chrissie said. 'I was drunk. I didn't know at the time but I was pregnant and drunk. I drove through the stop sign. It is my fault that I got run out of town. My fault that my father couldn't look people in the face. My fault that Dave was wiped from this world.' She paused, pulse racing, pounding, gathering breath. *Count, one, two, three.* She stared at the blind again. 'My fault that his parents lost their only child and only chance of a grandchild. My fault I miscarried. Everything. It's called taking responsibility, facing up to the truth. I live this truth *every day*.'

Her repeated attempts to get out of the sessions had been met by protests from her supervising doctor, the bouncer, as well as her father. It was one of the reasons he'd agreed not to visit for a while. Apart from her family and the hospital the only people who knew about it were James and Maria. Gina too, she could only assume, since James told her everything. Chrissie eventually figured it was easier to go through the motions than fight about it. Just turn up each time and get it over with. But still, it was torture.

She sat silently. What had Dr Darcy meant, the harm people, *me*, do to others? Was she causing her father pain; she thought she was preventing it. The new worry added more space junk for her mind to race around as she lay on the sofa. Her judgement skewiff. If she questioned too much of the past or had to think differently she might not be able to cope. To hell with Dr Darcy, she had to stick with blocking it out.

'Time's up.' Chrissie had stood when the wall clock ticked over its final minute and had grabbed her jacket and satchel. She hadn't looked back as she rushed out the door.

A noise near the kitchen window startled her now, snapping her back into the moment. Something had been knocked over in the side path below. *Skinny?* After two days? She jumped up and looked out. Nothing, of course. Disappointed and angry at herself for allowing a small hope, she sat at the table and stared through the metal grid of the fire escape, the night shadows moving in the wind.

Tonight was the first time she had time on her own to dwell on Skinny. More wine. *That cat!* He had weaselled his way in so quickly. The first time she saw him, she had woken, hungover, on the sofa and he was just there. His purring was like a diesel generator, curled up by her feet. The happiness of it had made Chrissie cry. And cry again now at the sadness of it. *Dead husband, miscarriage, shunned by the town, bereft father. Yet a damn stray cat makes me cry!* But he had become her lookout, a small grey being who came to check on her progress. He had even braved what cats hated most: one night he had leaped on the side of the bath, balanced on the corner, as he stretched his long neck to meow loudly at her, submerged. In her fright to sit up, she had splashed him and he had jumped but didn't run, just sat in the doorway, silhouetted by the hall light. Chrissie had rested her chin on the side of the bath and they had watched each other.

She pulled her gaze from the window to the overflowing rubbish bin. She checked the time, 10.30. It had to be dealt with or it would stink out the place by morning. She tied the bag closed with a sloppy knot, grabbed the two empty wine bottles and went down to the large bins out the back.

'Puss, puss,' she called. Her common sense said there was no point but the wine told her to give it one more try.

Why did Skinny even come here in the first place? Chrissie stumbled on the broken paving. Nothing in the yard but concrete and an old rotary washing line. No welcoming garden beds or lawn to chase the sun across. She noticed a new plate of dumplings. Mike hadn't given up either.

As she lifted the bin lid she heard a shuffle behind her. Then a clink against the concrete. Chrissie spun around and froze. Rubbish bag mid-air. Swaying, her head whooshed with too much wine.

About ten metres away, half hidden by the shadow of the laundry shed, was the outline of a man.

Chrissie was torn between making a bolt for the back door or calling out. She looked at her hands, too full to fight. But the bottles would come in handy. She dropped the rubbish bag in the bin and held a bottle in each hand. Just another creep looking for forty bucks for a hit. But the longer she stared at the shadow, she realised he was too still and in control for a junkie.

'Hey! Get the hell out of there!'

The shadow remained frozen.

'Hey! You against the wall!' After a few more heartbeats he stepped out. Chrissie kept her eyes on him, feeling more and more unsteady. She gripped the necks of the bottles even tighter. The man took a couple of steps towards her. The light from the bulb above the back door stretched weakly across the yard. He had street clothes on but he was too clean. He stood confident, shoulders relaxed, head upright, unlike the hollow-chested hunch of an addict.

She loosened her grip. Even through her wine haze, she knew who he was.

Deep furrows ran each side of his nostrils and around the outer corners of his mouth. Chrissie thought of a puppet, his lips and chin separate to the rest of his face. He pushed his baseball cap back, his eyes unreadable.

'Hmm. Andy Dorn, I presume. Better come in,' she said. She dropped the bottles in the bin and waved for him to follow her. *Keep your wits.* Don't spill too much. Sober up.

'Sorry about that. I was just checking out the place,' he said from behind. 'Thought I heard something out the back.'

Chrissie was sceptical. Maybe he didn't want to be seen arriving.

'Do you know any of your neighbours?' he continued. 'You're unit three, aren't you. Where's unit one? I always get confused when they subdivide these old houses. A place like this, I'd imagine the walls are pretty thin.'

What didn't he want anyone to hear? Chrissie didn't answer, she was concentrating on each stair, holding tight on the bannister. *Maybe he won't notice.* At least she hadn't taken her sleeping pills yet. *Shit, why did I drink so much?*

They were inside her flat now. 'Can I get you something? Tea? Something cold?'

'You gave me a bit of a surprise today. I didn't expect to have a journo ringing about Grange. Think I can help fill in a few details but first I need to see what you've got, quid pro quo.' His words were drawn out slightly longer than needed. Years of talking to slow-witted criminals, she thought.

Dorn gave the room a sweep with his eyes. She got the sense he'd checked the whole room and everything in it within seconds. Would he know she was drunk?

'Your guys have already got most of my stuff. The threat I got at work, you know about that, don't you?' *Keep it together. Something's off about this man.*

'What do you mean . . . *the threat*?'

'So, you can find out my address, creep around my yard in the middle of the night, but you can't do a quick search on your database?'

He didn't bite, his eyes blank. Slightly built, but she knew undercover came in all sizes. His hair trimmed neatly and a slight military air about him further blew his attempt at street cred.

'Cat's paw, eh?' he said eventually. 'You know what it means?' He walked towards her. *So he did know.*

'Doing someone's dirty work.' *Thank you, James.* 'Although it could be, you know, someone might cut off my head, I mean hand, cut off my hand. To stop me writing . . . I think the paw was from a cat that lived here.' Her voice broke on the last sentence. Chrissie quickly turned, fidgeted for a glass of water and faked a cough. *For god's sake, get a grip.* Her chest thumped more heavily. *Breathe.* She rubbed her palms surreptitiously up and down her jeans to stop the itching.

'The paw's popular in certain circles.' Dorn was guarded.

'Meaning?'

'Your first guess is probably right.' Dorn nodded. 'You're being manipulated. It's usually crim to crim – someone connected. Maybe you're not as innocent as you make out?'

'And here I was thinking I was overreacting.' *Stall. Don't tell him more.* 'How about telling me what you're doing here tonight and why you're so keen to come snooping around after hours?' Chrissie propped herself against the kitchen bench.

Dorn stood his ground near the sofa. 'You called me, remember?'

Chrissie could feel a chill spreading across her chest.

'OTR, right? You phoned me but I never followed up, never returned your call. Got it?'

'Yeah, okay, 007. I haven't seen you.'

'We're running an investigation at the port. Between us, okay? We've been there for about six weeks.'

'Who's we?'

'Let's just say joint forces. An offshore party has taken a grip. We've just got an op embedded. What we don't need is for you to come out half-arsed with some little story, ringing alarm bells and scattering everyone to the wind.'

'What sort of offshore?'

Dorn remained silent. He kept his eyes on her. Unreadable.

'You mean South American?' Chrissie saw his eyes narrow slightly. 'Tell me something I don't know, because my half-arse isn't as half-arse as you think.' *Thank you, Janice.* 'I've got enough to print, not the full story but enough.' *Bluff.* 'And that's what I'll do unless you're going to make it worthwhile to hold off.' *Take it easy.*

'It's "organised", yes,' Dorn said. 'Illegal cargo. Containers coming in, being discharged, warehoused maybe but then they disappear. We're still piecing it together, working out how and when.'

'What is it? In the containers.'

'You don't need to know – yet.'

'Tea, coffee, Brazilian?' *Shut up!* She couldn't help herself. His eye narrowed again.

'Yeah, something like that.'

'How much is coming in?'

Dorn didn't reply.

Fifteen containers, at least, Chrissie knew, according to Parenta's numbers. Maybe she was ahead of Dorn.

'Why bother?' Chrissie ventured. 'Who wants to smuggle tea, anyway?'

Dorn stayed silent.

'I'm starting to think this is bullshit,' she continued. 'So far you've given me nothing.' *Take it easy!* Chrissie poured more water. *Sober up.* She sat at the table. The breeze from the window cool on her face.

'Coca,' he said.

'Tea, cocoa, so what, why bother?'

'Coca. Coca. It's Cocaine.'

'Cocaine! Oh my god. No wonder they'd kill for it.' Chrissie's head was reeling. *Concentrate, concentrate!*

'We suspect the guy last week was in the wrong place at the wrong time. You wrote it up. That accident. But the surveillance is faulty, it's hard to get a handle on it.' The slow voice continued. 'No one's forthcoming. But we took a good look at him. Clean. Bad luck, that's all. Our guys thought he might have been making a nuisance of himself. Snooping. The woman, we don't know about yet.'

'Bad luck? You think people getting murdered is bad luck!'

Dorn walked towards her. 'I've put my cards on the table. Now it's your turn.' He sounded annoyed. 'I want to know who you've been talking to. Why you're looking into this. If someone like you can work it out, chances are my op is blown. I'm not mucking around. I need to know.'

'You didn't tell me much I didn't already know. I want a guarantee, an exclusive,' Chrissie faced off to him. 'When you're ready to go public I want a head start, a drop. And I want another exclusive the next day with more details. Otherwise I've got to publish what I have now.'

'Let me make a call.' He walked out to the landing. Chrissie heard muffled words as he walked down the stairs and out the front door. She spied on him from behind her curtain as he strode to the other side of the street.

A cold shudder went through her. What if this guy wasn't who he said? She hadn't even asked for ID. Chrissie heard him coming up the stairs. Anxiety took over again. *Breathe; one, two, three.*

'We've got a deal.' Dorn walked back in. 'You'll get twelve hours head start.'

'Has to be midday to midnight,' Chrissie countered. 'Otherwise it's no use to me.'

Dorn nodded. He seemed to know the drill, Chrissie noted.

'Great, okay. But I'll have to get back to you first thing tomorrow, I need approval,' she was careful with her speech. 'I don't keep this stuff in my head, you know. Until then, your Detective Bannister has a copy of everything from our lawyers.'

Dorn walked towards her. 'You want to watch yourself. Maybe you got that journalist nose of yours caught in something you can't handle. You need to back off, leave it to the professionals.' When he reached as if to grab her wrist, she moved back suddenly and her glass smashed on the floor.

Now she was afraid. She couldn't think fast enough.

'I, I'm doing my job. I've got my sources to protect. Those two workers, killed, they had families, you know,' she stalled.

Dorn took another step forward. Before she could speak, her mobile rang. She lunged for it, didn't look at the screen.

'Hello?'

'Don't freak out. It's me, Mike. Don't say my name. Just say hi.'

'What?' She walked away from Dorn. She waved the phone at him, like a force field. He stayed on his spot, eyes narrow.

'Say hi, I'm your long-lost cousin. Don't say my name, just say hi.' Mike sounded slow and urgent.

'Oh, hi,' she obeyed.

'That guy outside on the phone, he went up to your place. He's bad news. I heard a smash. You okay?'

'I . . . don't know.'

'I can't come up, he might recognise me. Tell him your cousin has arrived. Coming to stay but not sure which unit number. He's arriving now,' Mike said.

A lifeline. She grabbed it. 'Oh, you're nearly here, great. Ring the bell for unit three. I'll come down and let you in.' Chrissie ended the call. 'Sorry, have to cut you short. My cousin's arrived.' She straightened her back, took a deep breath. 'I'll get back to you, I need to clear it with my editor.' She walked to the door and held it open, brazenly. Her head was thumping. The door handle felt like fire in her hand.

Dorn hesitated.

'Don't use the number you have for me again. I'll phone you,' he said as he strode past her.

It worked. Chrissie wanted to collapse with relief but followed him to the front door. She looked along the street. Coming along the footpath was a guy carrying a gym bag. Hood pulled low.

Dorn didn't hesitate, heading off in the opposite direction without looking back. As the hooded guy got closer, he walked in the gate and up the little path. Chrissie quickly stepped back to slam the door shut, then hesitated at the exaggerated deep voice.

'Hey, cuzzie.' But it was the big smile that gave Mike away. 'What the hell are you doing mixing with underworld trash like that?'

CHAPTER 33

Chrissie stood in the dim light inside Mike's apartment, a pile of takeaway containers rinsed and stacked neatly on the bench. No leftovers for Mike. *Or food poisoning.*

'He's a cop,' she said.

'Cop, my aunt. He's bloody underworld!'

'No, he's Federal Police. Andy Dorn, he's got some operation at the wharf. It's mixed up with my story.'

'He might be a cop but he's dirty. I've worked for him on a couple of lost and found jobs. Recognised him straight away. Andy Dorn, huh? I knew him as Gram. Better tell me what you're up to.'

Her thumbnails started their work, digging hard. Her breath shallow.

'But how would he have known what's going on at the port if he wasn't a cop? He must be involved, he must be legit.' Her legs started to fail. *He could be involved but not a cop.*

Mike checked through the window, down the street. Dorn had gone. 'Sit down before you fall. Phew, you're stonkered. I could light that breath up, dragon lady!' He steered her into his apartment. 'When did you first meet this Andy Dorn?'

'Tonight was the first time. But I spoke to him on the phone earlier. Okay, now as I say it, I'm stupid. I don't even know if that *was* Andy Dorn or if Andy Dorn is even real. No idea what he's supposed to look like. I didn't even ask for ID,' Chrissie groaned, slumping on Mike's sofa.

'Where did you get his number? Or did he contact you?'

Chrissie's faced crumpled.

'I got it from that guy I told you about, at work, the one I thought was applying for the job at Grange.'

'So he could be leaking this information to get in good, get hired for this job? Man, I hate this corporate world crap,' Mike shook his head.

'He's also the guy who, well, I don't know, who's been trying to get rid of me, put me on the wrong track, he keeps me off kilter. Shit! I think I've stuffed up.' She crumpled at the realisation.

'Come on then, let's have a look-see what the world has to say about dangerous Dorn. You can be sure this guy knew you were shickered.'

'Oh god.'

Mike pushed aside his room divider to reveal the desks, walked around the room, picked up cords, connected plugs and flicked switches.

The computers, screens and modems had to be connected and restarted each time, he explained. 'I don't want to be hacked.'

He grinned at her. 'Then this little baby,' he held up a USB drive, 'double encryption'. The screens popped to life.

Chrissie got up and wandered the room as Mike typed at the keyboard. She preferred to pace. *Try to sober up.* 'The first screen will run diagnostics on what's happening on the second screen. Make sure no one can come at me when I'm live. It helps me see what their detection software is doing.'

'Do you ever hear me walking around or my music or anything?'

'Like tonight when you smashed a glass? Yeah. Those big tough girl boots of yours are the worst.'

'Cost me good money, thank you!' She tried for normal.

'Ahh, here he is!'

And there on the screen was a photograph of Andrew Alan Graham Dorn, Senior Constable. It was from an old graduation photo and article in the *Police Gazette*, almost twenty-three years ago.

'That's him! At least he's real.' Chrissie stared with relief. 'But why did he come skulking through the backyard?' Suspicious still. 'What do you think he was going to do if I hadn't seen him, or if you hadn't phoned me?'

'Perhaps he knew I lived here, too,' Mike offered. 'He's connected, that's for sure.'

'What sort of work did you do for him?'

'He needed me to find something. From memory he was probably drug squad then.'

'Yeah, that would fit because my story has a drug connection, too. Coke by the look of it.'

'I never heard from him again.' Mike sat back in his chair. 'I just assumed he got found out, either by the cops or the crew he was with. Looks like he got promoted instead, maybe he cleaned up.'

'How easy is it to electronically block security cameras?' Chrissie looked away from the screen.

'Easy.' Mike didn't bat an eye, just kept typing. 'You want me to block something?'

'No, not me. At the wharf, they've got, or supposed to have, the whole place under surveillance but Grange says someone's tampering with the cameras. This guy Dorn said the same thing.'

'Yeah, super easy. Especially in those places, they use webcams – cheap to install, put them anywhere, no wiring. Nothing special to block. Why don't you ask your new boyfriend?' he teased. 'I'm sure handsome Detective Bannister might like to know about your midnight caller.'

'He's just being thorough. He wouldn't want anything to do with me, if he knew about –' Chrissie stopped short. *Sober up.*

'Knew about what?' Mike jumped on her slip. 'You know you're gonna have to tell me all those secrets one day. But look, here,' he motioned to the screen again. 'More recent. Says he's in Homeland squad. Big Kahuna. It's got Border Force, Feds, Austrac, drug squad, anti-terror, security intelligence. Jesus! Even Signals. Now that's a hamburger with the lot!'

'What's Signals?'

'Nobody really knows, 'cept my world – cyber. Got the name from Morse code in the old days, technically defence department, not cops. But they're all pretty murky these days.'

'Hey, do you think you could do me another little favour?' Chrissie gave Mike her best fake smile.

'Cost ya!'

Chrissie needed more than just a story about cocaine, she needed to link the importers to the deaths of Mas and Remi.

She looked at her phone: 11.56 pm.

'Is it too late to call someone?' She was already tapping the number.

Chrissie knew, as soon as the cops swooped at the wharf, nothing would be exclusive. The picketers, bystanders, workers, they'd all be filming it on their phones. Despite Dorn's promise, she'd be lucky to have thirty minutes head start before other media would cut and paste her online version and repackage it.

She needed a trigger to make the cops look harder at Mas's death. Dorn had already brushed over Remi's accident, collateral damage, and he'd probably do the same with Mas.

'Janice, hi. Can you talk?'

'Sure. I'm still watching the tele. Everyone's in bed. Night owl, me. How are you going? Any progress?'

'Getting there. But couple of things. If a shipping agent is listed as the receiver, can we find out who the end customer is?'

'Sure. That's all public. Not classified or anything. Tell me which agent and which cargo and I'll get it for you, or you can search the records.' Janice seemed cool as a cucumber.

'Great, thanks. Also, the security footage for the yards. Is there a way I could get a look?' Chrissie asked, almost holding her breath.

'The Port Authority runs all the external cameras. We don't record over anything, it's archived, time and date, vessel too. The terminal operators send us their footage, warehouses, crane cameras, internal areas, but mostly our cameras. I've had to request it a few times, insurance claims. I'd need approval for that, though, and it'd be strange for me to ask out of the blue.'

'Of course, no, no, no. That's fine. Thanks, Janice.'

Chrissie turned to Mike.

CHAPTER 34

As soon as she woke, Chrissie knew it was a good day. Her thoughts immediately jumped to the work ahead, she raced to get dressed.

She phoned Bannister's private number and arranged to meet that morning but first, she had to report her late-night visitor.

Chrissie pounced on Maria as soon as she arrived. Saturday morning was no different to any other day in the 24/7 news cycle.

'Cocaine! Jesus, Chrissie, great get!' Maria punched her walking stick in the air, the duck's head raised high.

'But it's still officially unsourced,' Chrissie said.

'Still good. But, look, I'm also worried about you,' Maria said. 'You felt threatened by this guy?'

Chrissie explained the ruse she went through with Mike.

'But I'm not so sure now. I might have overreacted. I mean he's a cop, so nothing was going to happen.' She looked away. *I was pissed out of my brain and couldn't do my job properly.*

'Okay, your call, but hell's bells, Chrissie, don't take risks,' Maria said. 'And good news, our persistence has paid off, we're definitely running the fallback feature on Monday. But if you can pull this cocaine angle off that would give us a huge front-page splash and then we could point to the bigger story inside. It'll earn you a lot of brownie points around here and a bloody great scoop to start the week for our readers.'

'Monday it is. Ready or not.'

—

Chrissie had one more thing to do before she headed over to meet Bannister. Tentatively, she began the email.

I'm sorry. Sorry for making you worry. For everything. I can make it up to you. Maybe Christmas?

'*Maybe Christmas?*' No, better. '*How does an Aussie Christmas sound?*'

No, stop it. Stop trying to sound so chirpy, so coping.

I'm sorry. Sorry for making you worry. For everything. *I can't even begin to think what you've been through. I was just surviving. How can I ever begin to make it up to you?*

She stopped thinking it over and pressed send on the first version, remembering the last time she'd seen her father and her frantic packing before he took her to the airport.

Bondy. Such an unusual name. She couldn't remember how it had come about. The small brown bear must have whispered it to her that first day. He was the first present Dave had ever given her, all those years ago. Chrissie tucked him in the corner of the suitcase. He fitted perfectly, in front of her work shoes and behind the cords and plugs and chargers.

The timer?

She spotted her favourite book, in it went. The *Portable Dorothy Parker*. She went to the dresser. Still in the original tissue paper she slid out silk pyjamas. Men's style, button front, cuff and collar. The palest dusky pink. She had saved them for good. Now they would be for every day.

The timer?

The photo of her mother, taken when she was in her early twenties. Before marriage and kids and the cancer that took her. Hair tied back with a scarf. A-line skirt and fringed leather vest. Posed beside a boyfriend's new Holden Monaro.

The timer?

Of course. The quilt. Room had to be made for it. The broken photo frame, her last picture of her and Dave.

The timer?

She took another long look around. Ornaments, jewellery, cosmetics. Old clothes, memories. She didn't need any of it. She reached in the cupboard. The timer: 34 days, 11 hours, 27 minutes. She slid it in and closed the lid of the case. She had everything.

—

Waiting for Bannister at the police station, she felt like a criminal. The cameras and the extra high counter made her feel small and judged. From the outside, the station looked just like its neighbouring city office buildings, staff bustling in and out, except the clientele in the waiting area soon gave it away. They had a certain look about them. Chrissie realised it was Saturday parole reporting time.

Bannister ushered her beyond the security door and stepped to the side as she went through a scanner. She followed his long legs, wide shoulders, hair always tousled. They walked through a large open-plan room, full of buzzing phones and people. It could have been a newsroom. Hunting for information, following leads, testing people's stories. No wonder journalists and police either hated or loved each other, too much alike. Chrissie was shown into a smoked glass partition room, she sat opposite a row of photos of hatted and uniformed commanders. The only window faced a multi-storey car park building.

'You were mysterious on the phone,' Bannister said. That smile again.

'Have you come up with anything from the information I gave you?' she countered. 'Anything about the story I was working on? Did it ring any bells, cause any fuss?'

'And here's me thinking you were finally going to ask me out.' Bannister sighed.

Chrissie felt her neck start to prickle. She knew the redness would creep up to her face and he would see it. She coughed and shuffled through her bag, got up to look at the photos. For a second, she felt herself respond to the flirting but dismissed it.

'What sort of fuss?' Bannister let her off the hook.

'Well, I was wondering if you cross-referenced it with any other investigations, other departments. Did you happen to find anyone else working on something connected – water police, major crime? That sort of thing.'

'What's happened, Chrissie?' Bannister was better at stone-walling than she was. *Journos and cops alike.*

'Last night I had a visit from a guy, Andrew Dorn, a federal copper by the look of him but I'm not sure about him. He told me he's got an operation at the wharf. It looks mixed up with what I'm writing about.' She had to take a deep breath now. 'But I heard Dorn's connected, underworld or undercover. Drugs, car imports, electronics, maybe, don't know. He came on pretty aggressive. Maybe I read it wrong, though. I was pretty, um, tired.'

'What do you mean aggressive? You mean . . . ?' Bannister sat forward.

'No, no.' Chrissie's face grew even redder. 'He was hinting that he was prepared to do anything to get information. A court order.'

Bannister nodded. Paused. 'What do you want from me?' *Why didn't he ask me what Dorn wanted?*

She walked to the window, distracted by the car park across the lane, bonnets and roofs peeping over the low concrete wall. *Does anyone else know or care about Remi and Mas?* The thought made her furious. 'Jesus, do I have to spell everything out? You haven't made any progress, what have you been doing?'

'Hey! What did you tell Dorn on the phone? It must have been pretty interesting for him to turn up like that.' *More stonewalling.*

'Enough with the questions. I want some answers. Is this Andy Dorn on the level? Is he legit, is he honest?'

'Yes, he's legit.' Bannister ran his hands through his hair. 'He's Homeland. They've pretty much got the run of the place. That's about all I can tell you. These counter-terror laws can be switched on any way they want. Come on, sit down, Chrissie.'

He waved her back to her chair. Reluctantly she took a seat.

'Dorn got in touch with me yesterday arvo, must have been straight after you spoke to him. Didn't waste any time,' Bannister said. 'I filled him in on what we had, some of what we got from you, the allegations of fake accidents, the theft, the cat, even your food poisoning. Guess he decided to play dumb. See what you'd say.'

'Yeah, dumb all right.'

'He was once drug squad, undercover,' Bannister said. 'I don't know his full record but he's top rank now, joint force. Keeps a very low profile.'

'There's something else I left out . . . about the guy who died, Remi Basill.' *Have to trust him.* 'He'd been in touch with me but not just about the feature like I told you.' Bannister sat forward again. 'Remi had a theory about something dangerous at the wharf. About, ah, his friend, Masina Weber. The crane driver. He was trying to look into it. I think it got him killed. Got them both killed. She was running away. Maybe she'd found out about the cocaine. Maybe Remi had too?' Chrissie stood again and paced the room.

'And you just kept this to yourself?' Bannister's voice had hardened. Their eyes locked. He broke their gaze first. 'Look, Dorn's taken over this investigation, me with it. I report to him on this now. He's obviously mentioned the coke. You and the paw, and *The Argus*, have been wrapped up in Dorn's operation. So all I can say is, back off, we've got it covered.'

—

As Chrissie walked back across the newsroom floor her phone started ringing. She smiled when she saw the caller ID.

'Want to take a look at the final safety report about Masina Weber?' It was Hel Carter, from the maritime union.

'Sure do. Thanks.'

'It's going to stuff Grange's allegations, that's for sure.'

'Really, why?'

'Check your email. It's about to bounce in. There was a witness to her death. Grange, not such a reliable source, eh? Think that should put an end to any fake accident angle you're trying to push.'

Shit!

CHAPTER 35

Chrissie couldn't keep still, swivelling her desk chair back and forth as she waited for the Safety Bureau report. She could see the finish line. The story was within her grasp. Finally she would be able to show them all. Prove to the newsroom that she was good at her job. Make Harry eat his resentment. *Make good her mistake. Ease the guilt. Reveal where the truth lies.*

The newsroom looked empty, despite it being a Saturday afternoon, the biggest production night of the week as the bumper Sunday edition was put together. True to her word, Carter's email arrived within minutes. Everything tallied with the draft that Grange had given her almost two weeks ago now, except for one important detail. A witness to Mas's accident had come forth, Daniel Kingaroy. *Kingi!* Chrissie devoured the new report. Kingi said he had signed over the crane to Mas at the end of his shift.

Kingi's statement was straightforward. He was walking away, had his back to the gantry, he heard a noise and twisted around to see Mas on the ground. He ran to her and called for help. No one else was nearby. Nothing suspicious. Did that debunk Grange's theory of a fake accident gone wrong? Not necessarily. Not if Kingi was involved in her death too. Chrissie recalled how he had stood over her, threateningly, at the pokies.

Chrissie switched to her laptop, plugged in the drive Mike had given her to scramble her IP details and forwarded the report to her website. Then she messaged her new best-buddy neighbour through her sadfacedgirl log-on.

How you going with the footage? Any luck? she asked Mike, then switched back to her desktop and pulled up the draft story to continue working.

The last hurdle for Chrissie, the biggest hurdle, was time. Time to write the story before the cops started making arrests. As soon as they swooped, nothing would be exclusive. Time to rewrite the angle around this new witness statement. And time to make sure she could get the story published before there were any more deaths. She had only tracked the story down by working in her own time. She'd be lucky to have thirty minutes head start before others would cut and paste her online version and repackage it.

Mike didn't take long to respond.

What? You want me to crack the Port Authority? Despite the question, Chrissie could imagine him already firing up his computers. Before she could type a reply, he shot back another message: **What happened to Miss Ethics, the last bastion?**

You're a persuasive man, what can I say?

What are you looking for? he typed.

I'm not looking for anything. That would be unethical and against my code of conduct. But if *you* wanted to get a look at what happened in the yard when someone was killed, well, hey, that's up to you.

That's like looking for a needle in a haystack.

What if I've got the date and time? She began writing dates, times and names. She knew the details of Mas's death by heart.

You got everyone doing your dirty work, have you? He added a laughing emoji. But Chrissie's stomach sank, she squeezed her eyes tight. *Dirty work. Cat's paw.*

The footage for the whole site, across all the yards was never checked, she typed. **You're looking for Mas when she fell from the crane. The safety report said the crane was out of range of the cameras but I just thought we – I mean you – could check anyway?**

Why don't you log off now, Miss Ethics, and I'll let you know. Could take a while, like way past your bedtime.

—

But under her door when she got home that evening was another USB, wrapped in a note. 'It's on your website. Take a deep breath. This stick will also plug and play so you can drop anon. Nothing traceable.'

She sat at the table and opened her laptop.

The footage was in colour but washed out. There were more than thirty camera locations throughout the yard. To find the right one must have taken Mike *hours*, she realised.

What she assumed was Mas's crane wasn't in direct view but it could be seen on the edge of two locations.

Remi had told her the protocol was for the crane operator to wait in the cabin for the new shift member and then sign over control in the high-rise cabins. But the cabins were small, so instead they often waited on the platform or even waited on the ground.

According to the sign-over sheet, Kingi signed out that day at 3.30 pm. But Mas never signed on. On the edge of the camera someone could be seen climbing down. Chrissie checked the time on the footage, 3.03 pm. Could it be Kingi? He must have left early, Chrissie thought. The sign-on records must have been altered. She pulled the chair closer, adjusted the angle of the screen.

When the man got to the ground, he walked off screen towards the main gate. Within seconds two people arrived from the other direction, from inside the yard, and slowly climbed the crane's leg, their faces obscured, their bulky clothes and safety vests identical. Whoever they were, they were definitely not 'crane fit', they lumbered, slow and heavy, up the stairwell. They were not regular staff, Chrissie realised. *Not Mas?* But maybe Mas knew Kingi had skipped off early and was covering for him. Who could be with her? The two figures sat in the control box. The footage jumped to 3.24 pm and a third person walked across the yard from the main entrance. The thick long plait clearly visible – *Mas!* Chrissie pressed on her stomach to force away a sudden queasiness. She watched as Mas climbed the stairwell. About three-quarters of the way up, one of the two above came out on the top platform. *I've been on that platform, looked down to that stairwell.*

Chrissie's stomach was churning now, her neck hot and prickly. She shifted on her chair as she watched with dread. Mas stopped. It looked like she had a discussion with the person above before she continued slowly up. Whatever was said must have reassured her to keep climbing, Chrissie thought. *Did she know them?* When Mas reached the platform, the second person came out of the cabin and then – Mas began to struggle with them. She threw a useless punch, turned around, waving her arms in a wide arc above her head. Waving for help, calling, waving for someone to see her.

The figures bundled her between them and simply lifted her over the barrier. Her body could be seen as it flew. Falling. It bounced against the stairway about a third of the way down, then bounced again and caught on a rail. Mas hung from her waist. Floating. Chrissie tapped pause on the keyboard and pushed back from the computer. She gagged, bile burning her throat. She swallowed and closed her eyes. *Breathe; one, two, three.* She leaned forward bent over, trying to put more pressure on her stomach, to ease the threat of vomit. After a few minutes she sat up again, pulled the chair closer to the screen. Pressed start again.

The two men walked down the stairwell. When they got to Mas, they casually flipped her over the rail again and she smashed on the ground. Chrissie bolted for the sink, tears already blinding her. But she just dry-heaved, dragging in a ragged breath whenever she could. She twisted the cold tap and scooped a handful of water over her forehead, another and another. With shaking legs, she returned to the table.

The two men didn't stop to look when they reached the bottom of the stairwell, they just walked, strong and sure, back the way they came. Neither looked around. Neither looked back.

Chrissie stared at the footage as it continued: seagulls played in the sky, Mas's discarded body on the ground. A huge wave of sadness filled her chest as she carefully sipped the air.

The witness statement was a lie. Kingi had said he had waited for Mas on the ground, against the rules but common practice. He said he had walked away at 3.30, the end of the shift, while Mas climbed up. Then he had heard a noise behind him and he turned to see her body on the ground. He told everyone, truthfully, that he didn't see her fall. 'She must have tripped, somehow,' Kingi said, 'no other explanation.'

What he didn't say, as Chrissie had just learned, was that he had left early.

But the recording Mike had done for her wasn't finished. The slide bar still had a few minutes to run. She pressed start again. There she was again, Mas, crumpled on the ground. Then Kingi could be seen coming back into the edge of the footage: 3.38. He stopped about ten metres from the body. Then sprinted and kneeled beside her. He didn't touch her but he wanted to, his hands hovering above her. Then his head was in his own hands. Within seconds she watched him do a backward crab walk away. His mouth distorted around ugly shouts, Chrissie could hear them in her head, despite no sound on the recording. Eventually people came running. The footage finally stopped.

Chrissie sat looking out her kitchen window. Mesmerised by the bland steel fire escape handrail, the perforated steel platform, a miniature version of the one she had walked up with Mas, the one Mas had been pushed from. Chrissie had to drop the footage on Bannister, anonymously. *Finally getting it told.* The key to Mas's death and a high likelihood the two men on the tape were involved with the cocaine. Could those men also have been in her place? Attacked Skinny?

But she couldn't let Bannister or Dorn know she was connected to the footage; that could expose Mike, and possibly her, to hacking charges. The cops would have to assume the footage had come from a whistleblower at the Port Authority or Grange or the union.

It was almost 8 pm. Chrissie caught the train into the city, waiting near Police Central. She found who she was looking for. Lycra head to toe. Built-in padding on his knees, bum and elbows made him look like a rubber man. The nearby Collins Street financial district kept these couriers working all hours, all days. Chrissie stepped in front of him and he came to a skidding stop, twisting the front wheel to avoid her.

'Fifty bucks to take this envelope to the station and get it signed in, urgent delivery for Senior Detective Jason Bannister. Must be signed in.' The bike courier took the cash and envelope without a blink.

—

She heard from Bannister early the next morning – Sunday – about ten hours until deadline, she noted. Today every minute would count.

'We got a tip-off last night. We've interviewed someone about your woman's death,' he said. 'Apparently this witness said he was approached by two of the casuals. Told him his shift would finish early.'

This new waiting period was the danger zone for Chrissie. She knew her media rivals would be much better connected with the Feds than she was. They had had years to build up a rapport, besides there would soon be cops shouting the odds all over the wharf as they made arrests. The risk of another journo finding out and losing her exclusive after all her hard work to get justice for Mas and Remi was all too real. Despite her fear, she also didn't want to risk any further complications with the story, she had decided to wait until after it was published to ask Dorn about the threats to her and Skinny.

But, for now, Chrissie let out a small sigh of relief. It would only be a matter of hours until Bannister and Dorn also matched Mas and Kingi's shifts and narrowed down the vessels involved. Dorn might have known the cargo but he didn't seem to know how and when it was arriving – or so he wanted her to think. He had lied almost as much as she had during their meeting.

CHAPTER 36

Today. The text from Bannister came just after noon. Chrissie was already at her desk putting the finishing touches to the inside-page story – not that they were ever truly finished, there was always a word to change, an adjective to remove. She phoned Maria straight away: 'The cops have started making arrests. We're on! They'll give us the details soon but I'm still not sure what to do about Harry and Jefferies. How are we going to handle this?'

'I don't want to give Jefferies a sniff of the cocaine angle yet,' Maria warned, 'or Grange may suddenly be looking for favours. I need to go straight to the editorial board.' Maria must have heard Chrissie's intake of breath. 'Don't worry, I'll persuade them. Although they won't be happy about coming in on a Sunday. Start working up a front-page draft. We'll need to give them a taster.'

'I just saw Harry,' Chrissie said quietly. 'Already looks like he's got a storm up about something, from the sound of things. But space-wise, I'll need at least three hundred and fifty words for the front splash, about nine hundred inside. We have to run them both or we'll lose –'

'I'm coming in,' Maria interrupted.

Chrissie looked around, a smaller staff on a Sunday but still hectic. The attitude in the newsroom towards her had changed in the past week. Twice she had been asked if she wanted to join people for lunch but both times she'd declined, too wrapped up in work to take a break. Funny, how the death of a cat had moved people more than her rumoured suicide.

Harry's less hostile attitude had also made a difference. But Chrissie still kept her distance.

The roster cycle meant everyone was on rolling shifts. Even James.

'Harry seems happier with you. What's happened?' James asked as he sauntered in a few minutes later.

'Maria had a word. I'm assuming my reprieve is temporary. Though he did give me one of his contacts from that golden contact book of his.'

'You are in the good books. Who was the contact? What's happening anyway? You're not on shift today.'

'I'm on a roll, Jamie James. We're expecting something any hour. I've got twelve hours' head start.'

'Today! Oh, well done. So what's the story, after all this? Details, please.'

But Chrissie didn't have time to answer.

'Okay, we're off,' Frances, the photographer, said to James as she appeared beside his desk. 'We're tag-teaming at the footy queue.' She looked to Chrissie. 'They're lining up already after yesterday's result.' Frances had a huge smile on her face. 'Gotta love finals season!'

—

The hours dragged as Chrissie waited to hear from Bannister. Maria had arrived about an hour ago but there was not much either of them could do for now. Chrissie tried not to pace. Not only did she want to get the story published, she wanted people to know the truth. How would Vince and Al and the rest of Remi's family feel when they found out that he may have been murdered by drug smugglers? She looked up to see Harry walking towards her. She forced herself to lift her head and meet his gaze.

'I hear you had a bit of a run-in with my mate Andy,' his voice was deep and rough.

'It was strange, a bit menacing,' Chrissie replied, alert at his dangerous tone.

'Running off to your copper mate and blurting his name and everything you talked about is also pretty strange. Especially as a journalist who's supposed to keep her sources confidential. Especially when that confidential source was given to her as a bloody favour. What the hell were you thinking, O'Brian?' His voice had risen steadily to a shout.

Chrissie pushed her chair away from her desk, away from Harry. She was blindsided. But it immediately hit her how badly she had messed up. Harry's anger was valid. How could she? *Idiot!* She rubbed her palms together, the itch overwhelming.

'Oh god, I'm sorry. It was totally wrong. But Dorn threw me for a loop. He came on strong, rattled me.' She looked down. 'It's no excuse.'

'Shit, O'Brian. I virtually vouched for you by giving you his number. This was my contact. Your only saving grace is that he was already working with this Bannister. But bloody big mistake, O'Brian. Huge mistake.'

'He turned up in my backyard, middle of the night. I was putting the rubbish out. I'd had a bit to drink. I was under stress, hospital, this feature, the cat's paw – and you!' she fired back.

Harry glared as he stood over her. Should she stand? He could report her to the board for a breach of standards. To her surprise he walked around and propped himself on the side of her desk.

'Look. Maybe I could have been more understanding,' he said. 'I know, now, about your –' He was stopped by Chrissie's phone pinging.

Another text from Bannister. Chrissie held up a hand to Harry. She didn't care what he wanted to say. She guessed, anyway. But she could put off that uncomfortable conversation for a few more hours.

Check your email. Draft only, official statement at 11.50 pm. You've got your exclusive.

None of the other papers would have time to put it to print that late. She stood and looked towards Maria. 'We're on,' she mouthed and gave her the thumbs up. 'I have to get writing.' Chrissie turned back to Harry. 'You can discipline me later, just leave this story alone. Let me finally write it!'

Harry looked as if he might object. But he surprised her again. Silence, as he walked away.

Chrissie pulled up the email from Bannister and gathered up her notes. Not that she needed them anymore – she had a good idea of what it was going to say. She quickly finished the front-page lead. The full story of her investigation was done, the distrust between the main parties, the changing technology, the economic impacts and the high accident rate – despite these murders. Chrissie just needed to write in the extra cocaine angle. The artists were also working on a new graphic image to show how the cocaine was imported and distributed. It would replace the original that had illustrated the types of accidents.

EXCLUSIVE
INTERNATIONAL COCAINE BUST
SUSPICIOUS PORT DEATHS
By Chris O'Brian

Fifteen arrests have been made and Australia's busiest port is in lockdown after the newly established Homeland force busted an international cocaine ring with a haul valued at more than $480 million.

The joint counter-terrorism and border force investigation is also expected to reopen investigations into the recent deaths of two port workers, Masina Weber and Remi Basill.

Arrests have also been made in Brazil and Peru after a surveillance operation at Port Melbourne. The Homeland combined force said the crime ring had also established a cocaine processing and distribution centre in the Northern Territory. Simultaneous undercover arrests were made at the port and the Territory factory.

The swoop is the biggest cocaine bust in Australian history and has shut down one of the largest drug rings to operate in this country. It involved the importation of cocaine paste and subsequent processing into cocaine powder.

Three Australians, eight South American nationals and a US citizen were held overnight awaiting formal charges. A further three people were also in custody in Alice Springs, awaiting charges. All charges are expected to relate to organised crime operating from Grange Industries' terminals at the Port of Melbourne.

It is alleged the cocaine paste was packaged and imported as acai paste. Acai is a berry grown in the Amazon and is used in health foods. The shipments were landed in Australia and transported north. Once processed the cocaine was being fed into the Australian market. Australia has one of the highest prices for cocaine in the world.

The deaths of Masina Weber and Remi Basill were initially reported as workplace accidents. Remi Basill was killed last week after he was crushed. Crane operator Masina Weber died from a high-rise fall almost three weeks ago. Both cases are now being treated as suspected homicides. Neither victim is alleged to be associated with the criminal activity.

The Argus has been conducting an exclusive investigation at the port following the death of Ms Weber and Mr Basill. Our investigation has uncovered crucial information and helped lead to the arrests. Suspicions were raised by reports to *The Argus* about missing cargo and a surge in accidents as part of a story about the changing waterfront industry.

See our exclusive in-depth report today on pages 4 and 5.

The Australian Government's Homeland force is expected to hold a press conference this morning.

At last. Getting it told. Fixing her mistake.

CHAPTER 37

'Okay, fingers crossed,' Maria said, waving a copy of Chrissie's story and the draft police release, on her way to see the board. It was just after 4 pm. The afternoon news conference was over and most of the page and story placements had been agreed. The Monday edition of *The Argus* was its smallest seller of the week. The drug bust story would definitely boost readership. She looked at the clock: 4.12 pm.

Chrissie's scoop was going to be the front-page lead, the more in-depth story about the wharves was being spread over two pages inside. As the deadlines for each section of the paper started to tick by, tempers frayed and voices grew urgent. Harry had already had two arguments with reporters, he was on edge, too.

4.32 pm.

Chrissie was getting agitated. The noise level in the newsroom increased. Writing to deadline was not a silent process. Maria had kept the cocaine story out of the news conference, away from Jefferies and anyone else. Chrissie had watched during the afternoon as Harry had allocated stories to pages she knew he would soon have to pull apart and remake. With the main news piece finished, Chrissie only had a couple of hours left to finish tweaking or write out anything the board or the lawyers wanted removed.

She couldn't officially attribute the information until the police statement was released at 11.50 pm. By then it would be too late for the other papers to have anything in print. Her story would blow the competition out of the water in the morning. It would be packed with the detail of the smuggling, and the inside piece about life on the country's biggest dock. Now the romance, the mystery of the open seas and the history of physical work were long gone. Today's docks were all about machines against men. Performance targets and cost cutting. And danger.

5.16 pm.

The union allegations of missing cargo had been confirmed by Bannister. The cocaine gang shuffled the containers from the arriving ships and almost immediately onloaded to coastal ships up the east coast and around to Darwin. Once landed, they were no longer subject to customs checks, Bannister had said. Grange, too, was right to be suspicious. The high accident rate was artificial not because people were staging them but because the gang was hurting people, warning them off. And murdering them – for those who wouldn't be cowed.

Finally, Mas and Remi would be heard. Chrissie relaxed against her chairback, hands still. She had already written a breakout piece about the 'wharf family' – how the great-grandfather, grandfather, father and Remi had built a life around the docks. Now his young children would grow up without a father. Three generations before him had survived the treachery of Australia's most dangerous occupation but it was a cocaine gang that would end the Basill family tradition. Her profile interview with Mas also featured on the two pages. Chrissie smiled at the photograph of Mas with her big wide grin, taken in the control box, its glass ceiling above her.

5.45 pm.

Chrissie rubbed her palms and glanced around. The deadline stalked but the adrenalin rush was part of what she loved about her job. She looked up to see Harry take a call. Then he stood and called for Sam, the whippet, to take over the news desk and he strode to the management offices. *He's been called in!* Almost at the same time, James came across the floor. Before he even had a chance to sit down, Chrissie unloaded.

'Maria has been in with the board for almost an hour and a half. I've got a bad feeling about this,' she said.

'What's going on?' James dumped his bag and sat down.

'The story, it's running tonight. But Harry got called in just now. Something's wrong.'

'Crikey, you're tight for time with all this.' He shook his head.

'The cops are issuing a public statement after deadline, we'll be the only paper to have it. Here, I'll send you my splash. Don't tinker too much, though. It's tricky until I get the official wording.'

Can you also look at the big piece? It's pretty much done, it still needs a final tidy but I've got to crack on, file before 7.'

'You betcha patootie.'

Chrissie gave James a look.

'Sorry, I know. One of my soon-to-be American father-in-law's sayings. I've adopted it.'

6.23 pm.

Chrissie's desk phone rang. The old grey handset was a relic from the past, the digits on the buttons long worn away, the speed dial labels clogged with papers and scribbled names from previous users. Without even looking at the caller identification, she slumped back in her chair. The tone of the ring meant it was an internal call. Her stomach twisted. Chrissie stared at the phone and considered letting it ring out. If she didn't answer, she could just keep writing.

James leaned towards her, 'Chrissie. *Answer it.*'

CHAPTER 38

Caroline waved her through to the boardroom. Chrissie hardly recognised her. Usually prim and proper, tonight she was in sneakers and jeans, with long, loose hair and no makeup.

Chrissie nodded to Jefferies. She hadn't realised he had been called in too. *That means both he and Harry have known everything for at least an hour.* She gave a brief nod to the rest of the people in the room. Caroline followed her in and sat at the table, ready to take more notes.

There was always an odd number on any editorial board call-up, so the vote was never tied. Tonight, there were five, including two of the firm's duty lawyers, also in jeans. One of them in a black Metallica t-shirt.

A woman Chrissie guessed was Karen Walter, the corporate governance director, looked like she was on her way to dinner, wearing a twisted silver necklace and the Melbourne staple little black dress. The fourth was someone Chrissie had never seen or met before. Short and overweight, a face stiff with Botox and his hair heavily dyed.

Chrissie joined Maria at the end of the large polished art deco table, a relic from the paper's more prosperous days. She put her notebook, pen and phone in front of her.

'Chris, hi. This is some explosive story you've unearthed, well done.' It was Darren Brown, the chairman. The fifth board member for the night. Jefferies, Harry and Maria didn't get a vote tonight, observers only. She had seen Brown in the newsroom a few times but had never been introduced. He looked like a hawk, curved nose, eyes sheltered by heavy brows. 'Can you turn your phone off please?' Chrissie picked it up and held the button until it went blank. She knew it was not just to stop interruptions but also to stop her recording the conversation.

'Excellent investigation,' Brown continued. 'Very impressed. Thank you. Unfortunately, we've got a problem. I'm not going to beat about the bush. We're not going to publish it tonight.'

The anger grew up from her chest and over her face. She sucked in a loud breath. The Metallica lawyer pushed two letters across the table to her but Chrissie was too panicked to read. Harry held her stare, unemotional, stone-faced. She looked at Jefferies, and he looked back, relaxed and calm. Both were unreadable. She broke eye contact and looked again at the letters.

The top one was on legal letterhead: 'On behalf of the Australian Federal ...' She couldn't read anymore. Her hand trembled too much. She tried to bring the letter closer but quickly dropped it. It felt like sandpaper. The noise of the air conditioning was too loud. Caroline's fingernails were going click-click-click on her keyboard as Brown kept talking. *Oh god, not now. In front of these people. Breathe; one, two, three.* She hid one hand below the table and her thumb started counting. *Feel the pain. Here and now.*

She shuffled the first letter aside. *Here and now. Feel the pain.*

The second letter was from Grange Industries. The logo instantly recognisable, a globe circled by ships. Chrissie didn't attempt to read that one either. It didn't matter what they said. They had beaten her. *Breathe; one, two, three. Here and now.*

'It's nothing to do with your work,' she heard Brown drone. She looked up at him. His eyes genuine, his voice monotone, business-like. 'But this has been taken out of our hands.' Caroline's nails again, click-click-click-click. 'The story will not be published tonight. We're waiting on a hard copy of the injunction but it's real. The whole lot has been gagged,' Brown announced.

Jefferies stood and went to the credenza. 'Chrissie, this is nothing that you've done. We'll get through it.' He poured a glass of water and put it next to Chrissie. She looked at him without speaking. *I'm drowning and you give me water.*

'You'll see from the letter,' Brown again, 'we're legally hamstrung. A lot has happened during the past couple of hours that raised your story beyond the cocaine angle.' Chrissie reached for the glass but saw her hand shaking and quickly pulled it back. 'Grange was the initial applicant for the injunction but then this second injunction lobbed,' he said.

'Homeland. For reasons that we haven't yet had detailed, Homeland has applied and been granted a total media block. That means we can't even report that there was a story. Or that a story has even been blocked. Once you read those letters, you'll know as much as we do.'

'Chrissie, you're not saying much. What do you want to know?' It was Maria.

'This, this . . . It stinks. Something's not fucking right.' Chrissie looked up, she wasn't sure if she had said the words out loud or just thought them. Their faces told her: out loud. She had nothing to lose. 'How did Grange know about it? How can Grange block it? Which one of you?' She looked at Harry and then to Jefferies. Then a sudden intake of breath. She looked at Maria. *No! Get a grip.* She shook her head to clear the thought.

'We don't know how exactly and we'll be challenging, of course,' Brown answered. 'These new anti-terror powers, we're still coming to grips with them. And we're not prepared to risk a raid by them tonight. So we're playing nice, for now.' Brown kept his gaze on Chrissie, waiting for agreement. She didn't respond. 'We'll leave you with the lawyers but, to be clear, you weren't called in here to discuss the merits of our decision. The story is not running. The injunction lists *The Argus*, you personally, me, the managing director, editorial director and most of our board. No one here, including you, can even talk about this conversation. Total blackout.' Brown took a large sip of water.

'They've started interviewing the members of this gang. One of them said they broke into a journalist's home,' he continued. Chrissie gasped loudly. She looked around the table. Their faces set, they had heard everything, knew everything, a direct line to the investigation. Brown's voice remained low and steady. 'They think that was you. Maria said it could have been the night you went to hospital . . .' Brown's voice faded in and out. *Fuck!* Maria automatically moved closer, inspected Chrissie's face. It was blank.

'Until this is all sorted out,' he said, 'we think you are still at risk.'

CHAPTER 39

Chrissie had overcome it. Her worst fear. An anxiety attack at work. As she sat through the final debriefing, despite the threat, the tension in her chest started to ease. In such a confined space, with all those people, her breath had been so shallow it barely moved her chest but she had made it through. By the time they let her out of the boardroom, her plan was clear. She was on her mobile as she walked to her desk.

'What the hell?'

'It was Grange's doing,' Bannister hit back. 'We pushed it too but Grange sought the original injunction.'

'So, what's this total blackout bullshit? Grange can't do that – you must have done that,' Chrissie shot back.

'Something came up, last minute. So, yeah, the blackout was us. But I can't do this on the phone. Can we meet? I want to talk about the break-in at your place. About your protection.'

'I'm too pissed off.'

'And you'll be nice and friendly exactly when? I can fill you in on a few other things. I'm assuming you guys are challenging? But what about tonight, I can get a patrol organised –' Bannister began.

'This is all crap. I'm fine. Tomorrow. My place, midday.'

—

'I'm taking you for a drink now, my girl. No argument,' Maria said as soon as Chrissie got off the phone.

Chrissie realised Maria must have been waiting for her the whole time she had been at the debrief. Maria wasn't even supposed to be in today. No one had waited for her or been that kind for a very long time. Tears threatened.

'Nah, I'm stuffed. I'm going to fall in a heap.'

'Not taking no. You're coming.' Maria grabbed Chrissie's jacket and bag. 'Come on.' She hooked her arm in Chrissie's. '*I* need a drink.' Maria was pulling the guilt-plea; Chrissie just nodded.

'James, the story's been canned. Grange got an injunction,' Maria announced. 'We're off to drown our sorrows. Coming?'

'Jesus H. Christ.' James searched Chrissie's face. 'Yes, I'm long done. I was just waiting for Chrissie.'

Two people had waited. More tears threatened.

She wanted a drink but she wanted to drink at home by herself, curled up on her sofa . . . with Skinny. But there was no avoiding Maria. As the three waited for the lift, Harry walked out of Jefferies' office. He hesitated. Then stopped.

'Haz, we're off for a drink,' Maria said, leaning heavily on her stick.

'O'Brian, can I have a word?' Harry surprised her.

Cornered. She looked down at the lino floor to avoid eye contact. She rubbed her hand down the strap of her satchel. Every grain and notch of the leather felt angry. *I don't want your words of destruction. Not tonight. Give me one more day before you tell everyone.* The elevator chimed, the doors rattled and shook as they slid open. Chrissie stared inside, longingly, hoping to get away. The antique lift had been totally refurbished, a grant from the heritage council, mirrors gleamed and bounced light everywhere.

'We'll wait downstairs.' Maria broke Chrissie's silence and bundled James in the lift. The doors took forever to close as Chrissie stood frozen. Helpless to force her way in the lift, helpless to turn towards Harry.

'I know your story, O'Brian,' Harry said quietly. 'You were born Christaline Mary O'Brian.' *Christaline: strong, intelligent, trustworthy, the keeper of secrets.* Her mum had chosen it. 'Your married name Watford. The accident, the drink-driving, you, Christaline Watford, convicted.' Chrissie rubbed her hands down the front of her jacket, her knees started to give way as Harry levelled the words at her. It had to come out, she knew. But not today, not now, among this latest failure. Her scoop was canned, weeks of investigation wasted, Mas and Remi's killers still out there, Skinny, the food poisoning, pill popper, suicide risk. Now everyone at work would know about her. Drunk driver, husband killer, baby killer. Failure. *Another crash landing. I'll have to leave.* Did she have the strength to face them?

'Sit down.' Harry seemed to hiss again as he grabbed her arm and walked her to the old black sofa near the kitchen. Chrissie followed, too exposed to resist.

She sunk deeply in the cushions. The broken springs made her knees fold up too high, her back pushed awkwardly forward. *I don't think I'll ever get up again.* To her amazement, Harry sat on the stumpy wooden coffee table in front of her. Eye level. A kinder face looked back at her.

'You've been going through a hard time,' he said quietly. 'I've struggled at times with drinking, think you might have too.' He waited but got no response. 'Anyway . . .' he tilted his head sideways at her. *Sympathy?* He was so close she could hear his old watch ticking.

What was coming?

'I'm just going to say this quickly because I'm busy, still got a paper to put out tonight. A hole on the front page to fill.' He puffed up his chest just a little. 'Oh hell, O'Brian. You're good, very good, all right? Just as well Maria kept you on that story. She gave you the support I should have. I was too, well . . . I should have put my own problems aside.'

Chrissie just stared. *He said I was good.*

'I owe you.'

He owes me? Or he owns me? What's he saying?

'This ban, this injunction tonight, it's not my doing. I know you have doubts.'

Then she found her voice. 'So how did Grange find out? How come they had time to get the injunction?'

'I know Maria's told you about Jefferies, he's always been a self-serving bastard.'

Chrissie nodded. It must be Jefferies, after all. Currying favour to get the new job? She couldn't think clearly.

'How are you with this break-in thing? If you're worried, the paper can put you up in a hotel.'

'No, no. No, thanks.' Chrissie was determined to get home. Pick at her failure by herself, away from any hotel staff.

'It's a great story, we'll fight for it,' he said, getting to his feet. 'I'll fight for it. You'll get more support from me from now on.'

Instead of striding off as she'd expected, he braced himself, offering a strong hand to help her out of the sofa.

'I suppose that's your idea of being a supportive boss, is it?' Chrissie managed a smile and took hold. Harry smirked. Not quite ready for jokes – yet.

'We're back to plan A.' He was back to business. 'Still running the two-pager fallback tomorrow.'

Chrissie just shrugged.

'It's still a great insight,' he tried to be positive. 'Paints an incredible picture of what's happening in that industry . . . We'll get to the bottom of the other, just not tonight.' Harry strode off. She could hear him yelling instructions as she waited for the lift.

—

Home at last, she knew she wouldn't sleep. Her couple of drinks with Maria and James did nothing to calm her. She was too hyped and upset to sleep. And they had both been too watchful of her, she had needed to get away.

Maria and James had done their best to map out a plan of action – an attempt to raise Chrissie's spirits – but they couldn't budge her disappointment.

'Come on, my girl, come and stay at my place tonight, we can get an early start,' Maria had said as they were about to leave.

'That's a great idea,' James chimed in but had immediately put his head down, as Chrissie saw straight through them both.

'Nah thanks Maria, I just need to hit the sack.'

Lying on the sofa now, she stared at the TV, mindless soft porn masquerading as music videos. Yet another woman called a bitch and a ho. Would *The Argus* get the injunction overturned? Would they push the legal challenge hard or would it suit the paper to let it slide? Would Jefferies get his reward, a cushy PR job or some other payoff? Grange would be pissed off at her now, too. There was no mention of the union staging accidents, instead her story focused on the automation, the impact on the workforce, the pickets, the dangers. The deaths. Helen Carter would also complain, she knew. There would be nothing blaming Grange for the missing cargo. Although Carter's research stacked up about the lost containers, it didn't imply fraud but it did imply Grange's new computer system was a lemon, adding to its financial woes and damaging its reputation. She knew but couldn't report yet that the missing containers were linked to the cocaine. The gang also responsible for the accidents and deaths – murders.

'Crap, crap, crap.' She flicked from one channel to the next. She switched the TV to an all-night news station and filled her wine glass again. For the third or fourth time, she searched her phone and laptop for breaking news, any reference to the port or cocaine. One strategy that Grange might take was to leak a spoiler. Get the excitement about the coke smuggling over with, but without any mention of Grange's terminals being involved. By the time the full story came out, the heat would be gone and people wouldn't care about the detail.

All clear. Nothing on the news links, she checked her Twitter feed. Searched Facebook. Nothing. She eyed the white pharmacy bottles on the kitchen bench. Tonight was supposed to be her triumph. To prove her worth, undo her mistake, the truth and justice for Mas and Remi. She walked over slowly then pulled the cap off the smallest of the three bottles and tipped out two small cream tablets. They seemed clean and pure in her hand. Her palm red and scratched, her fingertips raw and puffy. She had tried her best. She crossed the small hall and opened the taps for the bath then headed back in the lounge where she straightened cushions, neatened the coffee table and wiped down the bench. Chrissie still had the two pills clenched in her fist. She surveyed the room then walked to the big bay window. The sky was dark but a large moon showed a clear sky. Clouds usually sank and died in the cool night air, Dave had taught her. She flung the curtains across. Everything in order, nothing to see. She picked up the bottle again and tipped six or seven more into her hand and walked back to the bath. Full enough. As she looked in the mirror she emptied the palm-full into her mouth. In a single swoop, she filled a glass of water. The pills bitter on her tongue as she crunched through them. She lifted the glass and took a mouthful, swirling the water around in the mashed pills. Then she slammed the glass back down. Leaning over the basin she spat all the pills out.

Slumped on her sofa again, she pulled out the letter from her jeans pocket. Chrissie had slipped it out of the boardroom, nobody had noticed. But by then the large table had been littered with even more of their papers and excuses. *Still got a job to do.*

CHAPTER 40

Left, left, right.

Jab, jab, cross. *Again!*

Jab, jab, cross. *Again!*

This morning, Chrissie punched the media blackout over and over again into the red leather bag. It didn't add up. Something was wrong.

Left, left, right.

Jab, jab, cross, hook, cross. *Again!*

Why would the cocaine be going by sea to Darwin? Then down to Alice to be processed. Parenta, the transport boss, mentioned special access, the driver taking stuff to Alice by road, not ship. And Janice! A government contract? Environmental waste? Chrissie needed to follow up, find out the customers of the three agents.

Left, left, right. *Again!*

Jab, jab, cross. *Again!*

The sweat dripped under her chin. Large wet patches formed across her chest, under her arms and down her back

'Chrissie! Chrissie!' Her trainer Ken shouted. 'Keep your fucking right up!'

She heard but didn't stop. Correcting herself, bringing her right hand closer to her face as she hooked with the left. *Again!* Her eyes focused on the cracked and worn punching bag until she bent over, exhausted, her hair dripping. She hung her head and pulled apart the velcro on her gloves with her teeth, then straightened as she slipped each hand under her arms. Squeezing tight, she pulled the gloves off. *I'm outta here.*

—

It was Monday morning. The morning her exposé was supposed to run. The day the truth about Mas and Remi should have finally been known. Instead, Chrissie was slinking along Victoria Street, dodging boxes of fruit and vegetables, picking her way around the rubbish. The smell of the bakeries helped waft away the stench of the night before. But she was too focused to eat, turning into the lane without stopping. Only looking ahead when it was too late.

Of all the days, it had to be today. The two men walked towards her. She recognised Toothless from his shape. His friend she hadn't seen before. He was big. Steroids, she thought. Muscly, walked with his legs wide apart. The steroid guy seemed agitated; he shifted from side to side. Bannister was due at her place in a couple of hours. She needed to shower, to change, get her head straight to see him. *I don't have time for this.*

She saw Toothless point her out to his new mate. A target. *Why would he bother?* She reached in her gym bag for her wallet and pulled out some notes. She was more than halfway down the lane but there was still time to turn back. Toothless had dropped back. His usual apologetic self. Steroid guy was ahead. Chrissie was suddenly more on edge. Damn, shouldn't have taken the short cut. *But why shouldn't I?* It's my suburb too. She didn't have time to be delayed. She put the money on the blue stones and backed away to the side. She felt Steroids' aggression coming off him in waves now. He was advancing, almost on her. Could she slip past? Chrissie sidled along the wall, avoiding eye contact, but his arm shot out. She tried to dodge him but he grabbed her jacket and swung her around and against the wall, the bricks rough against her raw hands.

'Think you might have something else we want, bitch,' he growled, spinning her around and shirtfronting her. Chrissie looked to Toothless but he seemed just as shocked as she was. *Stupid, stupid, stupid.*

'Let me the fuck go,' Chrissie shouted in his face. He moved his head back but kept his grip. His other hand came up and slapped her head. Bang! The noise loud in her ear, her face stinging. Chrissie recognised the smell of him, the whoosh of air from his swing. The telltale chemical sweat of ice. There would be no talking him around.

'I've got a few more bucks in the bottom of my bag,' she tried to placate him. He swung her sharply around again and forced her arm high behind her back; it felt like her shoulder would pop out of its socket. He spun her around, bashed the back of her head against the brick wall then yanked her closer by the front of her shirt again.

'I've got a message for you. From Brazil.' *What?* Chrissie gagged for breath, she turned away from his eyes, their pupils dilated, their expression unblinking and full of hate. *He doesn't care if I know. He's going to kill me.* 'Meow,' he said straight into her face. He laughed at her stunned reaction. *Skinny!* 'Meooooow.' Longer, slower, louder this. 'They said you'd know what that meant. They wanted you to know, first.' He laughed again then punched her in the stomach. She folded in two, all breath left her body. He pulled on her bag and wound the strap around her neck tighter and tighter and then lifted her off the ground with it. She was slipping away. *They knew Mas was on to them. Then Remi. Then her. Skinny. I led them to all three. Now me.* Now she was floating up between the buildings, above the laneway. *Going home. Cumulus. Dave.*

'Leave her alone! Leave her alone or I'll fucking slash ya.' It was Demi. Chrissie was dragged back by the shouts. A box cutter glinted, clenched in one hand. 'Leave her a-fucking-lone. Leave her!' Demi screeched over and over as she jumped back and forwards waving the cutter. 'Leave her! Leave her!'

'Piss off, you crazy bitch,' Steroids cursed. He batted Demi across the face and she fell to the ground but at the same time he was forced to relax his grip around Chrissie's neck, her feet back on the ground. Demi bounced straight up, punching his back. 'Leave her a-fucking-lone. Leave her!' He was forced to let go of the strap as he fought Demi off.

'Come on, mate, let's split.' Toothless this time. 'She knows us,' he said to Steroids. 'I didn't know you were gonna do that ...'

Toothless pulled one of Steroids' arms but immediately stepped back again. 'Oh shit, man. Oh shit. Come on, man, I didn't know you were gonna . . .' Toothless pleaded, yanking at the big arm again. Then hands lifting Chrissie, trusted hands.

'Run, Chrizzie,' Demi rasped as she helped her up. Chrissie snatched her bag and ran, her legs shaking as the adrenalin fuelled her, only glancing back when she was at the end of the laneway. Empty. She stood leaning against the brick wall. *Breathe.*

Still propelled by shock but calmer now, Chrissie leaped up her front steps two at once. She barely had enough time. Two large lumps on her head throbbed, her breath ragged but deep, filling her lungs, giving her strength. Her shoulder too had eased but her arm still hung half dead beside her. She recalled the dead arms her little brother William and her would give each other as kids. It would come good soon. She had just over two hours before Bannister was due to arrive. She banged on Mike's door.

CHAPTER 41

'You owe me one hell of an explanation,' Chrissie said as she opened her door to the detective.

'And it's really nice to see you, too,' Bannister said. 'Good feature this morning.' He waved a folded copy of *The Argus* at her.

'Sans the coke bust.' She adjusted the scarf around her neck.

'You still had a great piece.'

'Half a great piece, thanks to you.'

'About time someone put all the pieces together about the pickets, been going on too long. Still, it'll cause a bit of a stink. I assume that's what you intended.'

Chrissie didn't reply.

'Here. This is a peace offering.' He placed a brown paper bag on the bench, tore it open and arranged the croissants. 'Chocolate, plain, almond, take your pick. And before you get stuck into me, it took me by surprise too. Dorn is an even bigger kahuna than we knew. Practically walks on water. He managed to shut down the whole thing.'

Should she tell Bannister about the attack in the laneway? Skinny, in the hands of that creep? The missing key? Not now. Not yet. She had to stay focused. Steroids was just a grunt, she knew, one of the gang but not the kingpin. Chrissie shifted the pastries to the coffee table and quickly sat down on a pile of cushions, waving nervously for Bannister to sit opposite, in her favourite spot on the sofa. The Arco lamp was on, issuing a soft glow.

'What, no tea?' He smiled at her. 'Think we need a calming brew after this week, don't we?'

She stood up and fidgeted with the leaves and boiled the water. He got under her skin, in a good–bad way. He wasn't put off by her briskness. She glanced sideways at him. His height and build and acceptance suddenly reminded her of home; she shook her head to get the image out.

He had already relaxed into the sofa, arm along the back, but sat forward when Chrissie handed him his cup. 'Where's your family, Chris? Is that a Kiwi accent?'

'Yeah, God's own, land of the long white cloud. My dad and brother live there. My mum died when I was young.' She kept it vague enough not to be traceable. She needed him to trust her.

Out of the corner of her eye, she saw her new anti-anxiety meds on the shelf. *Should have taken one before he got here. Need to block out the attack.* She closed the tea caddy and quietly tipped a tablet in her hand and coughed as she slipped it in her mouth. *Meooow.* Then took her own cup and returned to the floor cushions.

'I gather you haven't been in Melbourne long. I'm not sure you're seeing the best from this angle.' He nodded towards the street.

'Yeah, well, it's got a certain urban charm, if you squint. I've been here about a year now. What about you?'

'Ah, from the west, a place near Hamilton originally.'

'Hamilton? I come from a place near Hamilton but in New Zealand!'

'Knew there was something special about you.' He smiled. 'Family's in wool, sheep. Big fam, three sisters, one brother. Got myself a little niece recently. I'll probably head back one day. But I've been in Melbourne for ten-ish years. Promotion.'

A country boy. Damn it. He was her type, all right.

'Well, come on, what happened?' She was more abrupt than she meant to be. Back to business.

'The break-in here. Likely them but look, I don't know for sure. The interviews, we've got a few language, attitude, problems. Some of them seem to be willing to say anything at this stage.'

'No, not that. The story, the blackout.' Chrissie got to the point.

'This is all totally off the record. You know there's some almighty gag order. I can't talk, you can't talk. No one is ever going to hear any of this.'

'Yeah, I got the message. So, spill.'

'No, seriously. You keep digging, or let any of this out, and there won't be an *Argus* anymore. You and me? In jail. You can't even report that you've been gagged.'

'I've got my own lawyers to tell me what to do, thanks,' Chrissie retorted. 'Jeez, all this cloak and dagger, it's just another drug bust, for god's sake. And it's linked to those deaths. That has to be reported! Nothing to do with national security, more like national incompetency!'

He took another sip. 'Not as easy as that.' Another sip. 'There was something else just as valuable in those shipments. The coke was a by-product, shall we say. A parasite that attached itself.' Chrissie leaned towards him over the coffee table. The morning sun bright and strong through the kitchen window.

'So?'

'So, the cocaine paste was a side dish,' Bannister said. 'The main course was . . . well, we're finalising that still. But both from South America, sell for almost the same price per gram.'

'Heroin? E? So what? It still doesn't support going to these lengths.' *Doesn't add up.*

'Hey, this is still off the record, okay? Everything. But someone in Brazil, well, Peru probably, got greedy.' *Message from Brazil.* Her arms and chest shivered again at the laneway recollection. She tested her dead arm, better now, as she reached to adjust her scarf. 'The main course, the main cargo, had priority customs, no inspections, nothing,' Bannister said. *Special clearance, Parenta!*

'That's not possible, is it?' Chrissie played along. 'Not with all this anti-terror security at the port? How could that happen?'

'I'm only telling you because you're under the same gag as me. It was getting Triple A clearance, reserved for military, embassies, government, that sort of thing,' Bannister said. 'The receiver must be top brass, that's the reason for the blackout. Looks like the sender got greedy, thought this red-carpet treatment could be put to greater use. They expanded the shipments to include this coke paste.' Bannister put down his cup. Sat back in the sofa. 'It's not clear yet if the coke gang was acting alone or if a deal was done with the people in charge of the main shipment. It'll take a bit of time. But these Latino guys are thugs. They were all over the wharves. Reigned chaos, thought they were back in the Amazon, wherever. All on foreign work visas.'

Chrissie sipped her tea. Resisted reaching for her scarf again. The red mark from the attack still obvious but well hidden, for now.

'Nothing to do with Grange,' Bannister continued. 'It just came through their docks. They usually do the government work, military, diplomatic cargo. Nothing unusual there. But the containers still had to be unloaded and stored on the quiet. That's why the coke crew put their own muscle onsite, to protect their merchandise. We believe they're responsible for the homicides.' *Mas and Remi. Skinny. Hank, too?*

'So what happens now? When will they be charged?' *Justice!*

'We've got them, they'll go down. Good evidence for the murder of the woman already. I know you knew the guy, too. We're pretty close. We know where to look now,' Bannister replied.

'What's left for me to write?'

Bannister stood up and walked to the big bay window.

'You'll still get the cocaine angle,' he said. 'Almost word for word as the draft yesterday. As you know, they're already in custody. Everything has been kept under wraps, on the quiet. We took them in, one at a time, offsite, no attention. It'll stay quiet for a week, probably more.' Chrissie started to protest but he didn't let her. 'No one will get a whisper, don't worry. This lockdown is tight. Your deal will be the same, twelve hours head start. And Homeland will also give *The Argus* an official mention. Might get you a Walkley Award, or a pay rise. Bloody good for your resume.'

'Something, I suppose.' She liked Bannister. He seemed to play it straight. Pity the same couldn't be said about her.

'But you don't get anything on the other cargo. That is a national security issue. We're just trying to establishing if there was prior knowledge about the coke, if the diplomats or government involved knew or not,' he added, watching her closely. 'But either way, on that, it's not ever going public.' He looked straight at her.

'Yeah, okay, figured that would be the case.' She didn't flinch at the lie.

'You know you nearly stuffed up this whole operation. Lucky you're not getting an obstruction charge. Hell of a lot of people involved, lot of planning. The coke gang, too, had knocked out cameras, paid off staff, or frightened the shit out of them, ground crew, the works.'

'Was the union involved?'

'What? Course not! Neither the union nor Grange, apart from the contract Grange has for these diplomatic shipments. But the animosity between them all helped the whole thing,' Bannister continued. 'Neither sounded the alarm, not until they could work out what was best for each of them. Users, the lot.' *Users. Cat's paw.* Was she any different? Chrissie shifted on her cushions, took another sip, ready for the next question.

'How did Grange get to hear about it on the night? Who told them?' She had to find her leak.

'That threw us. We were putting through an injunction against publication on our own but somehow Grange's lawyers got in first. We let them run in front of us. We'll know more soon. They can't refuse to answer, national security, star chamber stuff.'

Chrissie just nodded. *That'll flush him out, once and for all. Jefferies? Or Harry?*

The tablet had already relaxed her. She thought of Mike, below, sitting at his computers, watching his screens.

She offered Bannister a refill. As she stood at the kitchen bench she unplugged the toaster and plugged in her iPod, pressed shuffle. Mike had downloaded some new music for her. 'Sick of hearing those same old sad songs of yours,' he had said.

'Collateral damage in our office, too,' Chrissie said as she half-turned to Bannister. 'I can't wait to know who the bastard is that leaked to Grange.'

He laughed now. A great laugh. 'You guys are priceless. You expect people to tell you stuff but you're angry as all hell if someone leaks against you! If you ask me, the media needs exposing just as much as anyone else. Present company excepted, of course.'

'Exception noted.' Chrissie sat down beside him, this time. Their eyes met. Hazel splashes in his deep brown irises. She could feel the warmth of him. She stretched behind the couch and gently switched off the lamp.

'Interrogation over,' she said.

—

A couple of hours earlier, Chrissie, panting from her escape from the laneway, had rushed into Mike's flat. He had noticed everything, but didn't ask why she was puffing and panicked today. The angry welt around her neck, her limp arm.

'I promise I'll tell you everything.' Chrissie had held up a hand to his worried look. 'But I need you to do a little job for me,' she rushed. 'I'm about to have a visitor.' She stopped to take a breath, heaving. 'And I want you to record what he says. Is that possible? Like, can you do it now?'

'Lady, that must have been some boxing session you just finished. But for you, crazy, beautiful neighbour? Anything.'

'First can you copy this and put it on that site you made.' She had handed him the blackout order from the boardroom. She had put it in her gym bag, worried about leaving it at home. Straight away Mike had cranked up the computers, then they were up the stairs to her flat.

'Two will be enough,' he had nodded, assessing the room. The devices looked like normal double adapters, he had put one in the toaster socket on the kitchen bench, the other in the socket for the lamp. 'Turn it on but dim it down low.'

'See if you can get your boyfriend to sit on the sofa, that'll be best for sound but I've got you covered most spots,' Mike had said. 'Oh, and I'll be able to hear everything, so not too much lovey-dovey, okay? I don't need to hear any of that business.'

CHAPTER 42

'Janice, hi, it's Chrissie. Did you read the story this morning?'

'Yes . . .' Chrissie braced herself for criticism. 'It made me cry, Remi's family, all the families. Mas. It's such a shame, all that tradition and history down the gurgler, what for, eh? Progress? That's not progress. Progress for who? For machines, for profits? What about people, have we all gone mad?'

Chrissie was taken aback, she didn't expect the emotion. She had temporarily forgotten it was always more than a story. It was people, their lives, that drove Chrissie to be a journalist, kept her there.

'It seems that way. I'm sad about it too.' Chrissie slowed down. 'Profit shouldn't ever come first. Look, sorry to ring again, I just wanted to follow up on those shipping agents and their customers. You're at work today, right?'

'Sure am. Of course, I've got it here. I'll email. Like I said, not classified or anything.'

'And one more thing. I was told that some incoming shipments are almost immediately being put on local ships and carried to other cities.'

'Yeah, coastal, short sea,' Janice said.

'I'm looking for cargo from the ships you gave me that could have been loaded again and shipped to Darwin or somewhere like that.'

'What's the time?' Janice paused. Chrissie could hear the rustle of her sleeve. 'Oh, yeah, quarter past one, it's lunch time, I'll do it now. Chrissie, thanks, you know . . .' She heard Janice's voice catch. 'Telling our story, it needed to be told and . . . you did a beautiful job. Mas too, she looked so lovely. I'll be cutting it out to keep.'

—

It was Chrissie's day off but a day off was the last thing on her mind. The list of customers arrived from Janice almost immediately. The eleven shipments from All-Sam were fairly evenly divided across the three Melbourne agents. Each shipment was either four or five containers, all up fifty-two. Chrissie read the names of the customers, nothing rang a bell. No familiar names or addresses. She snapped her laptop shut and slipped downstairs to Mike.

—

'Well, there's one odd one out,' Mike said after a few seconds studying the list. 'Take a look again,' he challenged her. Chrissie stared at the list but still couldn't see the one that stood out to Mike. She looked again but still shrugged.

'Bay Leaf Catering. See, there. It stands out as legit, not the other way 'round. You were looking for the dodgy one, weren't you?' He winked at Chrissie. 'None of the others are food companies. They're consultancies, equipment advisers, explosive experts, machinery. Now what would consultants like that be doing with a bunch of dried foods?' Mike sat back pleased with himself. 'Or more to the point, why would they be getting the red-carpet treatment?'

Chrissie patted him on the shoulder. 'Top of the class.' She searched each of the consultancies by name. Despite their diversity, they had one thing in common: the mining industry.

'Alice Springs!' she shouted.

'I reckon,' Mike said. 'And you know the only other big thing in Alice?' He paused for effect. 'Intelligence, cyber security. Pine Gap – or as we like to call it "the golf course". Anything to do with that place gets *special treatment*.' He returned to his screens. 'I've got a few mates who monitor that side of things. Let me see what I can find.' Chrissie took to her phone and texted Graham Parenta. She wanted to contact the driver he had talked about taking containers inland. The second email from Janice also arrived.

Sorry, Chris, nothing coastal involving those shipments, not even part shipments. All by land.

But Bannister had said the cocaine had gone from Melbourne to Darwin by ship. *A deliberate lie?* Or was Dorn lying to him?

'Hang on!' Chrissie jumped up suddenly and raced upstairs. She came back waving the green note she'd taken from the gauntlet.

Data breaches, geo blocks – smoke and mirrors. Rare to be safe. It's coming in under dark. Check the hardware store.

'It's coming in under dark,' Chrissie read aloud. 'Sounds like smuggling to me.' She handed the note to Mike.

'Rare to be safe – yeah, we know that and increasingly hard. Check the hardware store,' Mike said. 'I'm going to put this out there, too, see who hits me back.' Mike put the note on his scanner, Chrissie watched the blue light slide across the screen as it leaked out from under the lid. Her phone pinged. Parenta.

'Ha. I win. Old school. First to get a response,' she teased.

'You're in a good mood.' Mike raised his eyebrows. 'Nice private time with your visitor today?'

Chrissie ignored the jibe and read out the text.

He won't speak. Says boxes full of dirt. Destination: quarry West of Alice. Mackers he called it.

As she reread the text, her phone rang. Bannister. She pressed silent and it switched to messages. He'd only left her a couple of hours ago. *Clingy?* Then another text. Also Bannister.

Call please. Important.

Later. Got to find out about this Darwin shipping lie you've told me, first.

Chrissie searched for quarries near Alice Springs. Five. She passed her laptop over to Mike showing the results so far.

'What can you hide in a quarry? Chemicals? Environmental waste?'

'Hmmm. Add that name Mackers to the search.' He handed it back to her. 'I want to check something else,' he said.

'Oh, this must be it: where the containers are going. West of Alice, MacDonnell National Park. Mackers?'

'Think I've found ... Tyurretye.' Mike interrupted, then laughed. 'You know what that means? Tyurretye? It's the traditional owners' name for West MacDonnell National Park. You win, again.' He bowed slightly.

—

'Hey, look at this!' An urgency in Mike's voice, unlike his usual calm.

Mike and Chrissie had spent almost the whole day in Mike's flat, making connections and searching the darknet: Alice Springs, mining companies, quarries, diplomatic customs clearances, cocaine, heroin, South America. The streetlight outside Mike's front window had just come on.

'Your dangerous Dorn looks to be in trouble,' he said. 'I'm getting a whisper out of the Feds that Dorn is being held. Told you he was dirty.'

'Bloody hell, what for? Is it about the cocaine? Shit!'

'Too much of a coincidence if it isn't,' Mike said. 'Here, have a look.' Chrissie propped on the side of Mike's *Starship Enterprise* chair and read the messages. Part of an ongoing investigation.

'Bannister! Shit, I should have called him back.' Chrissie listened to the message he had left hours earlier.

'We've had a pretty nasty development,' Bannister's message started. 'You're not in danger, it's just that, um, my new boss might have been involved in the, um, issue. Look, I can't explain on the phone but I've put a patrol on your street, just precautionary.

This whole thing is going to take a bit longer than originally planned. Call me.'

She raced to the window as she started to tell Mike but he waved her to be quiet. He was hunched over the keyboard, head switching back and forth between screens. Chrissie took a quick glance out the window, nothing, then looked over Mike's shoulder. Dysprosium and Thulium. Looming shortages.

'Jesus, full-on,' Mike said as he pulled down article after article.

'What?' Chrissie was impatient.

'Have you ever heard of rare earth elements?' he asked, then stopped and stared at his screen.

'I think so. Those minerals, shocking stuff, third world kids forced down mines to get them, used in,' her eyes flew open, 'mobile phones.'

'China's one of the biggest sources,' Mike said. 'But they're also mined in South America – ring any bells, lady? And here, Australia. They're vital for military and medicine. Not just mobiles, without them even desktops would be great hulking mainframe things, no X-rays, no radars. Whoever controls this stuff is king. Global spook stuff. Man.'

'Especially in the wrong hands,' Chrissie said.

'Whose hands are the wrong hands?' Mike said, back working on his screens.

'That's the shipment! The dirt!' Chrissie said but immediately second-guessing herself. 'But wouldn't that involve massive loads of dirt, not just containers?'

'Just half a gram is all you need for something like a phone,' Mike said. 'Supposed to be the most expensive material in the world. Pure forms are small, easy container lots.'

Bannister knew! The second cargo was just as valuable as cocaine.

'That's what your tipster meant,' Mike said. 'Check the hardware store! Think of all the hardware that uses the internet these days, not just phones but cars, security, banking, planes!' Chrissie stared at him as she realised the full impact from a shortage.

'Boom! Got it! Smoke and fucking mirrors . . .' Mike pumped his hands in the air. 'No wonder that Homeland Hamburger mob is involved. It's us, we're stockpiling these ingredients, these rare earth elements. Australia is importing it, stashing it up at Pine Gap with our US of A buds. Up there in the desert with all the other massive piles of dirt.' Mike sat back in his chair.

'Hidden in plain sight,' Chrissie whispered as she flopped back down on Mike's sofa. 'I'm having a drink.' She laughed. But she was suddenly wary. The laneway attack. Ordered by Dorn? Acting for the cocaine crew. Next time he wouldn't use a simple thug to do his dirty work. Or was it actually Homeland, who wanted to shut me down?

'This is massive,' Mike said. 'Too big for you, lady. Too big for me. We've got to get this out, out everywhere. It's the only way you'll be safe.'

CHAPTER 43

Bright blue Melbourne sky. Its intense colour still caught Chrissie by surprise. Australian skies went on forever. Big skies, she'd often heard it said. No clouds today. Maria and Chrissie crossed the sun-bleached forecourt and into the cool of the church, their footsteps echoing in the foyer. Today, Saturday, was the day – the wedding of the decade, as James had dubbed it. They arrived early. Maria insisted on getting a good seat. Chrissie noticed heads turn as they walked in. Maria's height was set off perfectly by her newly spiked hairdo and large blue perspex earrings. Her colourful kimono-inspired dress stood out among the conservative guests, as did her shiny red Japanese sandals. Chrissie wore a sleeveless caramel dress with a floral water-coloured silk scarf and had gathered her hair into a loose bun. She almost approved of herself when she had stopped for a look in the mirror on the way out. *Not bad.*

St John's Toorak was the perfect venue for a wedding. It was one of the few things the two families had agreed on, James had said with relief. Its location, history and prestige made it a natural choice. Besides, James said, it had one of the longest central aisles in Melbourne and Gina wanted plenty of time to show off her dress.

St John's felt more like a cathedral than a neighbourhood church. Chrissie was in awe of the interior. Its timber vaulted ceiling gave her an unexpected sense of solid calm. She had usually shunned churches and religions most of her life. Not that she didn't believe in God or the supernatural, but she didn't believe in blind faith, a prerequisite for every religion she had come across.

The stained-glass windows, reds, blues, greens, purples, olive, turquoise, rust drew her attention. Their images portrayed pain and suffering but the light and colours made them extreme in their beautiful sadness. She was bewitched by them. Between the windows, the mosaics were equally enticing as they pulled her into their intimate depths. The muted soft stone tiled images were the opposite of the radiated attention demanded by the stained glass, but just as compelling.

The Resurrection, The Ascension, John, Peter, David, Joseph and Jesus. Men, Chrissie noted as she searched for women. There they were: the widow, the mother, the sister. Labelled by their relationships to men.

The church had filled quickly. The excited chatter had drowned out the background music. James and the groom's party had been at the front of the church for about ten minutes. He looked relaxed and happy as he joked with his best man and waved to guests.

'Everyone's talking about your cocaine scoop yesterday. Thank god, we finally got the bloody thing published,' Maria whispered next to Chrissie in the pew. 'All that effort, on-again off-again bullshit. But it was worth it. You did us proud, my girl.' Maria picked up the order of service. 'It's going to be a long one.' She began to fan herself with the thick brochure. 'Interesting about Jefferies. Fancy not going to Grange after all that palaver with the interview. Maybe they found someone better.'

'Yeah, well, he's obviously looking around. Only be a matter of time before he goes. *The Argus* powers aren't going to be too happy knowing he was considering it,' Chrissie whispered back. 'Although, I'm not quite convinced about the whole Grange thing. My money's still on Harry.'

'There must be ten grand worth of flowers in this place.' Maria gestured at the massed branches of pink and white crab apple blossom everywhere. Clear glass metre-high cylinders, complete with lit candles in their bases, held huge arrangements of green and white flowers at the end of every pew. Roses, lilies, tulips, fat hydrangeas, pure white daffodils, magnolias, slender delphiniums. White on white. Jasmine twisted around the short posts at the entrance to each pew and looped across to each one in front. A rope of sweet spicy scent that would linger for days after. 'How many people do you think are here, two hundred?' Maria asked.

'Close to two hundred and fifty,' James said. 'Don't think they're all here. Some are just going to the reception.' Chrissie's voice trailed off as the organ began a loud introduction. Everyone hushed and shuffled in their pews to get a good look as the main wedding party began to enter.

'That's Gina's parents, the Chamberlains,' Lou, the fashion editor, pointed out, leaning forward to whisper to Chrissie and Maria from the pew behind them.

A couple in their late fifties walked down the aisle. Her blonde coiffed hair and neat French blue silk suit and matching shoes oozed wealth. His posture marked him as a man used to being listened to. A lawyer, a very rich lawyer. Gina had followed in his career footsteps.

'Thought that might have been them. Gina's family is rolling in dough,' Chrissie spoke in a hush. 'I think James will be drawing double from his trust fund to keep up with married life. They've rented almost a whole floor at the top of one of those Docklands apartments,' Chrissie whispered back to Lou. 'How do you know them?'

'Oh, I do some consulting. James asked if I could help Gina with some of the outfits. Wait till you see the bridesmaids. Stunn-ing! I also arranged a session for Gina's mum and her best friend Sandra, they both flew in from LA together last week. They picked almost identical outfits! Often happens with best friends.' Lou smiled, reaching up and lightly touching the fascinator nestled in her blonde chignon.

The organ began blaring from the pipes and filling the church. 'Canon in D,' Maria announced reading from the booklet. Two shy flower girls dressed in ankle-length frills and holding hands were shooed ahead of a cluster of bridesmaids. The little girls made their way hesitantly, glancing secretly at each other but then stopped partway, as they desperately tried to remember the rules. At the far end, James stepped out into the centre of the aisle. He bent with his arms wide. As soon as they saw him, they ran the rest of the way, spilling their flowers as each grabbed one of his legs to hug. His twin nieces were besotted with their uncle. A murmur of love went through the congregation.

In floated the bridesmaids in floor-length navy gowns. Silk organza, silver shoes peeping out at every step. Chrissie heard Lou flutter behind her at the sight.

Without warning, Chrissie was suddenly back at her wedding. She was caught off-guard by the memory, for so long she had practised to block it out. But she sat with it, let it come. They married in a tiny timber church on the lake shore. Her ankle-length cream organza dress, pale silk slippers and a bracelet woven of freesias. Chrissie's father walked her down the aisle, bursting with pride and a tinge of sadness as they clasped a photo of Chrissie's mum between them. The party afterwards went all night. Lamb on a spit, fresh trout from the river that morning, the world's biggest tiered pavlova wedding cake.

The music changed again: 'The Wedding March,' Maria read out, unnecessarily, in her favourite TV presenter's voice. Excitement rippled through the grand stone church. Here she comes!

Gina's waist looked minuscule against the balloon of her full-length gown. Studded with tiny pearls that swirled across the bodice and down to the floor, she had stepped out of a fairy tale. The off-white silk had a pearl lustre all of its own, her veil an heirloom by the look of the lace. Her procession was slow and deliberate. This woman doesn't have an ounce of doubt, Chrissie thought.

For the first time Chrissie felt like crying, not from grief or anger, but from love. Love for James and Gina. Love for Dave. As she stood watching the ceremony, she realised she could survive the memory of him. Her own wedding, their love, the recollection, it hadn't crushed her into the earth, as she had always feared.

She watched as Gina turned to James at the altar, she recognised the look, their glow, she allowed herself to see it. These two people had the best chance in the world, she thought.

The long service tested everyone's patience, the crowd was in a hurry to empty the church and greet the newly married couple. The front steps and lawn were awash with one of the wealthiest and privileged gatherings Melbourne could muster.

As the bells rang and the couple thanked their guests, Chrissie was stunned to see a familiar man in the crowd. James and Gina were smiling and talking to everyone as they made their way down the line of well-wishers to the limousines. Chrissie nudged Maria.

'That guy James is about to talk to, grey tie, he's one of the Grisham family, Jonathan Grisham. He's like the chairman, the founder of the Grisham Foundation. What's he doing here? I thought he lived in the States.'

'Look at this crowd, this is network city. Looking for the next connection, the next investment, who to curry favour with,' Maria shot back. Chrissie's stomach churned, she widened her stance to steady herself.

'He's supposed to have bailed out Grange recently,' Chrissie said. 'Cash injection by one of his venture funds, basically a takeover.' Chrissie's eyes were fixed on Grisham as James moved down the line closer to him. Her heart pounded heavily but her chest felt hollow. Then she saw the woman with Grisham, wearing a pale grey silk suit, almost identical to Gina's mother. Is that who Lou was talking about? *The two best friends.* The scene started to go in slow motion. She could feel her blood throbbing in her fingertips. Her breath had shrunk to small sips. She had to get closer. *Breathe!* She pushed through the perfumed crowd, sliding awkwardly, roughly, between the fashion and the perfect hair. She had to hear what Grisham was saying.

'Good work, James,' Grisham said, pumping his hand, then turning to Gina's parents. The pale blue silk suit of Gina's mother. 'Don't worry, we'll have them stateside by this time next year,' Grisham said. 'Make sure you get plenty of American grandchildren.' He smiled at his pale grey silk wife looking for affirmation.

Confetti rained down. Chrissie was swallowed by the shouts and calls of good wishes. *You!* The sounds of cheering and goodwill whooshed in her ears. She loosened her scarf, stepped backwards through the crowd, not caring who was behind her. *I see you, James Howard. You!* At that very moment, James looked up, straight at her. He started to smile but instantly recognised that she knew – his betrayal, his leaks. For just a second, he hesitated, then gave Chrissie a hapless shrug.

All around her, phones started pinging and buzzing.

'Christ almighty, look at this. It's all over the internet.' Chrissie felt someone grab her arm. 'Hey. You okay?' It was Maria.

'Yeah.' Chrissie took a deep breath. 'Just not good in crowds.'

'It's about the docks, some mining thing now! Implicates the government, US and UK, too,' Maria continued. The church bells pealed even louder. Maria's voice was drowned out. Chrissie watched the photographer darting around the newly married couple, as the wedding party made its way to the line-up of silver Rolls-Royces.

'Hah, should have known,' Maria said. She was back in full flight. 'It's tied up with your story. I never understood that media blackout bullshit.' She pushed her phone closer to Chrissie so she could see the screen, then pulled it back and kept reading. 'I tell you, every time I hear the words anti-terror, I think bullshit cover-up!'

Chrissie was still numb. *James! James?* She watched as the attendants arranged Gina's gown in the car. Gina, too.

'The government's secretly importing this stuff, stockpiling it, to put pressure on the big tech companies. No minerals, no mobiles, no bloody multi-billion-dollar corporations. Hah! Slap down, as they say,' Maria was on a roll. 'Amazing really. I've always thought this government couldn't organise a piss-up in a brewery. Just goes to show ya! Chrissie? Chrissie?'

But Chrissie had turned back to watch the two immaculate blonde women, the best friends, Gina's mother and Grisham's wife, their 'almost matching' silk suits, laughing and hugging each other. Their husbands might have their lapel pins, denoting their secret male power, their clubs and associations but they had nothing on the machinations of their wives. They made the decisions for their families. These women invisibly smoothed their husbands' careers. Made the introductions. Ensured their children were educated together. Their grandchildren, too. Ski, entertain, holiday, advance in life together. Gina would have been well-schooled. Power all around. Old power, new power. Female power.

Then she spotted him. Drawn to look closer by a tall regal woman, black hair piled high, orange sari sparkling in the sun. And next to her a younger version. Suri Parenta. Of course she's here, she's Gina's friend. But the air in Chrissie's chest got suddenly thinner, she could barely move as she watched the scene through the heads of the happy crowd. Suri kissed and congratulated Gina's mum, who quickly slipped an arm around Suri's waist. The young woman let her parents say hello to Gina's mother. Chrissie held her breath. They had met before, she judged from their greeting. Old friends. Kisses all around between the two silk suits and the two silk saris. Then Graham Parenta shook hands with Grisham. The shake went on too long, a double-hander. Much too long. Then she saw it, the backslap.

Chrissie nodded slowly. *Played. Double played.*

CHAPTER 44

The number 8 tram rattled its way to Flinders Street Railway Station. She couldn't face the wedding reception. *Not now.* She couldn't pretend to James or herself. Instead of another train trip through the loop, she decided to walk. Clear her thoughts. Accept.

Fitzroy Gardens was like a cool zone compared with the spring heat from the city pavements. Her favourite spot was the secret lake with its sculpture of the boy riding a turtle. Maria told her the bronze had been stolen once, in the middle of the night. Someone had waded across the lake and hefted it away. It was missing for a couple of years, eventually found abandoned in Richmond. A bit like me, Chrissie thought. Abandoned in Richmond. *No, not abandoned.*

She sat for a few more minutes, then lifted her bottle of water. A silent toast to Mas, home floating above her beautiful islands.

And Remi. A high school dropout, a father, a flawed man. Perhaps they're together now, after all. If it wasn't for their deaths, the cocaine, the stockpiling, the government blackmail would have succeeded, the truth untold. Or perhaps that's the wrong way around. If the government hadn't been trying to blackmail the tech companies, the drugs couldn't have hitched a ride, then Mas and Remi would still be alive.

Chrissie knew Harry would assign her to report about the internet whistleblower, she would be an automatic pick for some of the bigger stories now. The only question would be how the government would react. Outright denial? Or just muddy the waters; confess to part but not all? Or the third and most popular option: refuse to comment for national security reasons. The power of public pressure, she mused. Not quite a superpower but all she had.

At least Mas and Remi's murderers would be partly held to account. Not the masterminds, they never get caught, but the local thugs.

'Get yourself down to the Supreme Court on Thursday,' Bannister had said during the week. 'You might just be in time for a mention on the coke charges. Nothing doing on the homicides yet but you'll be able to eyeball them. They were the ones based at the port.'

'What about Dorn's involvement?' she had asked.

'Nothing's ever going to see the light of day on that. Ever. You know that, don't you? Chrissie? Ever.'

'Yeah,' she had said, nodding into the phone. 'But did he know, or order, Skinny, you know? The laneway attack?' She had eventually told him about the steroids guy.

'Dorn's put that all on the drug crew. Says he didn't know but your call to him made him take a closer look. That's why he turned up at your place so quickly that night – thought someone was stepping out of line and, of course, to find out what you knew.' Chrissie had pressed the phone harder to her ear.

'The paw wasn't enough, obviously,' she had taken a deep breath, 'they wanted me um, dead or sick, out of action.' She had turned towards the soft breeze coming through the open kitchen window. *Skinny.*

'From what we can gather, someone went back into your place, after you went to hospital. Apparently, had to wait until your hacker mate had finished cleaning up.' *Hacker mate, he knows!* Chrissie didn't reply. 'And yeah, I'd put the laneway down to them too, maybe Dorn knew in advance that time, they were all getting desperate. We're still investigating.'

Chrissie had attended the court hearing that Bannister had mentioned. She wanted to see for herself. But they were nobodies. *Six faceless nothing men.*

She stopped, now, near the garden's strange folly, a miniature Tudor Village. A party of little girl fairy princesses were on the lawn. What would it be like to be a mother of one of those princesses? Her hand automatically went to her stomach but quickly withdrew, instead lifting her silky scarf and allowing it to float back down. Possibly, one day, she could fit into a group like that.

The smooth streets of East Melbourne were her final buffer of calm as she headed back to the hardness of Victoria Street.

She would miss James. He had betrayed her, tipped off Grange that night, and other nights, no doubt. But she had already forgiven him. It didn't matter in the end, the story was already doomed, by Dorn's mob – both of them: his Homeland team, under the sanction of the government, and the drug crew that paid him to let them 'piggyback' on the rare mineral operation. But she felt stronger now. Perhaps she could cope with it all, forgive herself one day, too.

The distrust between Grange and the maritime union had worked in Grisham's and Parenta's favour. The territorial relationship between unions had been ripe for the picking. Grisham would have thought nothing of manipulating the strike, stirring up the international unions, to add pressure on Grange to accept his takeover.

Parenta was a survivor, too. In the next pay negotiations with Grange, Grisham would owe the transport union boss a favour. Ultimately, it meant more clout for Parenta, especially in the next round of union mergers and power broking. Carter, however, would not forgive or forget. They didn't call her Hel for nothing. Just like the corporate world, it was also eat or be eaten in union empires.

As Chrissie turned the corner from the bluestone lane, she stopped and quickly ducked back behind the brick wall. Bannister was standing on the street outside her house. She couldn't face him. She knew he would suspect her about the internet leak. She had calculated that he would just ditch her with an angry phone call, say she'd betrayed his trust. He couldn't actually *do* anything official. He had told her part of the story and she had the audio and the phone message to prove it. He wouldn't risk his career. He had become a complication, Chrissie tried to justify.

She would have to avoid him. Their brief fling at her flat was a mistake. *Could I ever be enough for someone again?*

Her phone startled her, echoing off the narrow lane walls as it rang loudly. She fumbled trying to quickly quieten the sound, he might hear it from where he stood.

'Hi Chrissie. Where are you?' It was him. Bannister.

'I'm still at the wedding,' she lied, as she watched him from around the corner of the lane. He seemed nervous, fidgeting and pacing.

'Oh. I've got something for you. I tried your buddy downstairs but he's pretending not to be home again.'

Maybe Bannister hadn't seen the internet yet? Or perhaps he'd seen it and knew it was the right thing to do?

'Oh, that's okay,' Chrissie fobbed. 'He'll be home for sure, just a recluse.' *Never open the door to a copper.* Even a handsome copper. 'I'll ring him, get him to take it in for me. Is it an update on the investigation?'

'Yeah, sort of.'

'Great. Thanks. Just leave it, Mike will get it straight away. I'll phone him now.'

'Chrissie? I wanted –'

'Sorry, I can't talk. I'm at the reception. I'd better go. Sorry.' She watched him walk back up to the top of the steps in front of her building. *Possibilities? Maybe?* He busied with something as he bent over in front of the door, then just as quickly he was back down and out the gate. Chrissie watched as he got in his car and drove off. *Maybe.*

She saw the box, sauvignon blanc written on it, as she walked in the gate. Wine? That was odd, she was expecting paperwork.

The wine will last a while, Chrissie thought. She was on the wagon. Her drunken run-in with Andy Dorn had shaken her. The realisation she could cope with her memories, her self-doubts, also added to her resolve – never the old Chrissie, she knew, but a different version.

As she neared the top step, she saw Mike pull back his curtain and peer around.

Chrissie smiled at him but he looked panicked. He knocked on the window and waved her away.

'Careful!' She heard his muffled shout through the glass.

Alarmed, she looked down at the box. It had been opened, the flaps crossed back over and taped up. As Chrissie peered at it, it moved. She jumped. Mike jumped too. Then she heard it. She raced to quickly pull the tape off and the flap sprung open. An angry hissing grey kitten poked its head out. She heard Mike's muffled voice shout, 'Skinny Two!'

ACKNOWLEDGEMENTS

What a thrilling, and slightly daunting, experience to write this final page of my debut novel. It really has taken a village to go from manuscript to published book. And the people in this village are amazing!

Let me start at the beginning with a big thank you to the Janes in my life, my colleague Jane for planting the seed, leading by example and encouraging me at every step and New Zealand Jane for helping to save me when my world broke.

Thank you, too, to my gang of *Financial Review* chicks, Nina, Katherine, Nicole and Jo for being my first readers, your honesty was everything, and Myfanwy for giving me that final faith.

Thanks also to the Victorian Premier's Literary Awards for shortlisting this unpublished manuscript and encouraging new writers (young and old).

Now, for the best movers and shakers in the industry: my agent Clare Forster (assisted by Benjamin Stevenson) at Curtis Brown Australia, for expertly advising and steering me through the publishing maze; my publisher Simon & Schuster Australia and the magnificent Fiona Henderson, Dan Ruffino, Michelle Swainson, Angus Dalton and their brilliant team.

Last, but never least, my big fat, mixed up, inspirational Kilmore Barrymore Douglas Owens family – past and present – especially Steve and Molly.

ABOUT THE AUTHOR

Karina Kilmore is a writer and newspaper journalist with more than 30 years' experience. Under the byline Karina Barrymore, she covered almost every major business scandal and financial event since the 1987 global share market crash and has written for US, UK, Australian and New Zealand publications. Her first novel, *Where the Truth Lies*, was shortlisted for the prestigious Unpublished Manuscript Award at the Victorian Premier's Literary Awards in 2017. Born in Wellington, New Zealand, she now lives in Richmond in Melbourne. She is working on her second book.